A d i r _____, 1969

Advance Praise

"I've always wanted to visit the Adirondacks in summer, to listen to the loons on a glacial lake, and after my death, to eavesdrop on my spouse. This is *Adirondack Summer, 1969,* a smartly written, page-turner of a novel. Proctor's characters, as diverse in background as the mountains, as the 60s itself, are believable in every sense of the word. They engage us in a clever totem of personalities, a mix of harmony and conflict. From the early chapters on, we cannot help but wonder what is coming next."

—Al Ortolani, Manuscript Editor, Woodley Press

"A modern-day fairy tale, *Adirondack Summer, 1969,* draws on a generation's collective memory to place readers back in that moment when playful childhood innocence meets uncomfortable adolescent awakening, supervised by the flawed adults we all eventually become. In Alan Robert Proctor's sensitive hands, we can smell the pines, the lake water, the camp food and the pheromones while an ethereal omniscience observes a theatrical cast of characters who've brought their own demons to the iconic American idyll of summer camp. Meanwhile, it's impossible for us not to know that the real America smolders just beyond the gates of this richly imagined place. As Proctor suggests, what becomes of that real America now depends on the better angels we can only hope are guiding the long-ago graduates of Camp Cravitzes all around the country."

—C.J. Janovy, author of *No Place Like Home: Lessons in Activism from LGBT Kansas.*

"Welcome to Camp Cravitz, a fine arts camp in the Adirondacks in 1969. A strong sense of story keeps readers turning pages as compelling characters—campers, staff, and the spirit of the director's dead wife—deal with life-changing events during the camp's last season."

—Mary-Lane Kamberg, co-leader of the Kansas City Writers Group

"In remarkable story form, Alan Proctor captures (unobtrusively) the uncertainties of 1969, pivotal year of war and collective grief over assassinations and political upheavals. By allowing characters to reflect the chaos of the time, actively and passively in a style reminiscent of John Updike, the author employs a unique setting, unique narration, and a protagonist (Myron) whose goals appear to exceed his means of reaching them. Proctor's assembling of summer fine arts camp characters of variety and depth is a meticulous exercise often exceeding what most writers have the patience and background to undertake ...."

—Norm Ledgin, author of *Diagnosing Jefferson* and *Sally of Monticello: Founding Mother*

"An America that we offspring of the Sixties lost to adulthood and the 21st century returns to vivid life in *Adirondack Summer, 1969,* a novel more sweet than bitter about the losses that visit every life. This is a closely-observed celebration of the adolescent summers and sleep-away camps that helped shape a generation. From the uniquely clear-eyed vantage of camp co-founder Deidre Cravitz, we're shown a microcosm of the American experience during the Vietnam Era, including the joys and cruelties of coming-of-age in a troubled and memorable time as well as events leading to tragedy during this turning-point summer at the camp. Alan Proctor has crafted a book that beautifully recalls who we were then."

—Michael Pritchett, author of *The Melancholy Fate of Captain Lewis,* Unbridled Books

"This is a novel with charm and considerable crossover appeal for the YA reader. Set in the late 1960s—a backdrop of the Vietnam War, and the moon-walk—the novel offers a ghostly narrator and a host of interesting characters, both sympathetic and foul. Camp Cravitz has been run for years by Deidre and Myron Cravitz. But Deidre is killed just before camp opens, and the question remains will Myron be able to pull the season off. Proctor has a gift for drawing a scene ... A good, entertaining, fast-paced read."

—Catherine Browder, author of *"Now We Can All Go Home,"*
  3 novellas in homage to Chekhov

Also by Alan Robert Proctor

The Sweden File: Memoir of an American Expatriate,
co-authored with Bruce Stevens Proctor,
compiled and edited by Alan Robert Proctor

ADIRONDACK SUMMER, 1969

a novel

Alan Robert Proctor

Westphalia Press

An Imprint of the Policy Studies Organization

Washington, DC

2018

Westphalia Press
An imprint of Policy Studies Organization
1527 New Hampshire Ave., NW
Washington, D.C. 20036
info@ipsonet.org

ISBN-10: 1-63391-715-0
ISBN-13: 978-1-63391-715-6

Cover and interior design by Jeffrey Barnes
jbarnesbook.design

Daniel Gutierrez-Sandoval, Executive Director
PSO and Westphalia Press

Updated material and comments on this edition
can be found at the Westphalia Press website:
www.westphaliapress.org

For Susan, my one and only.
And for Devin and Thomas: love's calluses.

Dramatis Personae

STAFF

Myron Cravitz, camp director

Deidre Cravitz, Myron's wife and camp founder

Jake Daryl, head counselor

Fanny Daryl, Jake's wife and nurse's aid

also:

Alex, camp handyman

Sonja, camp cook

Lila Mae, piano coach

Maria, camp life guard and guitar coach

Wally, counselor-in-training and Maria's
water-front assistant

Stanley, orchestra leader

Leon, drama coach

Popeye, fine arts coach

Robin, creative writing coach

Brad, canoeing and overnight camping counselor

CAMPERS

Reginald Farrouk, nearly 13 and precocious

Kurt Willington, Reginald's orphan friend

also:

Colleen, 16-year-old tease

Betsy, Colleen's side-kick

Rope and Scotty, 9- and 10-year-old pests

Shortstack, 10-year-old know-it-all

Cheryl, Reginald's heart-throb

Megan and Thea, 15-year-old twins

Angela, 14 and Kurt's girlfriend

Freddie, Angela's friend

OUTSIDERS AND TOWNIES

Sally Moffett, Deidre and Myron's neighbor

also:

Ratchet, town hardware store owner

Snake and Clarice, middle-aged townie couple

Hal, owner of the Wild Cat Bar and Grill

Ruby and Charlotte, Hal's daughters

Bruce, town fire chief

Emile, Myron's attorney

Haskell, on staff at Kurt's orphanage

Mr. and Mrs. Thurley, Shortstack's parents

Skip, Reginald's older brother

PART I

Chapter One

They recovered my body that afternoon draped around a river piling. But I'm getting ahead of myself. Let's begin a year before my death.

We had started late. Myron couldn't find his leather work gloves. I waited on the porch with a thermos in one hand, my small suitcase in the other. Inside, something clattered to the hall floor and then Myron's, "Oh, Lord," more of a whimper than a summons. I set my luggage on the stoop and went inside. The phone rang. Myron snared the receiver. I picked up the other line. "What?" he snapped.

"Myron, this is Jake—Myron?"

"Go ahead, Jake."

"How's my room? Last year the closet never did dry out—"

"It's been a dry spring, Jake."

"No mushrooms growing in the corners?"

"Deidre's pulling me out the front door, Jake."

"Right, just wanted to make sure, as head counselor, I got a decent room this year."

"You'll have the upstairs east bedroom," Myron said. "Positive. Goodbye, Jake."

Beside him in the car, I closed my eyes. I knew Myron wished I had done the talking. I could simultaneously ruffle and smooth Jake Daryl's irritating arrogance.

3

It was late May 1968. Myron and I were in our brand new Camaro heading to the Adirondack Preserve in upstate New York. Every spring the details of opening camp for the season distressed my husband. He wasn't the organizer, I was. He enjoyed helping me run the camp once it was in session and the children had accepted their surroundings, but I was the one who relished the coming chaos—organic, full of serendipity, and innocence.

"The enrollment's fine," I said. "We have most of the staff. The others will come. They always do."

"Did you get hold of the cook?"

"She'll be there."

"When did you talk to her?"

"It seems a lifetime ago, but she'll be there."

"What do you mean a lifetime ago?"

I glared at him and he knew why. We never talked about Devon and Caleb's drowning anymore, but the twins' loss still clung.

"Myron, think back. Remember this time last year? Same problems with personnel. At least this year we have Gladys."

"Who's—how old did you say, Deidre? Eighty-five?"

"She's a cook, Myron. What difference does it make how old she is. And she's seventy-five, not eighty-five."

"A geriatric cook who probably thinks the generation gap is a tourist spot on the Ausable River." He lowered his head toward me, "And with whom you spoke *a lifetime ago*." He slapped the phrase into perspective. I had brought it up, after all.

We drove through intermittent sunlight and shade. When the woods pressed close to the road, shadows leapt onto the car and then vanished in sun-lit clearings. A half-hour away the smooth, blue-green gauze of the Adirondacks swelled above the horizon.

Myron palmed his left eye and rubbed. "Yeah, last year around now we didn't have a drama coach."

"Exactly. We're right on schedule. I've had my shopping fling in Montreal. Gladys is finishing up in the Catskills. We've still got almost a month."

A month seemed plenty of time for preparations to me, but Myron had spent the entire semester writing and re-writing the new camp promotional brochure: 'Nestled in the heart of Indian country, an Adirondack fine arts camp for children beckons and develops young talent.'

"Oh, Lord," he thumped the steering wheel. "I hope drama's covered. I forgot to call him."

"Who's that?"

"Leon McAdam. Mount Airy Community Theatre? We met him at that weirdo party. He went on and on about the width of a river in *Last of the Mohicans*. How it would have been impossible for the Indians to jump into the canoe because the canoe was in the center of the river and the branches couldn't extend that far."

"Oh, yeah. Very theatrical fellow. He asked me if I smoked pot."

"It's your earth-goddess aura, Deidre. Makes the hippy-chicks jealous." He reached across the seat and tweaked my breast.

I removed his hand, "eyes on the road, please," and then remembered McAdam's overbearing, finger-fluttering egotism. "You didn't hire him?"

"He was cheap. Said he'd do workshops and *Annie Get Your Gun*. Remind me to call him tomorrow."

He hunched further over the wheel to avoid my testy look. I should have handled this hire. No, that's not fair. Although he didn't like to, my husband was fully capable—well capable anyway—of making decisions.

I turned to the window. Clustered at the road's brink, blue hepaticas darted past the front fender. Camp wouldn't begin until late June. The hepaticas would be gone by then, but trillium would be blooming, their green seeds ready to drop. Among the shadows and ferns, lady slippers would raise and bow their heads, the ground pine thicken and the partridge berry's white flowers open.

Across a clearing, an expansive stand of beeches shimmered. As a girl, I had carved permanent and earnest proclamations into similar smooth trunks: 'Deidre & Eddy,' and during one summer when Myron was visiting friends, and I was too old to be marking my territory, I carved 'Deidre Loves Myron.' When Mom invited him to dinner for my 18th birthday, I shortened his name to Mye (rhymes with sigh). At the table, my first words to him, "Pass the butter, if it's not too much trouble," meant to intrigue. I made my vowels breathy, my eyes tantalizing.

"How much trouble is too much?" Mye ambushed the butter dish before my father could scoot it to me. We talked for an hour after dessert and then long into the night on Match Lake's beach, the engorged moon rising over the still water. After that, I knew I would never find a more attentive man.

If only he'd been a more attentive father.

Myron and I had inherited the lake-front, log and stone lodge from my parents and assumed we would continue the hotel business and summer there with a growing family, but they tied my tubes when Devon and Caleb were born caesarean.

My parents worked hard to maintain the lodge. Every spring they resisted a small fortune the property's sale would bring. I loved Match Lake summers, idyllic days exploring the woods and lake, late afternoons listening—a curled cat forgotten on the ottoman—to the preposterous stories our paying guests embellished on the veranda while the empty wine bottles multiplied. At night, the stars' bright reflections crowded the placid water. And at summer's end, the aurora borealis danced its curtained slight-of-hand.

My father fished brook trout—brookies—from the brisk streams. He froze the dappled creatures in water-filled, Pure-Pak milk cartons. When we left the lodge in September, he stacked them in our Brooklyn apartment's laboring and glacially entombed freezer. The summer fish hissed in the winter pan. My mother softened the piscine wallop with rosemary and mustard.

Our car drifted into gravel. "Mye, watch the road please."

"I am watching the road. The windshield's dirty." He spritzed the glass and flipped the wipers, then fumbled between the seats for the coffee thermos. Empty. "Who's the W.S.I.?"

I glanced at the junipers receding in my side mirror. "I thought you were taking care of that."

"What!" The car swerved. His eyes raked the dashboard. "What about your friend, Marcia?"

"Marcia took the YWCA job. I thought you knew that."

"We're opening in less than a month and don't have a water safety instructor? They're harder to find than the damn cooks." Myron's grip tightened on the wheel.

I reached across the seat and diddled his ear's cornucopia.

"Cut that out!"

"You're doing sixty-five and climbing, love. Relax. Somebody will turn up for the lake front. Someone always does."

He eased back on the accelerator. "Why do we do this every summer?"

"Because you adore the children."

"They're brats for the most part."

"They're talented brats." And the family we never had, but saying this would only bring Mye's guilt to the surface, remind him of our children's cherub bottoms smooth and dead as soap floating in the tub's creamy water. I had screamed and snatched them out. Lifeless.

"An accident," I told him on the anniversary of their births. "Maybe it was my fault; I should have been with you. I'd never have left them alone in the bath." I managed a smile. "They were a handful."

The gynecologist had said, "I doubt you'd survive another baby, Deidre." He conferred with Myron but hadn't asked my permission to sterilize me and, at the time, with two healthy angels, I didn't care.

Myron discovered the cast iron tub in the Antique Attic, a filthy junk store posing as a boutique. "Look at the claw feet on this thing. Beautiful, isn't it?" The four-footed basin belonged upstairs in the lodge, but he hauled it back to New Jersey. The twins were only 6 months old when they drowned in it.

The car's headlights crinkled through the ground pine that nearly hid the dirt entrance to our reclusive neighbor, Sally Moffett—final landmark before the camp's long gravel drive. Myron turned at the camp's catawampus sign. "I'll need to fix that," he said.

After 16 years of opening for the season, Myron still followed my instructions like a child. But the man in him knew a good merlot, always there for me at 5 o'clock. We would sit on the porch after dinner, listen to the loons, and finally make love in the Stone House bedroom. No campers, no staff, nothing but the groaning bed frame to quicken our passion and bring Myron's gasping mouth to my ear. Moments when he forgot, and I forgave.

Montreal almost a year later.

I was having dinner in the hotel dining room with Sylvia somebody, a new acquaintance. She spoke French fluently. "I think the *maitre de* is flirting with us. He's cute. *Mignon*," she said.

I beckoned to the man. On his way to us, his white cummerbund skirted flower vases and bobbed across the rosewood paneling.

"*J' ai une faim de loup.*" Hungry as a wolf, I pouted when he arrived. My tablemate snapped her napkin into her lap. She glanced at me and then at the waiter who bowed a smidgen too immodestly.

"*Tu veux dire une faim de tigresse?*" Hungry like a tigress? He tongued mustache hair.

Sylvia smirked.

"*Non, non,*" I said, "*J'aimerais les crevettes roses.*" The shrimp did look good. His breath stroked my cheek. I added— perhaps a bit uncivilly—"*Ce sera tout.*"

He straightened up, eyes all business and slipped the *serviette* from his arm. "*Oui, Madame.*"

I opened my compact to check my eye-liner. I always considered my eyes (powder blue) my best feature. Myron said it was my long tresses of red hair. Not really red, more like auburn with flecks of wistful thinking, I told him. I angled the mirror to inspect my earrings and caught the *maitre de* staring at me from across the room. It was the last time in life that I smiled.

Each spring, before the rigors of preparing camp for the summer, I spent May's second week gorging on French food and shopping the boutiques in Montreal. My getaway—which Myron referred to as the Montreal Fling—offered the chance to practice French and pursue some innocent flirting with the usually proper hotel staff. After dinner and *She Stoops to Conquer* at the St. Denis Theatre (not as good as *Hamlet* the year before), I washed up in the fake granite sink and went to bed.

I left the city early the next morning on Route 138 heading toward the suburban hamlet of *Saint Remi* on the Saint Lawrence River's south side. *Saint Remi* is not a picturesque place, but I wanted a breather before picking up Route 15 which, in the United States, becomes I-87. Eighty-seven plunges south through New York and hems the eastern boundary of the Adirondack Mountains. A brilliantly clear day. In an hour I would be able to see Mount Marcy's 5,300 foot summit in the preserve's heart to the west. As a child, I had climbed Marcy many times and soaked my feet until they were numb in the tiny stream that bubbled out of Lake Tear-of-the-Clouds, the Hudson's headwaters.

The Saint Lawrence, like the Hudson, is a busy commercial waterway. As I skirted the riverside, a barge—low in the water and filled with scrap metal—navigated near shore. Light traffic. I tapped the Camaro's gas pedal. The coupé's powerful engine pressed me into the leather seat. The long approach to the *Honore Mercier* Bridge fell into a terraced valley, swooping down between newly planted pines and up again to the suspension cables' thick assurance. At the bottom of the hill, the bridge's crest dipped from view.

I daydreamed of showering with Myron after our first exhausting day of opening camp, his hands cupping my breasts, fingers slipping down my wet stomach and straying into what he called my cabbage patch, and then the two of us rolling into the Stone House bed that for 8 months had been empty of our sticky, desperate love.

Although I didn't know it at the time, the barge captain began to choke. Pain rose like reflux into his throat. He clawed at his left pectoral to yank out the agony spreading deep into his chest, raised his grizzled face and gritted tobacco-blackened teeth. His cry and the wheelhouse ceiling offered no release. He fell forward against the throttle on the instrument panel. His ship rumbled in response, churning toward the bridge's concrete pilings below me.

The vessel grazed the first piling and swung full force into two more, crumpling the bow and port side. Honeycombed lengths of metallic piping broke their straps and rolled into the water like runaway soda straws. Deck planks exploded. Twirling boards pelted the river.

The bridge pillars shuddered, buckled, and shed their skin to rebar. Concentric waves avalanched from the footings, and then the anchoring husks slid into the Saint Lawrence. The bridge—with me on it—began to sway and crack.

Ahead, I saw an older car's tailfins disappear in the adjacent lane. The Camaro fish-tailed toward the precipice.

And here I am. *Was* it a dream? The relief of again being conscious is so intense, I want to close my eyes and fall back to sleep. But I can't. Instead, I'm watching the grainy screen of a television set. The newscaster's face is grave. "A scream could be heard," she says, "as two cars plunged into the river. The late-model vehicle sank immediately and then resurfaced to sink again, almost leisurely, as reported by the eyewitness."

I look at my hands. They aren't there. I touch my face—no feeling, just a humid gauze of clouds, flight without velocity. Where am I going?

Our camp, the lake, and lodge are below me. Why have I come back to a bodiless intelligence? Why am I not with my dear, dead children? A punishment, perhaps. Or a reprieve? Why in *this* place, dead but not dead among my grieving husband and the campers, his 80 inherited children?

Of touch, I now know nothing. But I taste the camp's textures. As though scribbled in the air, I can read the silliness, endearment, and cruelty each townie and camp resident says or thinks. I wing, like a loon, through generations. I can pluck from time's möbius the whole shebang.

This is why I'm here—to tell the story: the jerky plots and brief luminescence of the living—the saga of Camp Cravitz that summer in 1969, and the lives changed through serendipity, love, and malice. When I finish the tale, I'll fly away.

Chapter Two

Myron pounded the long dining hall table. His fist startled the pretzel tray two inches closer to the edge.

"Quiet!" His staff's bickering labored to a halt. "People," he muttered, "tomorrow parents will deposit 80 children on our doorstep. We've got to be ready for them."

I had been gone less than a month. Myron doubted if he would ever be ready. He surveyed his staff with a haggard glance. Getting up in the morning and dressing exhausted him. He avoided mirrors, didn't want to see the thinning, sandy hair and raku-splinters around his gray eyes where grief welled. His body had shrunk. Clothes hung on him like afterthoughts draped on our—on his—bedroom chair.

Years ago my husband left our twins alone in the tub to answer the door. When he returned a few moments later, Caleb was under water. In his lunge to pluck him out, Mye fell against the bathtub's cast iron enamel lip. Later, I found my husband's face in a scarlet puddle—Devon and Caleb's lily-pad of elbows and buttocks were floating in the steep-sided bath. For days afterwards, the ringing in his ears plagued him—shrill and accusing. Stress always worsened his Meniere's syndrome. Now, under this new stress of opening camp without me, his disease pounced on his brain, a blizzard of howling. But the cyclone of his illness was usually brief. Quiet would return. He had to focus. Camp would begin in less than 24 hours. He—not I—was in charge now, like it or not. He clutched the table's edge and waited for equilibrium.

"Pay day," he began, "is every other Friday. You'll need to come to my office in Stone House to pick up your check. Days off are on the schedule on my door. Counselors of the day are also posted there." He paused. "I'm sorry I wasn't here sooner to attend to things. As you undoubtedly know by now, my wife, Deidre." His voice cracked. He gulped air struggling to regain control. "Deidre died recently."

In the unnatural hush, the counselors hung their heads and snuck glances at one another. At the far end of the dining hall, the cook shuffled among her realm of hanging utensils and scarred kitchen counter tops. She sang to herself—as she often did in the kitchen—her favorite Eartha Kitt song, "My Heart's Delight," and crossed to the stove. Her soft voice filled the silence.

Our head counselor, Jake Daryl, squeaked his chair joints. "You have our deep condolences, Myron," he said. "On the business end, the W.S.I. hasn't shown up yet. Her name's Maria Azavedo, from some third-world, banana republic."

Myron brushed at a tear that lingered on his cheek. "How's her English?" he asked.

"Her job acceptance was clear enough." Jake's pencil rapped against the edge of his clip board. "We'll have to cancel beach hours tomorrow and just hope Maria gets here pronto." My husband nodded.

The art counselor, who called himself Popeye, curled his bicep into a veined knot and smacked his neck with an open palm. "You use Cutter's or Six-twelve on these fucking black flies?"

Babble erupted from the table, typical mayhem for the first staff meeting. Most of the staff had worked together in previous years. A few were new, like the missing lifeguard, Maria Azavedo. Job descriptions were one-liners. I had liked it that way. The mix of talent and vague expectations kept things interesting. It offered new opportunities for the staff and new challenges for the campers. But now that he was in charge, the uncertainty terrified my husband.

When Mye arrived to open camp that summer, he felt my departed presence everywhere. I stirred in the empty cabins, hovered above his shoulder when he replaced the sprung bed springs, and alighted with him at night like a cotton throw on the bed. He thought I was an illusion that he wished would stay with him for the rituals that initiated every season: lighting the welcome fire in the massive Stone House fireplace; the first general swim in water so cold the campers' screams shot a quarter mile into the woods; the first week when older campers jostled for recognition and the status that accompanied choices for summer romance. But without me, the familiarity of the season's beginning seemed foreign to him now.

"If you have any maintenance problems," Jake was saying, "don't bring them to me, talk to maintenance. He's skilled in plumbing, carpentry, electrical work."

Jake's wife, Fanny Daryl, raised her hand. "You know that cute little trailer out past the barn? That's the maintenance quarters."

Heads turned to Fanny, then back to Jake.

"Maintenance gets a trailer for the summer," Jake explained. "Part of the contract."

After years of being left at home for the summer, Fanny was finally joining her husband to work with him at camp. Jake had grudgingly allowed her to come, but his skepticism chided: "what the hell will you do? Knit?"

Myron, however, hired her immediately. The camp cook had a 33-old practical nurse's license from a defunct junior college outside Rochester, and she hadn't plied her medical training in two decades. Myron charged Fanny with the dual job of girls' counselor and nurse's aide. He hoped this tactic would satisfy the state requirement for medical personnel on camp premises. Jake disapproved. He thought Mye was slipping. "You don't know a thermometer from a corn cob," he had grumbled at his wife.

Fanny fidgeted under the stares. She was determined to be useful. "What do you know about twelve or thirteen year-old girls," she had challenged Jake when Myron offered her the position, "how they think, what they want? You've never bled down there for cripe's sake or had the cramps so bad you'd like to curl up and die."

Jake asked, "did you want to say something, Fanny?"

The woman squirmed in her seat. "I'll try to be the best girls' counselor and nurse's aide this camp has ever seen."

Jake glanced at the vaulted dining hall ceiling. "Jesus, Fanny," he mumbled.

The screen door creaked open and thumped shut behind a lanky young man. "Welcome, stranger," Popeye drawled.

Braddock Stringer was so lean I could smell the distressed skin stretched too tightly over his bones. He set a large case by the door. "Mr. Cravitz?"

"Shit no, man," Popeye said pointing, "that's Cravitz."

Myron shook the lad's hand. "And you are?"

"Brad Stringer."

Myron regarded the wiry figure before him, his face blank. "Brad Stringer."

"Overnights, hiking, and canoeing?"

"Of course," Mye said. "Sit down, have a pretzel. Everyone, this is Brad Stringer. Why don't we go around the table and tell him who we are and what we do." The introductions were flaccid. Popeye said, "Art, man. Fine friggin' art." The drama coach, Leon, whom Myron had hired the year before to direct the season's musical, *Annie Get Your Gun,* announced himself with a bow and then swept an open hand to Myron's new music teacher, a student at Julliard.

"Piano," she said. "You left an instrument case by the door. A cello?"

"Nah," Brad said, "that's my sitar. I made the case myself."

The pianist lifted her eyebrows; the dark skin crinkled. "A devotee of Ravi Shankar, Ali Akbar Khan?"

"Right on. Ali Akbar played at Newport in '65. After hearing him, I had to have a sitar."

Jake crossed his arms over his chest. "Orchestra?"

"Right-oh!" A six-foot-four Brit rose gangling over Brad. "Stanley Throckmorton at your service. I shall attempt to coax from the sweethearts who will grace us with their presence tomorrow some of the world's great music. I suspect, as usual, we will be a bit slight on strings and over indulgent on reeds. Perhaps you and your see-tah," he glanced at Brad's instrument case, "might be recruited to play a violin line or two?"

"Sorry, I don't read music," Brad said.

"A pity." Stanley stroked his long chin, drew a nail across its prominence. "A bloody pity. Ah well, into the breach." He smiled broadly and sat down.

The creative writing counselor was jotting notes for a poem. Popeye cupped his hands around his mouth. "Yooohooo!"

Her pencil stopped. She looked up. "Sorry. What's the question?"

"Exactly," Popeye said. "That's the question: What are you?"

"Creative writing, poems, short stories. That kind of thing." She glanced from Brad to the others around the table and bobbed her head to phantom music and rhythm. Her short, brown bangs cut straight across her brow. "And if Popeye can stomach my superior intelligence, I'll also be helping him with silk screening," she said.

"Well, now that we know each other," Jake cut in, "is there anything else that demands our immediate attention before tomorrow night's staff meeting at 9 o'clock?" A chorus of moaning.

"I say, is there a camp project in the works?" Stanley asked.

"For the new kids on the block," Jake glanced at Brad, "every year we have a camp project. Last year we produced a dinner theatre musical." He chewed his mustache. "What was the name of that thing, Leon?"

"Annie Get Your Gun," the drama coach said. "Everyone participated—actors, musicians, costumers, waiters, strike crew. The youngest campers made pudding for dessert. A great success, wouldn't you say, Stanley?"

"Indeed," Stanley mused. "A bit dicey, though, when Annie started vomiting backstage. Another act and we'd have cancelled on account of rain, Ha, ha-ha!" Stanley smacked the table to seal his joke.

"How about an Indian theme this year?" the poet said. "Maybe a potlatch?" She noted the blank looks. "It's a party where the host gives his guests presents to show them up." She looked at Popeye. "Make them feel inferior."

"Why would the host do that?" Fanny asked.

"Status," the poet said. "The more valuable the presents are, the more important the host becomes."

"What about a totem pole," Stanley offered, "like your Indian chaps from the northwest make? The Haiku or Heidi tribe."

"High-dah!" the cook called from the Kitchen. She shambled to the double Dutch doors and pushed them open. "I just read an article in the paper about raising a totem pole in the Queen Charlotte Islands. That's where the Haida people live. First totem pole they've raised in fifty years. Supposed to be a dying art, carving totem poles."

"Fabulous!" Stanley said. "It's a sign. We're resurrecting a dying art and have an expert to help us along!" The cook grunted and turned back to the grill.

Myron surveyed his staff. Traditionally, the camp project was a mountain of work. Those who had been through its demanding preparations were calculating their load. He waited for their appraisal.

"The older kids could carve, the younger ones paint something on the pole," Popeye said.

"Maintenance isn't here to defend himself," Stanley added, "but he could orchestrate cutting a suitable tree and erecting it—although I haven't the foggiest idea how."

Fanny raised her hand. "We could have a pow-wow and bonfire."

"Sounds like we have a camp project." Myron stood up. "Before we break, I have a few announcements. Fanny, one of your campers is diabetic. I've got her name somewhere." He fingered a clutter of paper. "You may need to monitor her medicine."

Fanny's face paled. She raised her hand. Jake barred his teeth at her. She pulled her arm to her side.

Myron shuffled through the sheets. "Brad, a kid from the Upstate New York Children's Home will be in your cabin. Keep an eye on him. He may need some special attention."

Mye dropped his notes on the table. "Anything I've forgotten?"

My husband had forgotten plenty, but he'd hear about it soon enough from returning staff, the 'retreads' as we called them. Their help would be critical—and he knew it.

"All right." Mye consulted his watch. "Dinner's in an hour."

The chairs scraped back. Fanny extended a shy hand to Brad. "I'm Frances Daryl, by the way. Call me Fanny. Nurse's aide and girls' counselor."

The dining hall emptied. Our cook's song drifted out from the galley. The Julliard student lingered with a pretzel and strolled to the kitchen. Together they sang the chorus to "My Heart's Delight" with its ache of loving to distraction. Helpless love.

Chapter Three

Haskell glared at Kurt. "This map is worthless," the man said to the boy beside him in the front passenger seat of the car. "It says turn right after the first bridge. We've gone two miles. What right turn? Roads aren't even marked up here." A three-inch scar ended in a dimpled blemish on Haskell's weak chin.

Kurt figured Haskell was a complainer. Most adults were either complainers or glad-handers. Sometimes a smacker showed up. You had to watch your step with a smacker. They'd be talking calmly one minute and smacking the back of your head the next. The weirdest stuff set them off. Best to say, "Yes, sir. No, ma'am," to whatever they asked. Best to watch your back because they'd never hit you in the face; that left marks, the kind that got them fired at the home. Most smackers didn't last. But eventually, another always took their place.

The late June sun shimmered on distant water. Birds darted and swooped across a passing meadow, and settled at its periphery in the foliage. Kurt had yet to learn the names of the shrubs: partridge berry and ground pine.

So, this is the glorious Adirondacks, the boy thought. When they told him about the camp, he was okay with that. Better than staying at the home all summer. There were trees, mountains, lakes, and streams all over the place. Maybe there were mountain lions. That would be cool. Kurt had never gone to a real camp before. Most of the older residents went sooner or later. In his case, at 13, he was older than anyone else at the home besides a stuttering, booger-picking, 14-year-old girl. If you hit 13 and hadn't been adopted, they said you were un-graftable.

He'd been to the petting zoo near the home lots of times. He liked watching the 4- and 5- year-olds with the goats. Haskell gave each kid a paper bag of food to feed the animals. But the kids didn't watch their bags and the goats stole them, brown teeth ripping into the popcorn and raisins. The littlest ones, the ones still cute enough to be adopted, cried. Sad and funny at the same time, Kurt thought.

Once in the spring and once in the fall, they went on an all-home picnic. As an older resident, he helped with preparations and got special privileges. Table lights out at 9:30 instead of 9:00. Big deal. The dim, barracks overhead light always stayed on—a black circle of dead insects in the bottom of the plastic cover. Coffee on Saturday morning. Now *that* was something to write home about—if he had a home. Special privileges really meant special duties. He made and packed the tuna fish and egg salad sandwiches, a so-called *honor*. Kurt also sorted the mail. Some privilege. It only took a few minutes. Nobody got much mail.

He hadn't always lived at the home. The week before his sixth birthday, a scrawny, skittish woman and her husband took him in. Their round, backyard pool—water rippling the chest-high plastic sides—crowded their small yard. Where the lawn thinned under a silver maple, she had planted Bermuda grass to conquer the mud. They allowed swimming during his second year with them and cautioned him to clean his feet with the hose before entering and after leaving the water. They reminded him to use the plastic ladder which clung to the vinyl side like an insult.

When the woman wasn't watching, he'd vault over the three-foot rim, flood her new sod, and wipe out his army compound of plastic soldiers positioned within the tree's encircling hummock of roots.

"Use the ladder, Kurt!" she would shout from the back door.

"Sorry," he'd shout back. He wasn't sorry.

Kurt thought they were okay, but their real son treated him like crap. The older boy spit on Kurt's dessert when the adults weren't looking and punched him in the shoulders so often—middle knuckle spiking the fist—that Kurt had permanent, plumb-colored bruises at the center of both stringy muscles. Kurt didn't flinch. He had discovered early that recoiling from the blows pleased the bully. Kurt wouldn't give him the satisfaction.

Ahead, dense woods squeezed the road. As they approached a tunnel of trees, the light changed color. Haskell said, "Did you pack two pairs of swimming trunks like the letter said?"

"Yes."

"You're lucky to be chosen for camp, you know."

"So I've been told. Repeatedly."

"You're still on probation. Hey, look at me. You never look at me when I'm talking to you."

"I gave it back," the boy said evenly.

"That's not the point, Willington. You stole the watch in the first place. What's wrong with you?"

"I didn't steal it. I borrowed it."

"Yeah, like you borrowed the sweater?"

"He gave me that sweater. The jerk said that to pay me back for losing the food fight —which he started."

Haskell saw our sign nailed to the ash: "Cravitz Fine Arts Camp, Welcome!" and the camp entrance just beyond. He turned into the road surrounded by Ringer's Field on the right and our pasture of tall grass on the left. The road stretched to a line of trees and disappeared into them. He slowed the car and rolled down his window as the sedan bumped along dual ruts. On each of the front car doors, 'Upstate New York Children's Home,' formed a circle. Under the Great Seal of New York, and inside the circle in script: 'Caring and Teaching.'

"You'd better watch your *behind,* Kurt. Headmaster alerted the camp about you. Do us all a big favor. Just stay out of trouble. Okay? Why is it so hard for you to stay out of trouble?"

The four-door pulled a thin cloak of dust into the ballfield and rustled an isthmus of weeds behind our three, paint-shedding sets of bleachers.

Kurt was too old, un-graftable.

When he was little, before being adopted, he gathered with the others in the Day Room as the couples strolled the line searching for the perfect child. To prepare for the *showing,* as they called it, they matted his unruly red hair with fruity smelling oil so it would lay flat. His freckles were unfortunate. Not much could be done with them, as though erasing the galaxy of spots would somehow make him a better little boy.

The car passed the tennis court with its jagged stalks of garlic mustard Myron had clipped to green stubble. Beyond the court, Popeye was sweeping out his screened-in work hut. The dirt flew from the open door and settled on the stairs. Above the hut's entrance: "Art & Sculpture."

When his adoptive parents finally chose him as their foster child, Kurt Willington was happy—and terrified. The home delivered him and his new suitcase in a taxi. Within 5 minutes, they told him, "don't touch" pointing to the do-dads that filled their floor-to-ceiling shelves under the stairs. When he later broke a small glass horse, she spanked him on the backs of his thighs. Not hard, though, not like their real child's savage, relentless punches he'd endure.

They introduced him to visitors as "our other son, Kurt." They never told their guests he was adopted, but the visitors must have known. He was 6 when he went to live with them. He wanted to talk to them about his real mother and father, but they always changed the subject.

"You *could* have been our real son," she said. "We both have red hair."

That didn't help. Kurt's birth mother had given him away. What was it about him that made her do that, he wondered?

During third grade, his adoptive parents vacationed in Ft. Lauderdale with their son. On their way back the three of them were killed in a car accident. The woman's sister confronted Kurt after the funeral.

"You should have died too, sonny," she hissed. "If you hadn't gotten the measles and stayed with me the week they were gone, you'd be laid out in there with them." The home asked if she would take him in and the woman tearfully refused. "He tears up his room, deliberately breaks things. I won't repeat the filthy things he's said to me and my sister. She suffered long enough with him. Let someone else manage."

But there was no one else. So, they sent him back to the home.

The car crested our drive's small knoll. New arrivals streamed back and forth on the patchy grass and makeshift roads Mye and I had bushwhacked years before. Creeping autos dodged pedestrians in rheumatic starts and stops. My parents' rambling, two-story log hotel sagged on its rock and mortar foundation. Its porch—front lattice nudging the oval drive's crushed rocks—wrapped each side of Stone House in a broad hug.

Match Lake's fierce, silver expanse sparkled beyond the main house. On the far shore, faint vegetation smeared the horizon. Remote mountains hung in a slur above the trees. Kurt's eyes settled on the narrow beach. On-shore waves lapped at the pilings that staggered into the water under our worn dock. He unrolled his window and inhaled the water's breath.

Haskell stopped in the circular drive by the flagless pole. Brad Stringer leaned on the car's open window and introduced himself to the driver, then strolled to the boy's side.

"I'm Brad. Welcome to Cravitz Fine Arts Camp. What's your talent, Kurt?"

The home hadn't told Kurt he needed a talent. "I'm good at making tuna fish sandwiches—and defending myself."

Kurt held up his fist, slender fingers clenched, knuckles white under the pale skin.

Brad nodded. "Fair enough. Sometimes though, it's better to back away from a fight."

"For you, maybe."

I knew I was going to like this boy.

Kids arrived all morning, 12-year-old Reginald Farrouk among them. He had never been to an arts camp. The Chess Club Day Camp, yes. Young Friends of Mexico, *¡por supuesto!* Of course! And his favorite, Future Astronauts of America—for 3 years running—but never an arts camp, or an over-nighter.

His psychiatrist father had authored several well-known books: *Coping with Crisis; The Ape in Us All; Sock It To Me;* and most recently (and not selling well) *Sock It To Me With Feeling.* Dr. Farrouk felt Reginald needed time away from his parents and older brother. And the doctor's wife wanted to give their younger son the psychological space his artistic sensibilities required. Brookside Academy for the Gifted, while a fine school, didn't channel the boy's intuitive side.

"Reginald needs to be with others experimenting in the arts," Mrs. Farrouk told her husband after reading our camp brochure.

"Well, if he's going to be a physician, the experience might enhance his bedside manner," Dr. Farrouk said.

"Maybe *you* should have taken art lessons," she said.

Reginald and his father had driven all morning from New Jersey. Dr. Farrouk was more than ready to stop. When they reached camp, he got out and stretched to his toes. He stood up with a grunt and slammed the car door.

"Reginald, help me with the footlocker."

The boy squeezed over the seats into the station wagon's cargo space and helped his father slide the Kelly-green trunk onto the open tailgate. He jumped out and slipped his stout, dark-framed glasses off to clean the lenses with his shirt tail. Children swirled around him in smears of indistinct clothing and blurred faces. Duffle bags lolled on the sparse grass—like drunks sleeping it off in Passaic Park, the boy thought.

What a creative imagination this boy had. Although his eyesight was less than perfect, the simile was apt.

Reginald slipped the glasses back on. "Let's track down a counselor," his father said.

They headed for a wooden cabin with a roof Reginald surmised was moss. Gauzy strips and rectangles quilted our battle-worn screens. Trap-door shutters, propped open with poles, were ready to be slammed shut in cool or bad weather. Above the entrance, Myron's freshly painted plank—'Black Bear'—hung precariously.

Dr. Farrouk poked his head inside the cabin. With him, I sniffed the damp mattress, dirty laundry, balsam, and new paint aroma that—even here in death's dimension—leaves a fingerprint.

"Anybody home?" he called.

A tow-headed kid leaned out from a sagging, upper bunk. "Nobody's here right now 'cept me," he said.

"Who's in charge?" the doctor asked.

"Beats me."

"What's going on, dad?"

The man let the screen door bang shut. "Indeterminate," he said to Reginald, and then, "beats me."

"Comin' through!" Two boys burst past and dove into bunks. Moments later, Reginald heard them jumping from mattress to mattress. The springs shrieked.

Dr. Farrouk squinted through the screen. "The furies have arrived. I hope law and order isn't far behind."

On their way back to the car, Fanny, in her nurses' simulacra of white stretch pants and open white jacket, stopped them. "Who do we have here?" She hugged her clipboard.

"We have Reginald Farrouk. I'm his father, Lester."

"Frances Daryl, nurse's aide. Call me Fanny."

Fanny shook the doctor's hand, dropped her clipboard, and in the lunge to catch it jabbed Reginald's nose with her right breast.

"Clumsy me! All my life I've been clumsy." She stooped to retrieve the board. Reginald was already there. They bonked heads.

"This is terrible," she fretted. "I'm so sorry. Are you all right?"

"He's fine." Lester took the clipboard from his son and gave it to the woman. "No broken skulls."

"I'm okay," Reginald said.

"That's a relief," she said.

Reginald had never been assaulted by a woman's breast. Kind of nice, he thought. Forlorn curls of blond hair draped Fanny's ears and wan cheeks. Her eyes were crooked, the right intent on Reginald's mouth, the left on his ear. Inflamed threads of crimson rimmed her eyelids. Brown, pencil-thin cigarette tips poked from her white coat pocket.

Fanny held her hand out to Reginald as though reaching for a bit of food. He shook her fingertips. "Anyway, nice to meecha, Reggi. Do you have a bunk assignment yet?"

"Excuse me, my name has three syllables, Reg-i-nald," the boy said. "No, I don't."

"Okay, let's see then," Fanny ran her finger down the clip board. "You're in the Wolf Cabin for boys twelve and up." She confirmed this research with a finger-tap on his name and pointed to a cabin among pines. "Your counselor is Brad Stringer. Just put your footlocker by the bunk you want. I'll be around if you need me."

She departed waving two fingers. They watched her cross the road to meet a car in the oval drive. When she bent forward to greet the driver, she dropped her clipboard again.

Dr. Farrouk knew it was time to go. He shook his son's hand and then hugged him. "Write to your brother. He'd appreciate it," he said. Reginald waved to his father as the departing station wagon kicked up dust.

The boy's perceptions were delightfully straight forward. The nurse is a klutz, he thought. He didn't need Dr. Farrouk to interpret Fanny's inadequacy. "All my life I've been clumsy," she had said. Reginald could identify. Lately, his own body had been blundering through some physical dilemmas.

When his older brother, Skip, came home from boarding school, he had pulled Reginald into his room and shut the door. "Cop an eyeball on these, Squirt."

From the magazine's dog-eared pages, nude women in a contortion of poses seemed ready to wink at him. Others peered off into the distance, their downy, pubic hair ("intriguing muffs, huh, Squirt?") covered what the boy had decided was the mysterious triangle.

Reginald knew that breasts made babies' milk. "They're mammary glands, not ornaments," he had admonished a friend at school. And his own pubic hair had recently sprouted in wisps above his penis. He was maturing. But what did that mean, exactly?

Skip pointed to a reclining woman. "How'd you like to wake up with *that* suckin' the tootsie roll?" A quizzical thing for him to say. He asked his brother about it, but Reginald knew a brush-off when he heard it. "In a couple years, you'll be having the spasms like the rest of us and going all the way with the babes, Squirt."

Going all the way. Going where he wondered? In 2 years?—that was 24 months. He did the math: 720 days. Forever.

Viewing the pictures gave him what his brother called a 'hard-on;' Reginald speculated (he had muddled but ardent instincts) that the hard-on was an important piece of the puzzle. His penis crept up his underwear, strained against the cotton, and throbbed in time to his heartbeat. Pleasant—in an odd sort of way.

"You can't shoot pool with a limp cue, Squirt," his brother told him. Reginald would have an urge to pee, but couldn't until he wilted again. Sometimes at night, a similar urge would wake him. More than once he had grabbed his penis to keep from what he assumed would be wetting the bed. Embarrassed, Reginald asked his brother about it.

Skip was typically vague. "Wet dream, Squirt. Don't sweat it." But Reginald was mortified. He'd almost wet the bed. He'd finished seventh grade and was going into eighth, only two months away from being a teenager.

Reginald's father had defined copulation for him. They were uncoiling the garden hose after its winter storage in their Huntington garage.

"Yes, I understand," Reginald said. "But doesn't something happen when the man's penis deposits sperm in the woman's vagina?"

"What happens," his father said, "is love, Reginald. Sex. When two people care deeply for each other."

"Yeah, I know. But isn't there something that makes you get weird, makes you have spasms or something?"

"Spasms?" His father's slow motion chuckle always irritated him. "Don't worry about it. When the time comes, all the details will fall into place."

"I'm not worried, Dad. I'm confused."

36

His father peered down at him, "Son, how old are you?"

Reginald yanked the last few feet of hose off the roll. The classic example of a rhetorical question. He had learned in American Civics that attorneys used rhetorical questioning when quizzing suspects. They only asked questions they already knew the answers to. End of discussion.

"Almost thirteen. You know that, Dad."

"You understand everything you need to for almost thirteen."

His father was stalling. His brother was inscrutable. This summer, Reginald promised himself, he'd find out what they were—and weren't—talking about. This summer he'd go all the way if it killed him.

Hunched on footlockers, anxious campers waited for instructions on either side of our oval drive. Parents worked the travel from stiff necks or stood in pairs gawking at the swarming melee.

"Hey, Rope," a boy called.

"Scotty, you're back!" Rope submitted to Scotty's head lock and quick release.

"What's the umbrella for?" Scotty asked.

"Mom thinks I'll catch pneumonia like my cousin."

"I got a cousin with only four fingers on his left hand. Cut his pinkie off with a power saw."

Rope dropped the umbrella, clutched his hand, and sank to his knees. "I'm crippled forever." He grimaced and clamped his eyes shut. "Will my hand be all right, doctor?"

"Son," Scotty scuffed his voice to baritone, "you've had a close call, but I think I can sew it back on." He fiddled with Rope's clawed fingers. "There. And be more careful next time. That'll be a thousand dollars."

"A thousand dollars?" Rope snatched his umbrella and plunged it at his friend's stomach. Scotty howled, pirouetted clutching his belly, and crumpled onto the grass.

A blue Cadillac with Rhode Island tags pulled into the drive at the front of the lodge and stopped with a jolt. The back window scrolled down and a small suitcase emblazoned with a black horse flew out onto the lawn. A petite, 10-year-old pushed the back door open with her legs. "I thought this place would be bigger," she said.

The front doors of the Cadillac opened. Smoke curled onto the roof. The girl's father, a stout man with a dying cigar in plump, ring-adorned fingers heaved out of the car. Black chest hair bloomed from the open collar of his Hawaiian shirt. The girl's mother, a small woman, emerged in a skirt and matching suit coat.

The man shoved the cigar in the corner of his mouth. He held our thin, camp pamphlet. "It says here Match Lake's southwest pebble beach was formed by moraine deposits during the Ice Age." He rolled the cigar to the opposite corner. "The lake is five square miles bounded by white pine on the northeast." They both wore sunglasses.

The woman followed her lumbering husband up our thick wooden stairs to the dark interior of the lodge. At a long wooden table stacked with information, Jake Daryl interlaced his fingers and smiled unconvincingly at them. "Welcome to Camp Cravitz. Name please?"

"Our daughter, Maura Thurley," he began.

"She's small for her age," his wife interrupted, "but mature for her years. I assume she will be rooming with girls of similar interests and talents?"

"All our campers are talented," Jake said. "Thurley. Thurley. Here she is. She'll bunk with musicians, artists, thespians."

"What?" the woman gasped, eyes wide. "My daughter will not room with lesbians!"

"Thespians. You know, actors, drama. Theater?"

The woman softened; the whites of her eyes diminished. "I see, of course. Maura is a talented pianist. The literature said she would have expert music teachers and ample time to practice."

"Our piano teacher is a Julliard student. We have two music sheds and there's a Baldwin piano here in the lodge."

"A Baldwin," Mrs. Thurley exhaled the word with contempt, "Oh, my."

Jake asked where their daughter waited and suggested to her parents that they tour the camp. Maura would be shown to Hiawatha Cabin, and they could help her unpack later.

Outside, Maura was bantering with the two boys, Scotty and Rope. "This is my first summer at Camp Cravitz. Is it your first summer?"

"Guess," said Scotty. Rope giggled.

"Honestly," the girl said. "You're so immature. I'll bet you're not ten yet."

"Am too," said Scotty. "And Rope's almost ten."

"Rope? What kind of a name is that?"

"Short for Rupert. What's your name?"

"Maureen but everyone calls me Maura. You can call me Maura if you want. I play the piano. I'm small for my age, but mature for my years."

Rope appraised her. "I think I'll call you ..." he balanced his glance between Maura and Scotty who waited wide-eyed, mouth tight. "I think I'll call you Shortstack."

Scotty's laughter exploded in braying snorts. He turned and limped toward the boys' cabins, his left arm dangling. "Come Igor," he called back to Rope, "we must feed the monster."

I can't smile in this realm, but I remember the feeling of teeth exposed and lips parted. Shortstack and I watched them go. "Honestly," the girl said shaking her head like a midget matron.

Chapter Four

The stainless steel coffee pot belched through a second percolation. With his fingers, Myron circled a chink on his desk. The pitcher's reflection made his hand grotesque. He wondered about Maria Azavedo, the absent, 21-year-old life guard from Colombia, a vague, mountainous place that grew the coffee he had consumed all morning. He squinted at the spattered window. Did Jake give her the wrong starting date? It didn't make much difference. Rain had persisted since dawn and even the hardy avoided Match Lake in June.

Among the letters on his desk was a personal and gently reproachful memo from the Match village fire chief who reminded my husband that unauthorized placement of a hot plate in the barn dated from the summer before. Also a notice from the County Health Commission about unsanitary storage room conditions in the main dining lounge. Myron smiled at the dining hall's lofty title. Our handyman, Alex, called it: the mess. Lastly, a realty contract—with a note—requesting his signature to finalize the property's availability:

Dear Myron:

The funeral's simple elegance befitted such a strong and loving woman. Again, my most sincere condolences. I hope this last season without Deidre won't be too much of a strain on you. I know how much the camp meant to her. Please be assured the respect I will give in offering the property for sale is only overshadowed by the respect

I felt for the woman. She was a fine teacher as our son, Walter, has told us so often.

Please check the utility easement (item six). I believe all else is in order according to our earlier discussions.

Sincerely,
Emile W. Barr
Barr & Harcourt, LC

Enclosure

P.S. Give Colleen my love. At 16, my niece had other ideas for the summer, but I impressed upon her parents the unique opportunity two months in the Adirondacks would provide for their daughter. Colleen's feisty, but at heart very sweet.

Myron folded the letter and reinserted it into the envelope. He opened the contract, signed his name at the bottom, and slid the document into a new, stamped envelope addressed to Emile W. Barr. He tossed the letter into the plastic vegetable bin I had years earlier labeled "outgoing mail." That's that, he thought.

He pushed himself away from the desk, walked to the streaked window, and with his hand swept the condensation away to observe the lake. His warm breath obscured the pane in a widening iris. An arc of beach moistened over, then the pier, canoes, and jumbled pontoons fogged up until the lake itself vanished. For the time being, he would keep the camp's for-sale status a secret. No need to distract the campers or worry the staff.

"Myron?" Jake Daryl rapped on the office door and pushed it open.

"Morning, Jake." Mye motioned to the coffee. "I was just thinking about the waterfront. Have we heard from the W.S.I.?"

"Nope." A mordant smile exposed Jake's uneven teeth. "But when we do, you ought to make her queen for a day." Jake removed his tweed beret, slapped at his rumpled hair, and tossed his cap on the desk. The sandalwood candle—a gift to my husband—flickered. The homemade, mean-spirited card I had written said: "Happy Unfather's Day." During our marriage, it was the only time Mye ever slapped me. We both cried. I promised forgiveness. His hunger for it made me keep the pledge—mostly. Myron, for his part, offered hope: amulets we hung on every word and touch.

"Emile Barr's niece is here this summer," Myron said. "Colleen. She's sixteen. Might be good CIT material next year if ..." he paused. Next year. Where would he be at this time next year? Where would any of them be?

"I've got my eye on Betsy for the art hut," Jake said. "Third year in a row. She's almost sixteen, I think." Jake slipped a mug from the cup tree and filled it. "Bitchy weather. The black flies never let up, not even in the rain." He took a sip. "Decided on the camp project yet?"

The question annoyed Myron. He thought the camp project had been resolved. "I think the Indian theme will work. What were the options we discussed again?"

Jake sipped his coffee. "A pow-wow and bonfire would be easiest."

"We have a bonfire every year."

"Not on the beach. The counselors could dress up. Stanley could—I don't know, play the tom-tom. Leon could do a little dance around the fire, give a dramatic reading." Jake set his coffee down and tugged at his scrotum, "By the shores of Gitche Gumee." He thumped his chest, "by the shining big sea water."

Mye smiled at the spectacle. "We'd better leave out the Gitche Gumee."

"We could turn the pasture into a tepee village. Maybe use the old drop cloths in the barn."

"We threw those out."

"There's always—the potlatch!"

Mye sighed at Jake's sarcasm. "A bonfire and pow-wow are fine," he said, "but we need a project. Something the campers can sink their teeth into." He tapped quietly on his desk. "Didn't Stanley suggest a totem pole?"

Jake blew at his coffee's steamy surface. "Yeah. What a crock. That's all we need, twenty feet of graffiti." Daryl snapped his fingers. "I've got an idea. How many canoes do we have?"

"Five or six."

"And archery sets?"

"A half dozen. What do you have in mind, reenacting the French and Indian Wars?"

"No," Jake tried to sound patient, "what I have in mind is an Indian-style Olympics. Bow and arrow matches, Indian wrestling, canoe races, maybe some crafts."

"Canoe races are too dangerous, Jake."

"No more dangerous than archery."

"Some children don't swim."

"Kids don't do a lot of things. That's why parents pack them off to camp." Jake leaned both hands on the desk. "They swim if they're taught. They drown when the lifeguard's away." He blew out the candle and straightened up. "If she ever shows up, this Maria woman's supposed to be an expert."

Myron snorted with anger. I always knew when Mye's irritation was about to surface. "Someone was at the door." He raised his voice, "I was only gone a minute or two."

"Get over it, Myron. It's water under the bridge, an unfortunate lapse in judgment. One of the twins should have been in the crib. You should have taken the other one with you when you answered the door. You said so yourself. Am I right, or am I right?"

Myron looked out at the rain. "Why is it a crock?"

"What?"

"The totem pole. Popeye could teach the older kids to carve. The younger campers could paint. This is a fine arts camp."

Jake bit and released his lower lip. "It's a bad idea because we'd have to cut down a damn tree. Who's gonna do that? Your handyman Vietnam veteran? Number two, we'd have to haul it up here with—let me think—the camp bus? Third, can you see some of the ding-a-lings in this place with a Bowie knife carving their initials, much less an eagle or buffalo or whatever the hell you put on totem poles? And then," Jake snuggled into his cap, "we'd have to hire the Match Lake fire department to put the thing up for us." He took a final gulp of coffee. "Besides, none of the Indians around here made totem poles. Thanks for the coffee. Let me know what you come up with."

Myron doubted Jake ever talked to me with such condescension. At the front window, my husband watched him stride up the muddy road to the dining hall. Myron lifted his coffee cup. "To the totem pole," he muttered at Jake's receding back and drank.

The next morning, Myron drove to the library in Tupper Lake. He rummaged through the Periodical Index, reproduced on the library's new Xerox copier machine two *National Geographic* magazine articles, and checked out *The Wolf and the Raven: Totem Poles of the Queen Charlottes.*

"We're building a totem pole," he told the librarian.

"That's nice. It's due in six weeks." She stamped the book on the inside front cover and slid it back to him.

From the library, he went to the Tupper Lake Hardware Store, a wood-shingled building with two China-white rockers at the end of a long, unpainted front porch. Poking from lengths of stove pipe, artificial irises slap-dashed across the banister. A carved, life-sized Indian hunkered by the door, its leg shackled to an iron ring secured in the planking. I remember when I first saw that poor Indian in his leg-iron. I couldn't have been more than 12.

Inside, 100 varieties of do-it-yourself optimism overflowed from crowded aisles and wall shelves: shovels in barrels;

bins heavy with nails; stacked raingear; pairs of sour-smelling leather boots; peg-boarded spanners; cheap, $1 screw drivers; pliers filling buckets.

"I need twelve, one-inch brushes, twelve, two-inch brushes, six, three-inch brushes," he told the proprietor who glanced at him inquiringly.

"Anything else?" the clerk asked.

"A gallon each: white, black."

"Snow Drift," the salesman said. "Midnight."

"Red."

"Sunset Brick," the clerk lifted the handle and heaved the can from the shelf onto the counter.

"Blue."

"What kind of blue? We got Blueberry, Twilight."

"Blueberry's good." The store owner moved his step stool for each new color. "Green," Myron said.

"Moss or Deep Sea?"

"Do you have something," Mye swept his hand across paint-can row, "that's dragon-scale green?"

The clerk smiled. "Let me see. How about Old Irish Pasture?"

"Perfect. And yellow. No, that yellow, the canary yellow."

"Sunburst Yellow," the salesman read from the label. He took the green and yellow cans from the shelves and swung them onto the front counter. "What else?" he asked enjoying himself.

"A couple dozen packets of garnet sandpaper, grades sixty to one-eighty, five gallons of kerosene. Wood carving mallets and tools."

"I got chisels."

"Are they beveled on the back?" The clerk showed Myron what he had. "No, I need wood carving chisels. Adzes and gouges and V-tools and cabinet makers' scrapers."

"You'd best try Saranac Lake for things like that."

With both hands supporting a box piled with the purchased items, the proprietor jammed his chin into the paint brush bag to steady the load. He eased himself down the porch steps toe-tapping one tread at a time until he found the bottom. After loading the paint, the kerosene, and a second box, the store owner slammed the car's trunk.

"I hope the project goes well. Don't be a stranger now, Mr. Cravitz. Come back and see us again."

Myron stopped last at the Saranac Lake Art Shoppe. "This isn't one of those hippie art colonies." The sales clerk waved a dismissive hand, "you'll have to go to Syracuse for things like that." Myron decided he'd make a special trip that week to Syracuse or Albany and visit the college art departments for information on supplies. He would personally design and carve the totem pole's crown.

Driving back, Myron remembered the cool, bright-hazed mornings before camp started when he and I had sipped coffee on the Stone House veranda overlooking the lake, steam from our cups rising like fog above the calm water.

"We'd better get the tar paper off Eagle Feather's west side so it can air," I had said. "And for once, let's get the bus fixed *before* camp opens." I had suddenly put a finger to my mouth and stopped the white cane rocker.

"Listen," I whispered, "loons!" To Myron, the reedy calls were an old argument's redundant stalemate, Pandora's box freeing a millennium of sorrow. The echo skimmed the lake, died, and then welled up again. "Listen!" I remember feeling—radiant, I think.

Once, after soaking up what Mye called the loon's melancholy, he asked me if I believed in reincarnation.

"I don't always vote a straight party ticket," I said.

"What does that have to do with it?"

"Well, I'm open-minded, but it seems we've had this discussion before. You were about to be locked in a public stockade for disturbing the peace in some little Massachusetts town. I was trying to placate the mob that gathered to fling dirt clods and spit at you. The first time we met you said, wasn't it? As I recall, 1660 or thereabouts. Funny thing is I don't remember the intervening 300 odd years."

"I'm serious. The person you were in Massachusetts helped me. Now you're Deidre. After you die, you'll become someone else." He was sorry as soon as he said it.

"Some of us," I said, "don't have time to become anything." Devon would have been 10, probably taller than her brother, Caleb, typical for girls at that age. "My father never told me I was a particular twinkle in his eye before my birth, if that's what you mean," I said.

"That's not what I mean. Look, where does a flame go when it goes out?"

I massaged my temples. "In physics, not my favorite class, I learned that for every action there is an opposite and equal reaction. So, I guess the flame's energy is converted into the energy needed to make it go out." I patted under my chin with the backs of my fingers. "Is that right?" I asked myself.

"Think metaphysically, Deidre. Where does the flame go when you blow it out?"

"Ah, I see what you're driving at. In other words, do I believe in reincarnation?" I set my coffee cup on the railing and raised my palm. "Agnostic."

"I think it's highly possible, likely in fact."

"So you've said before."

"It's logical." Myron rocked forward in his chair, upended the curved back runners, and pointed to the shoreline. "Do you believe that tree at the edge of the lake gets bigger every year?"

"The white birch? Sure, because I can see it grow."

"No! You see the results of its growth. It grows much too slowly to actually see it happening."

"What's your point, love?"

"Continuity." He let the rockers drop again. "Just because the body dies doesn't mean its spirit perishes too."

Myron always had a way of charming me into corners.

"Mye," I said, "when this body drags though its final summer up here, it's not only going to die, it's going to turn in all copyrights."

That finally made him smile. "Okay, but if I go before you do, plan on a few visits from a former Massachusetts citizen."

Of course, Myron survived all of us. And now I visited him in moments of lassitude, in remembered frivolous conversation that wrenched his heart. He vowed that our memorial must be more than the three white alabaster slabs in New Jersey.

Myron slowed the car for the familiar deep curve around Hickory Hill. He lowered the visor against the sun. *The twins died a long time ago,* I said to him in a language still new to me. My words—debris—swirled in his head.

At the hillock's bottom where the north and south running highway carved its own valley, Myron passed into a long stretch of cool shade. His Meniere's tinnitus—like cicadas—flew toward him, far away but closing in. The insects' wings buzzed his ears, muffled his hearing, and then a train whistle shrieked. He had no control over it and could only wait for the shrillness to retreat on the winding track of his disease.

Poor Myron.

He checked the rear view mirror. Only the highway's swath parted the lush growth. Mye eased the car onto the shoulder and let it roll to a stop. He recalled that he hadn't eaten since morning. Too much salt at breakfast? That sometimes worsened the symptoms. He took several deep breaths as the wailing changed pitch.

I'm right here, I told him.

Then he saw the bear loping gracefully out of the woods into the still, wet meadow. Its shaggy, black belly flattened the tall grass. The animal stopped and reared on hind legs, majestic, fearless. It sniffed the air, dropped onto all fours, and disappeared into the forest. The cicadas swarmed back into the brush. The train in his head derailed and plunged into a quieting canyon.

Chapter Five

Reginald hunched above his sketch tablet, feet folded under him. The bed springs squeaked as he sat up to consider his next sentence to his brother, Skip. Above him, the upper bunk's pendulous belly grazed his hair. He waited for the springs to calm before crouching again:

> I've also signed up for the drama workshop and *Summerbook*. Robin, the creative writing counselor, says my poems are freaky but cool. Popeye (art) says I show a talent for sketching (duh!). I'm working on a charcoal and ink of Stone House. That's the main building where the older girls live upstairs. There's a huge fireplace that smells a little like Uncle Jack only better and a porch all along the back of the lodge where you can see out into the lake. It's really great here.
>
> Leon (drama) is weird, clinically weird, you know what I mean? Like, he tries to hide his really loud farts by giving these boring lectures in the performance barn. "Breath is the essence of acting," he says, all the time farting, "just as sight," (faaaaart, fftt, fart) "allows us to understand Picasso's soul." Does he think we can't hear him? The man could use a few sessions with dad.
>
> We've just started rehearsing a play called *Butterfly Girl and Mirage Boy*. Cheryl Mariano plays Butterfly Girl. It's about an Indian girl who sees and hears an invisible boy. Cheryl studied drama

and diction at the Children's Studio in New York City.

Reginald unfolded his legs and thought about Cheryl. She was an eighth-grader going into ninth, a bit taller than he was with blond hair she flung around like a shampoo commercial. On the cusp of narcissism, he thought. When he got to know her better, he'd tell her about Narcissus.

"She sure is beautiful though," he said under his breath and crouched again:

> Here's a poem I wrote. You see, the toilets and showers for the older girls are upstairs in Stone House. I was in the upstairs lounge fooling around on the piano. The bathroom is right down the hall and Cheryl went in to take a shower. I could tell because she had her towel, and shampoo and clothes all rolled together. She didn't quite latch the door. It swung open four or five inches.

> > I was waiting to see you
> > step naked from the tub
> > After your shower.
> > Would you ask me
> > to shut the door and leave please,
> > or invite me in
> > to see your mysterious triangle?
> > Now after walking back to my bunk
> > In the rain,
> > I realize my dreams will never come true
> > until I make them.

> I've also created the Farroukian system of counting from one to ten in case you're apprehended

by aliens (who will surely know advanced mathematics):

> Fart
>
> Forest
>
> Transform
>
> Obscure
>
> Sketch
>
> Cheryl
>
> Playful
>
> Lake
>
> Idiot
>
> Peanut butter

You have my permission to use this advanced mathematical code on any future correspondence. I'm already on page "obscure," so I'll say "adieu" or "a don't" which is a Farroukian salutation that means "so long for now."

REGINALD (written and mailed in the year: fart, idiot, Cheryl, idiot).

I wish I had met this boy when I was living. My transubstantiation is panoramic but fleshless. The virtual eye beholds, but you can't eat the peanut butter. At least the smells of life still linger in my memory's plasma, olfaction's symphony.

Yes, the camp held a symphony of aromas. I could smell the sycamore bark Myron lit into a curl of smoke. From the fireplace, he moved back to his chair. Moments later the younger kids, sweaty from an after-dinner game of capture the flag, stormed in. They tumbled at his feet in the large Stone House foyer and faced the catching blaze. The older campers lounged on the veranda overlooking the lake or drifted off together into the cooling dusk outside. I remember Mye's awkward attempts at keeping up with the children when he and I first opened the camp. He had since learned not to try, and let the younger staff wear them out.

Myron inhaled the children's crushed grass and wild onion smell. He clapped his hands, pulled their eyes to him, and began reading from his library book, *The Wolf and the Raven*.

"Long ago the Haida did not know how to carve, so Master Carver taught them." Their attention settled on his gaunt face. "Master Carver wore a wooden headdress—carved and painted—and a blanket shirt woven of mountain goat wool ornamented with designs. Under the shirt, his body was painted with totem figures. A halo of bright light shone around him. Human faces covered his finger nails, each with a different expression."

Scotty nudged Rope and bug-eyed his fingernails.

"Master Carver told the Haida, 'Tonight go to bed as usual and pay no attention to anything you hear. Don't look until the sun is up.' During the night the people heard chopping, but they covered their heads and restrained their curiosity as Master Carver had instructed them."

Rope pantomimed destruction with an axe. Myron snapped his fingers at him. "In the morning," Mye read, "the corner posts inside the house were painted with animal and human figures. Outside, three carved poles had appeared, one at the entrance to the house and one at either corner—all carved and painted. The people were amazed. These were the first such beings they had ever seen." Myron's young audience listened, spellbound.

Scotty and Rope thumb-wrestled.

"Each day for ten days, Master Carver pointed to one of the faces on his nails and explained the expression behind it. Thus, lesson by lesson, he taught the Haida their carving secrets. He showed them what medicines to take and what training would be necessary to become successful totem pole makers."

My husband shut the book. "Does anyone know who the Haida are?" Heads wagged. The fire popped. A young girl cried out and then, giggling, buried her head in her hands.

"The Haida," Myron said, "now everyone say it with me: HIGH-dah, are Indians, Native American people, who live on islands along Canada's west coast. Several tribes who carve totem poles live there, all the way up to Alaska. Who knows where Alaska is?"

"Alaska's a state." Rope said.

Scotty slapped the back of Rope's head. "He didn't ask that blubberbrain."

"Alaska was purchased from Russia," Shortstack pronounced, "and is located on the West Coast of America quite a ways above San Francisco. I'd say about 10,000 miles above San Francisco." She flicked her tongue at the two boys.

Rope drew his hands up into paws and began panting. Scotty scratched his friend's side. "Good doggie!" Rope rolled onto his back and got the leg going.

Mye reached across heads to quiet Rover's leg. "Maybe not 10,000 miles, but, you're right, a long ways. Your counselors have told you our big project this summer will be making a totem pole. Who can tell me what a totem pole is?"

Shortstack's hand shot up. Myron saw other tentative fingers. "Yes?"

"It's sort of a tall, skinny statue," a boy said, "made from a tree trunk with birds and animals and stuff on it. The animals are standing on top of each other."

"Uh huh, good. Anyone else?"

Shortstack's hand went up again. She waved and flapped. Myron relented.

"A totem pole," she began, eyes focused upwards as though the answer was inscribed on the squared rafters, "symbolizes the Indian religion like a cross symbolizes our faith."

"Not if you're Jewish," Scotty said to Rope.

"Not exactly—" Myron hedged.

The crestfallen girl slouched and retied her shoes.

"—Totem poles mean different things," Myron said. "Sometimes they're like history books and tell the story of chiefs and important events in village life. Sometimes they're monuments to fallen heroes. The animals carved into the totem poles are symbols of the stories and heroes."

Mye was losing them. "Anyway, we're going to build a totem pole and I want you all to think about the symbols you'd put on the totem. Who can think of some good symbols?" Several hands went up, Shortstack's not among them.

"My brother plays symbols in his, in his school band," a young girl said breathlessly.

"No, no," an older boy said, "he means if you're—say a lion—you're king of the forest."

"Grilled-cheese sandwiches are kinda symbols of lunch." Rope looked at Scotty. "Right?"

"So you see," Myron broke in, "there are many symbols we could use on the totem. Starting tomorrow, Popeye's giving wood carving lessons to those taking art if you're twelve or older—"

"I already got a knife from my dad and I'm almost twelve!"

"I carved a balsa airplane once."

Myron shushed them. "If Popeye thinks you can responsibly handle a carving tool, he might make exceptions." Myron raised his voice as commotion spread, "For those of you under twelve—" He was almost shouting now as they scattered into the twilight, "—Popeye will need lots and lots of totem pole painters."

"I'm gonna carve a rocket ship." Rope launched his hand with sound effects as the foyer emptied. I watched the boy's believing eyes as they tracked the phantom rocket's lift off. In his mind, it gathered speed and punched through the ceiling. I followed it into a gathering hubbub on the second floor. The plump girl opened her dorm room door as a pillow blurred across the opening and caught her roommate, Colleen, in the face.

Freedonia stepped in and pulled the door shut behind her. "What have I walked into?"

A pillow fight, I wanted to tell her—one of camp's adolescent rituals. The six young women whose lives intersected that summer sparked a gap in my own protected youth. If she had lived, I like to think my daughter, Devon, would have been in there swinging with them.

"Come on in Freddie. We're just getting started. Have some ammunition." Colleen slung a pillow at her.

From behind, Betsy cuffed the back of Freddie's dark, fleshy knees. The girl went down on her bottom shaking the wooden floor. She began to laugh, a heaving noise like a car trying to start, and settled on her back. "I give up!"

Colleen sprang from the bed and smacked Betsy hard between the shoulder blades. Two bobby pins lost their grip. The girl's hair tousled over an ear. Betsy squared her shoulders and pillow-pummeled Colleen's crossed forearms.

"You die, villain, die," she snarled. The two 16-year-old girls fell grunting and squealing onto the bunk.

Megan, ready to join the fray, hefted a cushion. Thea, her 15-year-old twin, wrestled it from her sister and stuffed it up the back of Betsy's T-shirt. "Got your Wonderbra on backwards, Betsy?"

Freddie lumbered to her feet, yanked the pillow from her bunk, and pelted Thea's backside.

"Hey, one hit, one hit," Thea complained.

"You mean there's rules?"

A brief civility. Megan pillow-stripped the adjoining bunk and toppled her sister with a wicked backhand. Thea fell against the dresser and knocked the curling iron to the floor—a piece of plastic flew off the handle. The twins paused, panting.

"That's gonna cost you, Meg," The two girls circled each other in a tight pivot, clutched pillows cocked.

"Cat fight, cat fight!" Colleen brayed.

"What's it gonna cost, Tee?" Megan taunted, her braces glinting.

"Your ass," Thea spit back.

"How would you like two fingers where your eyes are?"

"How'd you like my foot where your brain is?"

Angela, a frail and sullen 14-year-old watched from her bed. She slapped her book shut. "How'd you like to give us who want to read a little peace and quiet? This is so childish."

"This is so childish," Thea mocked. She shot-put her pillow at Angela. "Who do you think you are, Madame Curie?"

Thea was unarmed.

Megan whacked her sister in the solar plexus and then all hell broke loose. Pillows flew from bunk to bunk, their mass swirled feathers, whipped up pigmy tornadoes. One of the missiles nicked Betsy's mirror which skidded off the dresser onto her bunk. Freddie and the twins hunkered into repetitive thwacking. The large girl alternated diagonal sweeps between Thea's hips and Megan's knees; her pillow spat fluff. The twins retaliated on Freddie's back and shoulders. Betsy was smothering Colleen against the wall. Colleen swung both fists straight up and exploded Betsy's weapon in a blizzard of confetti.

"Snow storm!" Angela shouted and then grinned from the safety of her upper bunk. Her roommates batted at the flurry. Feathers clung to sweat.

Colleen and Betsy collapsed into each other's arms, "Oh, God, let me breathe."

Colleen shouldered Betsy away. "Watch those groping hands, mister."

"Don't you wish," Betsy said.

"Yeah, we've been watching you watching Popeye, Colleen." Megan flopped on her bunk. "You know why they call him Popeye?" Megan didn't wait for an answer. "Because your eyes pop when you check him out, Colleen." The girls laughed. Even Angela snickered.

Freddie worked her jaw. "Somebody really creamed my ear."

"Don't you wish," Colleen said. Nobody got it until Angela said, "That's all you ever think about Colleen. There are other things in life besides sex, you know."

Colleen crossed her arms on her chest. "Well, Angie, once your skinny hormones kick in, maybe you'll understand."

Angela turned away. She already understood more than she wanted to, more than she should.

As the whiteout cleared, Thea picked feathers from her face. With her breath, she launched them from her palm onto the floor. "Hey, that reminds me of this joke about an elephant and a tight rope walker—"

"Clean-up time." Colleen, the Stone House spokeswoman, cut her off.

The other girls across the hall called Colleen Mother Inferior, which amused her. Catholic school girls were prudes. Smart, but prudes. At 16—"seventeen technically if you count in utero like the South Koreans"—she had corrected Betsy, Colleen was the oldest female camper. Rumor suggested she had lured a dozen men into bed and destroyed a perfectly good marriage. Actually, the number was a fraction of that and the marriage was premature and on the rocks anyway, but Colleen relished the mystique that the gossip created. Some older girls demanded specifics.

"Billy had a great little apartment," she demurred, "with shag carpet and lava lamps. Drove a red, '65 Mustang convertible." Colleen had paused to let the details grab hold.

"Wow!" Megan and Thea said.

"Really cute. Black wavy hair. Tall. And big. Know what I mean? Big!"

Megan narrowed her eyes. Thea's brows shot up.

"Didn't last long, though. His wife found out about us. We had a real knock-down, drag-out." Colleen sucked on her cigarette. "He wrote me for months after that. But in the end, I knew it would never work." She blew smoke from her mouth like hard words on a cold day. "It was an age thing. Then in April," she confided, "on the anniversary of our first time together, Billy-Boy sent me a rose, a single red rose."

"Wooow!" Thea and Megan's envy elongated the vowel.

Physically, Colleen had matured early. She cut a better figure than I did at her age. Tight jeans helped: slender thighs; young hips; flat stomach; long legs. Her vanity was as ample as her bosom. She discovered early in adolescence that her nipples would harden and soften according to the prevailing temperature. She thought the phenomenon worked to amazing advantage braless with sheer or thin, warm weather blouses that grazed her skin. Earlier that month, she had arrived late for her art lesson wearing a tight cotton peasant's blouse. Her teacher's scolding, flirtatious eyes dropped repeatedly to her breasts. Older men tended to openly size her up. Most boys her age would stare and then glance away, embarrassed. *Not* a turn-on.

Colleen's advanced state of sexual awareness and its mesmerizing power over men delighted her. But it hadn't kept her from being dumped at our fine arts camp for the summer. Her mother's brother—Myron's attorney, Emile Barr—talked her parents into sending her. Emile's son, Walter, had attended our camp at Colleen's age. Walter had recently graduated from college and, at 23, was (according to Colleen's mother) an up-and-coming teacher at the Saltlick Art Institute in Virginia. Cousin Walter was the "successful alumnus" as Emile pointed out by reading aloud to Colleen's parents the portion of the camp brochure that glorified him.

"My parents swallowed every crumb of Uncle Emile's hype," she complained to a high school friend. But Colleen knew better. Her parents wanted her away from home for 2 months. Her moods were unpredictable, her behavior wild.

"Maybe a creative arts environment would encourage your talent for visual mimicry," her mother had said hopefully.

"I draw, Mom. I just draw things. It's no big deal. And I don't have to go to some kid's camp to practice my visual mimicry, as you call it."

"Your mother and I think it would be best," her father said.

"What about practicing with the clutch?" Colleen whined. "You promised. You said once I turned sixteen we'd practice using the clutch so I could get my license in the summer." Colleen knew what her father's cold stare meant.

"Well, I'm not going!" She stamped to her bedroom and slammed the door.

Three months later, Emile drove her to camp.

The girls snared feathers which Angela and Freddie stuffed into a ruptured pillow. "We're actually going to build a totem pole?" Thea said.

Megan slapped at the debris in her hair. "What in the world for?"

"It's the camp project." Betsy batted her eyes and gleefully rubbed her hands. "Oh, golly, golly, golly. It's going to be fun!"

"You won't see me down there bustin' my ass," Colleen said.

Angela threaded hair behind her ears. "Everybody's supposed to help."

"Says who?"

"Says old man Cravitz."

"Cravitz can't make us," Betsy looked from girl to girl, "can he?"

Colleen punched the pillow's ballooning nap. "What's so hot about a totem pole, anyway?"

"It's part of the Indian theme for summer." Freddie pulled at her socks.

Thea stood up and began a shuffling hop from foot to foot. *Hi*-ya, hey-ya, *hi*-ya, hey-ya." She stopped and faced Colleen, torso erect, arms folded over her chest. "Me Chief Smoking Totem. Tradum Manhattan Island for cigarette."

Colleen rummaged in her drawer and held up a tampon. "Have a cigar." Thea cracked a smile.

"Hey, Smoking Totem," Betsy said, "what'll you take for ten minutes alone with Popeye?" The girls giggled.

"Hmmm," Thea scratched her chin. "Chief Smoking Totem tradum for Corvette and learner's permit."

"How come they call you Smoking Totem?" her sister, Megan, asked.

Thea pulled the rumpled coverlet from her bunk, shook it out, and draped it over her shoulders. If she had a talent, it was spinning and acting out intricate tales—tales set in jungles, on dirigibles, in farm houses haunted by the disassociated body parts of previous owners. Truly focused, she could convey her little brother, jittery on before-bed sugar, into sleep with a yarn so compelling and complex that her enraptured sister and parents would peek in from the bed-room doorway. The girl had read about the famous Indian storyteller, Te Ata Fisher—'Bearer of the Morning'—who performed for Kings and Presidents. Thea was ignorant of Native American cultures but that didn't lessen her aspira-tion to be Te Ata's successor.

"Many moons ago," she began, panning an arch in the air, "my father, Chief Baggy Britches married Skinny Knees. But the ceremony was not a happy one. The bellies of our hungry village rumbled. Starving children skulked through camp fighting like cats for meat scraps. Grown braves forgot they were warriors and dishonored our tribe by stealing from one another." Thea solemnly crept among them, "A terrible thing to see."

"Then, one night when the moon had been buried in the earth for one long campfire, a spirit appeared to my father." Thea raised her index finger toward the window. "The spirit pointed his bony arm to the farthest wigwam out beyond the swamp where Gritchysneeze the hermit lived. 'Your tribe has lost its way,' the spirit said, 'Salvation is with Gritchysneeze, the hermit. He is wise, but deceitful, so be-ware. Beware!'"

Megan repeated her sister's incantation, "Beware. Beware!"

Thea walked to Angela's bunk, her mantle dragging pillow feathers. "Chief Baggy Britches woke his new bride and told her what he had seen and heard. They both agreed they should act quickly. So, wrapping themselves in a smelly buffalo hide, they tiptoed out into the moonlight—"

"Why did they tiptoe?" Freddie whispered, her afro still speckled with fluff.

"Spirits," Thea thrust her face close to Freddie's, "are powerful and everywhere." Thea turned to Betsy. "They crept through the forest until the moon had slithered into the bare tree branches. At last, they came to the dark swamp where they saw a faint light."

Colleen lit another cigarette, forbidden in our dorm rooms, and blew a smoke ring into the center of Thea's intimate stage. The girls watched it circle in on itself and expand, roiling up like a bubble under water.

Thea suddenly thrust her arm through the smoke. "'Behold! The spirit has led us to the hermit's wigwam. The answer our hungry people seek is here at the dark swamp's edge.' My father told my mother to wait for him by the twisted oak in case the spirit had tricked them and was luring them into danger. Chief Baggy Britches saw the fire shadows dancing on the walls of Gritchysneeze's wigwam. He softly scratched on the hide."

Thea's voice cackled, "'Who is scratching on my wigwam,' a wizened voice demanded."

The twin scanned her roommates' faces. They leaned closer. "Now my father," Thea said, "was a brave warrior, but he didn't recognize the spirit who told him about Gritchysneeze. And spirits can play mean tricks, so he was cautious. 'It is I your chief, Baggy Britches.'"

"'Go away!' said the voice."

"'No way, Gritchysneeze,' my father answered, 'I am your chief. Let me enter.' Then the voice said, 'You banished me to the swamp for poisoning the Raven Claw River with—'" Thea was momentarily at a loss, "'with—'"

"With stewed tomatoes," Angela suggested.

"—with stewed tomatoes. This swamp is my domain. You have no power to command me here!' My father, an honorable chief, couldn't force his way in, not even to old Gritchysneeze's place, so he decided to trick the hermit. 'Very well,' he said. 'I am leaving.' But instead of leaving, he hid behind a tree, and when the hermit came out to see if he had really gone, my father slipped into his wigwam through the open flap."

Thea raised her arms, palms out, and lifted her eyes. "Inside the gloomy wigwam, Baggy Britches saw a huge totem pole which glistened with strange animals and figures. The wigwam smelled like—Chef Boyardee. Baggy Britches crept closer to the totem and realized with a gladdened heart that the spirit had been right! The hungry tribe's salvation was right in front of him. He reached out and touched the totem pole. He licked his fingers. A totem hotdog!"

Thea threw her arms up in victory. Her cloak slid to the floor. "A giant, kosher totem hotdog! The hermit's wigwam, a sort-of lunar cooker, had transformed moonlight—"

Betsy booed. "We want our money back!" Colleen turned thumbs down and hissed. Angela and Freddie applauded.

Thea bowed deeply. "Thank you," she said throwing kisses, "thank you!"

Hunched behind a bunk, Thea's sister Megan finished preparations for her own show. She completed the last concentric rings, recapped the lip gloss, and stood up facing Thea. Megan had removed her bra, unbuttoned her blouse, and stuffed the two front tails wide apart into her jeans, buccaneer fashion. Smeared, lip-gloss war paint encircled her breasts. Dark sunbursts radiated from her areolas. She ground her shoulder in jerky, exaggerated circles. The small breasts shuddered. "Me Princess Titty-Totem."

The girls' laughter roared down the Stone House stairs like kerosene on a fire.

"Sounds like the girls are enjoying themselves," Myron said softly to the hearth's landscape that had settled into flickering coals.

Alone now, Myron pulled his chair around to face the warmth. He and I had spent many hours before bed staring into similar embers and listening to the crackling insinuations. A wisp of green smoke curled up from copper wire embedded in a charred length of wood. A long hiss escaped. Shapes in the cinders moved in and out of form: a bird with one wing; a smiling fish. When the last log burned through and dropped, the head of a wolf and then a bear's skull shimmered. The bear's jaws yawned open, incisors red, and then orange. Its single eye throbbed with heat.

Myron leaned forward in his chair, picked up the tablet and pencil next to his book on the floor, and began to sketch the animal. Above the cleaved jaws, he added a snout and rendered the head in circular strokes. He outlined a stubby ear and an oval eye knowing the ashes would soon claim the bear.

The tension of the sketch pleased him: wire and sky. In the gloaming light, he drew quickly. His pencil remembered the bear in the meadow on its hind legs, paws raised. He tried to recall my words which his shrieking tinnitus garbled when the animal reared up. Lyrics to a forgotten song? It doesn't matter, he thought. 'The muses at my ear dictate in strange tongues,' as Rodin put it.

Mye lingered at the fireside with his drawing. Darkness fell. Kurt had remained sitting in the corner under the bookshelves with his back against the knotty pine cabinets. The boy's voice jumped out of the silence.

"Where do you get the wood for this totem pole?"

Myron turned to search the shadows. "Oh, Kurt. I didn't know you were still here."

"Do you chop down a tree, or what?"

"Yep, only you use a chain saw. The Haida liked cedar because it was plentiful and resisted rot. Let's hope ours doesn't resist carving." Mye thought his humor lost on the boy in the shadows. In fact, it wasn't; Kurt's mouth cracked a smile.

"How do you get a whole tree back to camp?"

"With help. Would you like to help?"

Kurt snorted. He rose up from crossed legs and sauntered to the porch door. "Good luck." The door banged shut then creaked open like a dog growling in its sleep.

The Meniere's disease sprung its tiny trap. Pinging stones skittered down cheap metal roofing. The din's quickening whiteness sucked Myron's eyes shut. It would pass. He waited ...

... A ringing, pure as heat, pricked the squall. The humming faded into static. Myron pushed himself up by the armrests and unhooked the heavy iron poker from its stand. "That boy's too young to be so down on life," he said aloud. Myron spread the coals. As he worked the poker, the noise in his head became grainy and soft like the ashes.

Give him time, Myron.

He heard my reproach, which I hoped was gentle, but he didn't believe he heard it. "You were always so patient with the children, Deidre," he said to the darkness. "Unlike me." Myron stabbed at the last struggling flame. "Kurt's aloof. He'll come around. My problem is finding a good-sized cedar."

I wanted so much to help him: *There's a stand a mile down shore—*

But the clarity of my words startled him instead. In the gloom, he stumbled against the chair. The poker fell to the stones with a dull clanging.

"Mr. Cravitz, are you all right?"

Myron's eyes darted to the corner where Kurt had been moments before and snapped back to the smoldering fire, and then came to rest on Brad Stringer's face nearly obscured in the doorway.

"Sorry if I startled you," Brad said. "You okay?"

"It's you, Brad. Yes. It's this damn ringing in my head. I'm fine—"

Brad relaxed. "The rest of the staff's waiting for you in the dining hall. Should we start the staff meeting without you?"

"No, I'm coming." Mye stooped, replaced the poker and

groped for something else to say. "How are the boys in Wolf Cabin, Brad?"

"No problems." Brad held the door for him. "Kurt talks in his sleep."

They thumped down the porch steps and crossed the lawn in the night's damp air. Under a full moon directly overhead, Brad thrust his hands into his front pockets. "This morning you mentioned something about finding a cedar for the totem pole?"

Myron stopped. "Yes?"

"Well, there are two or three large white cedars a ways down shore, maybe a hundred, two hundred yards into the woods." Myron stared at him and then peered down the lake's silvery shoreline.

Brad shifted uncomfortably. "I just thought you'd like to know."

In the pearl moonlight, Myron's shadow—a small animal cowering at his feet—yearned to bolt into the trees. "Yes, I heard you the first time."

"The first time?"

"Didn't you tell me that before?"

"I don't think so."

That night Mye listened to the wind. The restless sounds of the buffeted lodge woke him over and over. Beyond the window, pines blustered. Their fitful shadows scurried over his blanket. Throughout the building, his charges slept while he hoped for the ringing to start, for his disease to bring my voice (could it be?) back to him. At breakfast, he over-salted the already salty scrambled eggs. He sat solemnly now in the wicker chair on the veranda, half a green banana on the wide arm rest. The morning remained windy. Cloud shards scudded from the west.

"I'll bet you're going to miss this place," Emile Barr, with Barr and Harcourt, Attorneys at Law, said. He had arrived early to assess the camp site and prepare for a prospect interested in buying the land. A short, powerful man, Emile's tonsured and mole-dappled pate reflected on-again, off-again sunlight. "Will you be reinvesting the money in another property?"

"New York and the feds will get a lot of it," My husband said.

"Despite the taxes, this is valuable real estate, Myron. When it's sold, you'll have enough to build your own studio in Jersey. Paint and sculpt full time like you've always wanted—"

Myron wished a thousand starlings would interrupt the lawyer's swashing prattle and alight on the branches of his diseased auditory nerves. He hoped my voice would puncture the birds' urgent calls.

Deidre, tell me what to do, he pleaded silently. These woods are yours, not mine. How do I keep you? Talk to me!

I hesitated. I had already startled Myron by the lodge fireplace the day before.

"—You could travel," Emile was saying. "There are lots of places to go in this wide world, Myron—"

Deidre, we can't escape each other. Damn it, talk to me!

74

"—You could go to Europe, visit all the famous museums. The Louvre, the Tate, the Prado—"

I don't want to sell. I have to. Without you, the lodge is a cancer. My life here is empty. Deidre, say something, please!

"—Maybe take one of those Aegean tour ships to Mykonos or Santorini—?"

Have I left something undone? I'm not losing you again. Deidre?

The birds' chorus invaded his head like a sudden wind. I pitched my voice high and pure as an old radio's electric hum. *Build the totem pole, Myron. For me—for Devon and Caleb.*

"—How does that sound, my friend?"

Mye sucked breath into his belly and then sobbed in quavering gusts. His torso shook under the flannel shirt I had ordered from L.L. Bean.

Emile put an awkward hand on his client's shoulder. "That's it, Myron. Let it all out," he soothed. "Losing a loved one is about the hardest thing to bear in life."

When my husband finally rubbed his tears away, face ravaged and puffy with grief, and the sleepless night, he wore a gaze men indulge alone, a mad gape, half-smiling, and resolute. It sent a shiver down the lawyer's back.

But Emile was not an artist. Myron had invoked the muse, and I was learning how to answer.

Chapter Six

Jake thought some days were shit right from the beginning. Fanny's wheeze-dried smoker's cough twice woke him from a sound sleep. A 14-year-old across the hall threw up all over her bunk. The acrid, vomit odor would linger for days. The breakfast biscuits, as usual, had a left-in-the-rain texture.

"The older kids aren't stupid," he told Stanley that morning. "There's a black market in snacks. Customers are popping up like mildew." Our head counselor's eyes surveyed the campers in the dining hall. "Granola's a dime an ounce. They've cornered the canned meat and dried fruit market. Parents ship it wholesale. They sell it retail."

"Capitalism, old boy. It's the American way," Stanley said cheerily.

"The damn snack hut doesn't help. Candy bars, gum, sugar, caffeine."

"All my favorites."

"Yeah, well that's because in jolly old London, all you guys eat is fried fish 'n chips."

"In point of fact, the lamb tandoori and chicken curry masala are famous in London." Stanley stood to gather his tray. "And I'm from Canterbury."

Worse than last year, Jake thought. Besides fat-soaked breakfast sausages and rubbery eggs, peanut butter was the only daily protein available. Peanut butter a la mode:

a tablespoonful drizzled with honey. P.B.V.D.: peanut butter spread on soggy French fries. Jake could only speculate what the "V.D." stood for. A Willington hoagie: peanut butter and apple sauce between two slices of white bread, so named for Kurt Willington's savvy when it came to doctoring up institutional food.

Willington was a problem. Jake told anyone who'd listen. "The kid's a drifter." He caught up with the piano coach walking to the lodge after breakfast. "He's disrespectful, Lila Mae, belligerent, a trouble-maker."

"Kurt goes to workshops," Lila Mae said. "I've seen him."

"He wanders in. He wanders out."

"That's not a punishable offense, Mr. Daryl."

Maybe not, Jake thought. But it was disrespectful. Kurt would slip up and blow it one of these days. Then he'd nail him. "Deidre was a bitch," he said to Lila Mae's sashay as she retreated to the lodge, "but it wasn't like this last year when she was around to kick ass."

I guess he was right about that.

Back in the bedroom, Jake swept his keys from the ceramic tray and pocketed them. That morning, Myron had told him Maria Azavedo would be arriving at the bus depot in Tupper Lake. About time she showed up, he thought. He preened in the mirror and pinched breakfast snippets from his mustache.

Fanny clopped up the broad wooden stairs into the second story hall. She cradled a cardboard box lid heaped to excess with antacids, aging aspirin, colored pills in plastic bottles, and gauze bandage in yellowing paper.

"Hi, Jake. Look what I found in the storage shed." A thin, brown cigarette bobbled between her lips. She hurried into the bedroom, left eye squinting against smoke, and spilled the clattering bottles onto the bed in a cloud of exhaled vapor. She flicked her ash to the floor.

"Have you seen our sicky? I'm worried about her. I don't think she slept much after upchucking last night."

Jake snatched the butt from his wife's fingers. "How many times have I told you not to smoke in the lodge?" He threw it down and crushed its red punk under his shoe.

"Sorry. I forgot to put it out before I came inside." Fanny watched her husband sidle back to the mirror. "So you haven't seen her?"

"Nope. I felt queasy myself yesterday. I don't think the— what was that crap? Chicken salad? It wasn't right. Tasted bitter."

"Mr. Cravitz should really talk to Sonja. I don't know how the food's been in the past, but lately it's pretty..." Fanny searched for the word. "Yucky." She sat next to her rescued medications. "And I wish he'd get a real nurse up here." Jake looked sharply at her. "Sorry, but it's true," she whispered. "What if someone really got sick? What if someone was bleeding or dying or something? I wouldn't know what to do. It's a good thing Liz can give herself insulin shots."

"The money's not bad, Fanny. Besides, the cook's an LPN."

"Yeah, but how long has it been since Sonja was—one of those?"

"Once a nurse, always a nurse, even though she's the cook. That's all the law requires a nurse on premises. And it stands for licensed practical nurse." I'm wasting my breath, he thought. "Maybe you two should switch jobs. You make a mean plate of scrambled egg shells and burned bacon."

Fanny picked at the brittle wrapping on the gauze bandage. Her mouth quivered.

"Just forget it," Jake said. "I've got to pick up the lifeguard. If our intrepid leader wants to know where I am, remind him *he* sent me to get her."

As he left, Fanny grabbed her brush from the rickety night stand and yanked it through her hair. "You don't appreciate me, Jake Daryl," she said to the dresser when he was gone. "I've given you everything momma said a husband would want. You can be so cruel!"

Half way down the stairs, Jake heard the brush clatter to the floor.

The parking area, a muddy field of cars, pick-up trucks, our faded yellow bus, and a motorcycle, bordered the derelict tennis courts. Jake's sedan—roof, hood, and trunk losing top paint—languished next to our handyman's Harley Davidson. A skull and crossed bones pictograph dangled from the cycle's headlight—"Don't Touch" scrawled underneath.

A slipshod, wire fence ran along the lot's northwest end and hedged what had previously been the Rabbit Farm—now Ringer's Field—where the campers romped through capture the flag, touch football, and other free-wheeling games with improvised rules and equipment. Jake considered The Rabbit Farm a ludicrous vestige of past summers when Myron and I didn't know any better. It's true, we had tried to raise rabbits that burrowed under the encampment at will or were otherwise dispatched by foxes, owls, and the occasional coyote or wild cat. Among our staff, only Jake knew the Rabbit Farm's history.

"Incompetence surrounds me," Jake sulked. This is the last summer, he promised himself. Our head counselor churned from the lot slinging mud from his car's back wheels and shoved the sedan into second gear.

I need to explain the origin of Jake's cynicism. He had met his downfall, Robley, on the basketball court next to the high school where Myron taught. My husband's school was a block east of the Majestic Dry Cleaners where Robley worked nights for his father, who owned the place. Robley was older and, so Jake thought, wiser.

"That's what you get for trusting a crook," I told Jake after his release from community service.

"Buddy boy, it's a piece of cake," Robley said. He had invited Jake to his apartment to discuss a business deal with 'real money in it.' Robley stacked his *Playboy* magazine collection next to the sofa under the James Dean poster tacked to the front room wall. Whenever Jake visited his older friend, he thumbed through the worn, 1953 issue with Marilyn Monroe on the cover. Robley stored his cigarette pack in his T-shirt's rolled-up short sleeve. Definitely cool, Jake thought.

Robley handed him a beer—technically illegal since Jake wouldn't be 18 for another month. That was cool, too.

"My dad's given me complete control of the Majestic and it's goin' nowhere," Robley said.

"I didn't know my dad," Jake said.

"Yeah, boo-hoo. You spent your impressionable youth in an orphanage."

"If I owned a business, I could make a lot of money." Jake drained half his bottle.

"Not me, man, I'm not cut out to spend my life cleaning up other people's shit." Robley mimicked an elderly matron, "Now, Mr. Angelo, make sure you get that spot off the cuff and don't forget that little oil stain next to the zipper. Oil stain, my ass. The dick-head pissed his pants. I watched my dad bust his balls hiring people, firing the fuck-ups, going in late at night to check on supplies." Robley took a long swig. "The dry cleaning business ain't for me."

"So, hire some guys to run the business."

"That's what I'm sayin', Jake. Listen to me. You hire them, they fuck-up. Then you gotta hire somebody else who's a retard. It's a vicious cycle."

Jake slurped his beer. "Why can't you do it?"

"Because I stand to get the insurance money. I'm the owner now. What's called an interested party. If they suspect arson, I'd be the first person the cops would check out." Robley put a comforting hand on Jake's shoulder. "All you gotta do is light a match and make sure nobody sees ya. It's a piece of cake."

Jake finished his Budweiser and belched. "And I'd get part of the insurance money?"

"A cool three grand."

Jake would like to have an apartment like Robley's someday. A place to score with chicks, listen to music, watch TV. Anyplace would be better than the dank basement room the home arranged for him. And with three thousand dollars he could buy a car. Once he finally finished high school, he'd be king of his own castle.

Unfortunately, when the building burned, Jake's 18th birthday had come and gone. They tried him as an adult with no previous arrests and sentenced him to 2 years probation and community service, part of which as a summer janitor at the courthouse in Tupper Lake. Robley got sent up-river for insurance fraud and conspiracy to commit arson.

Myron lost his best suit in the blaze. My silk evening dress was reduced to singed scraps. On a camp-related business trip to Tupper Lake the year after we lost the twins, we befriended Jake, the conscientious janitor—a hometown boy who'd made a mistake.

Life wasn't easy for him. His community service included working for the road clean-up crew, stabbing, and bagging filth along the highway. In the summer, he sloshed toilets and mopped floors in the court house. When his probation and community service ended, Myron and I hired him. We watched him closely and kept him busy. During the winter, he worked down-state at the Pizza Palace and rose to assistant manager. In the summers, he kept coming back to the Adirondacks and eventually became indispensable to Myron.

I never really trusted him, though. I knew his smarmy thoughts before he did. "It really ticks me off," he would tell Myron. "What kind of psychic power does she have, anyway?" Jake had learned from his troubled youth that power was short lived. He figured if you didn't use it to gain an advantage when you had it, the tables would turn.

The bus, carrying our tardy life-guard, arrived 20 minutes late. When it pulled into the Sunoco Station that doubled as Tupper Lake's depot and Maria Azavedo stepped off into the idling diesel fumes, Jake's gonads clenched.

My current view on sexuality's tangy insistence is second-hand. I had to admit though, Maria was beautiful. While the driver retrieved two bags and a scruffy black guitar case from an almost empty storage bay, Miss Azavedo stood tranquilly on the blacktop. Her dark, languid eyes surveyed the landscape. Black hair cascaded in ringlets down a terrycloth top. Jake's licentious scrutiny darted over the young body and almond limbs.

"Maria?" he inquired politely and descended the parking lot stairs.

"*Señor* Cravitz?"

"No, I'm Jake Daryl, his associate. I hope you had a pleasant trip." He stacked her bags and guitar in the trunk with exaggerated vigor while she waited for him to open the car door. She slid into the seat. The slash on the side of her matching blue terrycloth shorts puckered open just below her hip.

Exceptional, Jake thought.

Maria woke up the next morning to American rock 'n roll crackling over the camp loud speakers. She knew the song, *Monday, Monday,* by the Mommas and the Papas. As she struggled out of her quicksand bunk, she realized it was, indeed, Monday. She slipped a thin wrist through her watch band. Her cabin girls coughed and groaned as they woke. In 4 hours, at 11 o'clock, the lakefront would officially open.

Maria had been warned that the entire camp might descend upon her, sun-burn prone and swim-crazy. She had endured Jake Daryl's leering congeniality: "I know you'll do a bang-up job. Come see me with any concerns." Why did Americans use phrases like "bang-up"? she thought.

Myron's rambling instructions after breakfast bewildered her: "extend the dock with pontoons, tie them together first, of course, check the wading bottom for glass, set up the ropes and make sure everybody knows the rules." Then he had handed her a silver whistle on a string. Despite her job description—which was inarticulate—she tried to point out that the rules had never really been explained, but Myron's other chores tugged him away. She was on her own—the lakefront officially hers. Maria changed into her swim suit and headed for the water.

During the summer between her freshman and sophomore year at *Universidad de Los Andes,* Azavedo lifeguarded from a chrome chair seven feet above the side of an indoor, chlorine-scented pool. The *Los Lagartos* Country Club catered to Bogotá's upper crust. But Match Lake, stretching before her like the stark plateau east of her birth-city's last *calle,* intimidated the young woman. Robbed of the standard 25×15 meter boundaries, this new job perplexed her. At which point did the lakefront begin—or end? Where did Mr. Cravitz want the pontoons placed when he said, 'beyond the dock'? Did she have staff? And why did her letter say to arrive at camp on the last day of June when orientation (she had just been told at breakfast) was on June 25th? Camp had been functioning for 5 days.

Maria could hear her father's indignant voice: "*¡Americanos*—a wolf's instinct, a goat's sense. They promise riches, deliver sand. And when you complain, they're hurt and wonder why you distrust them! *¡Contrarios!*" She climbed onto a granite outcrop near shore—a roost I had often occupied—faced the water, and hugged her knees.

On his way back from checking the barn for fire code violations, Bruce McIntyre, the Match town fire chief, paused to take in the lake's blue calm. Seated on the rock, Maria's swim suit exposed to the waist an unblemished cappuccino back. I was pleased that Bruce remembered me sunning on the same perch the summer before. We had only known each other for a few seasons. The fire chief strolled over to her. "Nice day," he said.

She turned into the sun to face him and raised her arm to shade her eyes. "Yes. The water's beautiful."

"You must be the life guard." Bruce stepped closer and shaded her with his body.

"Maria Azavedo." She extended her hand.

Bruce shook the slender fingers. "May I?" He skirted the boulder and sat next to her. "I'm Bruce McIntyre, the fire chief. Here on business. Fortunately, everything—except the hot plate in the barn—seems up to code."

"Up to code?"

"Not in violation. According to fire safety rules."

"Ah. I hope my water safety rules are also up to code."

"Like no swimming beyond the floats?"

"*Sí.* Yes. And watching the ones who can't swim—but think they can. I suppose that is most of my job."

"My job's teaching high school physical science," Bruce said. "Being fire chief's just voluntary."

Maria sensed the conversation would soon become personal. She was accustomed to the flirting American men scattered in conversation. Displaying her mother's ring (worn on the third finger of her left hand) usually deflated their eagerness.

"Why do you say *just* voluntary?"

"Well, there's not a lot of call for firefighters out here. If there's a big blaze, Tupper sends in their trucks. Match only has two and they're both fifteen-year-old rattletraps."

"You're not proud to be fire chief of these," Maria hesitated, "rattletraps?"

"Proud? I guess so. Someone has to do it. I just like teaching a lot better than hosing down singed pot roast. Like I said, the real McCoy is rare in Match."

Maria gazed at the cloudless sky. During the rainy season, the Colombian sky was seldom blue. Fog draped the mountains every morning, sometimes for weeks on end. "I like studying in America better than in Colombia."

"What school?"

"Amherst. I transferred there last year. Someday I hope to be a medical doctor."

"You must be very bright, Maria."

The chief of fire flirted well. "Physical science. Is that geography?" she asked.

"Geo-physical science, botany, health. In high school, one

teaches a smattering of everything. But what I really like is geo-physical history. It always wows the students, the better ones anyway. This rock we're sitting. Guess how old it is."

Maria cradled her chin in her left hand so Bruce could see the ring. "Maybe twenty million years?"

"Much, much older. The ground under Match Lake was once part of the Laurentian Shield. Imagine a whale breaching a calm sea. The shield, a tectonic plate, uplifted the earth's crust and formed the Adirondack Mountains over a billion years before I was born in Schenectady or you were born in ..."

"Bogotá."

"Heart of the Andes, right?"

"Correcto, Professor."

Bruce smiled. "Geologically, Match Lake's a fledgling compared to old-geezer granite we're sitting on." He slid off their sofa-sized boulder. "The Ice Ages, dozens of them, advanced and retreated from the north and scoured valleys into eventual coves that filled with melting ice." He gestured to the lake. *"Voila!* The Adirondacks by then were already ancient. Older than the Rockies, the Himalayas, the Urals, the Pyrenees."

"Older than the Andes, yes?"

"Far older. How do we know when mountains are truly old?"

I was impressed with Maria's patience during Bruce's impromptu lecture.

"When their shoulders are smooth and round?" the young woman said and slipped her right hand over her left with its prominent ring. Maria, too, was flirting.

Bruce grinned. "Yes! A good analogy." He plucked a stout stick from the pebbled sand. "One hundred million years after the mountains burst from mother earth, mammals were a future miracle of adaptation and the Ice Ages hiccoughs in the last outposts of geologic time."

He scored a long line into the beach. "Another five hundred million years, give or take, before ripple-backed Trilobites swarmed the seas scavenging the bottom for plant sludge." He flicked a cross-hatch off-center right of the stick's meandering scar. "A hundred million years after that," he made another mark, " before the Nautiloids, tentacles bristling—visualize a bouquet of squirming flowers—preyed on the Brachiopods clustered among sponges where translucent jelly fishes, big as umbrellas, floated in the shallow seas."

Maria lifted her eyebrows and cocked her head. "¡Caramba!" she said—a polite expression of astonishment. What she meant was, "get to the present, I'm *dying* here!"

Bruce made a mark farther to the right near the ragged trough's extremity. "Another thirty five million years" and Maria repeated with him: "'give or take,' and simple fishes twitched themselves onto the alien shore to breathe the moist, ozone thick air. Thus, Maria, we begin the quarter-billion year descent through cold blooded reptiles, the dinosaur's reign," he dimpled the sand, each prick closer to his time-line's terminus, "warm-blooded sloths, marsupials, Lilliputian-hoofed mammals, primates, binocular arboreal apes and finally Homo Sapiens. You and me,

Maria." He stabbed the channel's end. Maria applauded delicately.

"I get kind of wound up sometimes." Bruce smiled bashfully. "Time for me to go." Our fire chief scattered his time-line with the stick. "A billion years of history is a lot to absorb in a single morning. Nice to have met you, Maria. Good luck at school." He waved to her as he mounted the small rise into the meadow. It was still early. Maria shut her eyes and thought of home.

I was a Homo Sapien once, descended from the diatomaceous muck. I contemplated destiny and recorded victories and forfeitures of intelligence with indiscriminate hope.

"Maria, right? Didn't mean to sneak up." Maria opened her eyes. A tall, large-nosed boy with pimples veiled in lotion beamed at her. "I'm Wally Van Dusen, your assistant." Wally's black nylon swim suit exposed a lank physique devoid of body hair. Two lines of side-burn fuzz disappeared into the straight brown mop hugging his head like an inverted bowl. "Were you asleep?"

"Absorbing history," Maria said.

"What should we do first?" Wally asked.

"I'm not sure." Maria stood up on her ancient granite hump and gestured to the beached pontoons, canoes, and ropes. "What do you suggest?"

Wally found her accent charming. "Let's lash the pontoons together and put them in the water. It's chilly, but only for the first 5 minutes. This is my third year up here, second as a CIT. That means counselor-in-training. I finished my senior lifesaving last year, working on Eagle Scout this year." Wally sensed her uncertainty. "Don't worry," he said, "I'll show you the ropes. This place is only crazy when you fight it. 'Relax and float downstream' as the Beatles say." He slapped his thighs in a quick, three-quarter burst and appraised her confidently. "Ready to get wet?"

Eleven o'clock came and went. Most campers who wandered down to the lake ready to swim settled for wading knee-deep. They browsed the water near shore, skeptical of the older few who braved its 65 degree temperature above their waists. Scotty and Rope eased into the lake tiptoeing through the bottom ooze, their skinny arms drawn up, elbows akimbo.

"I've been in bath tubs colder than this," Rope said shivering. He smoothed the surface water's shallow warmth with his hand.

"If it's so warm, why don't you swim out to the ropes and back?" Scotty said.

"I could if I wanted."

"You're chicken." Scotty flapped his elbows, "Rope's chicken of a little cold water! Bwok! Bwok-bwok-bwok!"

"I'll race you out and back," Rope said. "Ready?" He eyed his friend who puffed his cheeks with air—and froze. Rope pushed him away, sucked a deep breath and plunged in screaming. His soprano skipped the quiet water like a flat stone. Maria awoke from a sun-soaking stupor and rocked to her feet. Wally was already sprinting toward the lake.

Scotty, jubilant and bouncing, jabbed at ripples where Rope had disappeared. "Shark attack! A shark got him!"

Two Stone House girls, Angela and Freddie, shrieked and lunged for shore pulling panicked waders with them. Wally churned into deep water and upended, feet sliding out of sight.

As Wally went down, Rope came up, "Holy crap, it's cold!" He disappeared again, a shadow gliding toward the floats that marked the swimming area's perimeter. Wally surfaced just missing sight of the boy's legs as he went under.

"He's okay," Maria yelled, but Wally was gone, his quick breath and deep dive rescue technique finally in use. Rope thrashed up for air twice before Wally reappeared. The 9-year-old smacked the line and launched a racer's crawl back to shore. He cruised past Wally's hair-plastered face which floated like a detached scowl on the surface.

Despite the cheers which greeted him when he stood up and stumbled for land, Rope maintained himself with humility. Maria, who had already captured Scotty, caught Rope by the arm as well. "Do that again and you're both grounded for good," she warned them, her accent adding a touch of malice.

Rope thought her grip on his bicep surprisingly strong. "I couldn't help it, it's freezing," he protested.

"It's not so much you," she said to Rope. "It's you," Maria tapped an index finger on Scotty's forehead. "Shark attack. *¡Madre de Dios!* Go dry off, both of you."

Elated, the two boys tramped up the grassy bank. Summer's first shit-kicker: a life guard in action; near panic. "You won fair and square," Scotty said.

Rope scrubbed at his hair with a towel. "Remember last year?"

"Yeah, the fat guy you pushed off the dock into the canoe."

"Punched his foot right through the bottom!"

"Yeah, and Robin's jitterbug on the beach when Fang slid into the cave between her boobies!"

"Our best garter snake ever!"

"Remember the guy who threw up in his tuba during parents' concert?" The boys grimaced.

"Yeah, those were the days," Rope said.

The trees, a stand of about a dozen Atlantic white cedars were where our neighbor, Sally Moffett, Brad (and I for that matter) said they would be, a 100 yards from the lake shore just inside Sally's property line. Myron remembered seeing them years before when we had first toured the camp and surrounding woods. The 1950 big blow toppled most of the remaining large trees in the state preserve, white cedars included. But this stand on Sally's land survived, one of the few left. During our years summering in the Adirondacks with other people's children, Myron had taken titans like these for granted. They were as predictable as the seasons among the squat undergrowth that annually bloomed and withered. The large trees had never mattered. Now he was thankful for their resilience.

The morning after Myron's meeting with his attorney, Emile, our handyman, Alex, invited Sally and Mye to lunch at the Wild Cat Bar and Grill in town. The woman offered condolences for my death and then came straight to the point. "I suppose you'll use professionals to cut the tree down," she said. "There's a good arborist in Long Lake."

Alex meant to be reassuring: "I spent a year with a tree surgery firm after the Army," he told the woman. "I've even got my own saws."

Hair disheveled, eyes like augers, Sally drilled into Myron's gaze. "I'll allow one tree considerin' the historic nature of the project," and then turned her scrutiny to Alex. "But make sure it comes down clean. Don't take two or three others on the way. Those big trees are kinda' like children to me, the children I never had." Her tongue, an albino eel, slithered onto her upper lip through a gap in her front teeth and then retreated into the cave of her mouth. "You're gonna owe me one, Mr. Cravitz."

Sally was never neighborly. One day many years ago when I was frolicking in the woods near my parents' lodge, we stumbled upon each other. She apprised me silently and then sawed through some ugly fungus growing like shelves on a tree trunk. "Don't hunt 'em unless you know what they are," she said. "Chicken of the Woods. Orange on top, yellow underneath. Good with olive oil and garlic." She stopped as though she had said too much. I stood mute and still. "On second thought, don't hunt 'em at all. I knew a man, picked and ate what he *thought* were Morels."

"What happened to him," I asked.

"Died a month later. Organ failure." She smiled and added, "Pick lady slippers instead, lassie." And then her hard look returned. "But don't touch my ferns."

It was a casual schooling. Every time we serendipitously met in the woods, Sally taught me something about its wonders. Years later, I didn't realize her husband, Delmore, repeatedly beat her up until she stopped me in the Tupper Lake hardware store and showed me a shiner, big as a coffee mug. "He got the worst of it," she said. A few summers after the twins died, Delmore left, and Sally settled into aloof independence.

The locals called her Shotgun Sally. Most folks in Match found her ornery. But Myron and I appreciated her directness and the way she parted company by saying, "suspect I'll see you again, if gravity maintains." Rumor had it she was rich as a gold mine, but you'd never know from the way she talked or the overalls and work shirts she habitually wore.

Within the blue line that defined the Adirondack Preserve's 5 million acres, private and public property zigzagged in a labyrinth of ownership. Sally's land abutted the camp on the west end down to the lake shore. Besides a thin wedge of public land that cut into her estate from the northwest, her ancestral territory ran for miles along both sides of the lake to the south and far to the north where the white pines towered during the lumber baron days. Most of these evergreens didn't survive, lumbered out long ago for ship masts, planking and, later, wood pulp. Trees were burned for potash and the ashes shipped to Canada for gun powder. But a few white cedar stands had been preserved through luck or superstition. On her vast property, Sally knew where every surviving giant, as she called them, loomed above the surrounding forest.

Myron studied the picture in his *Pocket Guide to North American Trees* and then looked up at the shaggy, tea-brown trunks that leaned across one another like Roman columns. Near the center, the largest and straightest cedar gapped his view from ground to sky. The sparse, top cone of fan-shaped foliage fell in continuous illusion across the scudding cloud bank. My Lord, it's huge, he thought.

Myron pressed a heel into the soft soil. He thought of his 10th-grade English students. "I went to the Garden of Love, and saw what I had never seen," he said to himself. He knelt and uprooted a tiny seedling. Dark loam clung to the root hairs. "A chapel was built in the midst, where I used to play on the green."

"In what way is 'The Garden of Love' similar to or different from Blake's poem 'The Tiger?'" he had asked his big-knuckled boys who slumped over their desks. The students—his immature academic seedlings—eyed the clock in sporadic lapses of patience.

"'Tiger, Tiger burning bright, in the forests of the night,'" he read, "What do you suppose the Tiger is, and what does Blake mean by 'the forests of the night?'" The second hand swept slowly around the clock face, feet dragged across the gritty floor.

"Yes, in a way it's about good and evil," Mye nodded his appreciation to a square-jawed student. "Thank you, Mr. Spencer. Is the Tiger evil? 'What immortal hand or eye dare frame thy fearful symmetry?'"

The school boys remained mute and pondering. "Well," Myron continued, "if the Tiger is good, what is the lamb? 'Did he smile his work to see? Did he who made the lamb make thee?'" The full-grown hands scratched at the half-grown faces or tapped the desks. Were they thinking about the Tiger and the lamb or an alluring teen-age girl?

"'And the gates of this chapel were shut, and Thou Shalt Not writ over the door; so I turned to the Garden of Love, that so many sweet flowers bore.'" A boy named Peter discreetly picked his nose with his pinkie. "Come on," Myron urged them, "what basic thread is contained in both of these works? 'And I saw it was filled with graves, and tombstones where flowers should be.'"

"Yes, thank you, Mr. Meeker. Religion. Religious dogma. And what constraints did religion seem to place on Blake? 'And priests in black gowns were walking their rounds, and binding with briars my joys and desires.'"

And what constraints did Myron place on these boys whose immediate future consisted of lunch and the meager pleasures of walking past the Sweetbriar School for Girls on the way home for a chance viewing of uniform skirts short above the knee. "Good, but what do you mean by 'restrictive,' Mr. Spencer?"

The class period's confines were interrupted by the bell in the midst of the boy's groping explanation. "Tomorrow," Mye had called to them as they left in a tumult, "there will be a test on these two poems." His authority rested on the terror of the spot quiz.

Myron fingered the dark root hairs and the soil trapped within the fibrous heft of his unearthed, diminutive tree. He recited from the Haida carver's blessing: "Oh, cedar tree! Soft wood, but firm, so straight the split runs 40 feet without a knot. Reddish brown when new, silver gray when old." His students would have grasped those images more quickly than Blake's. He amended the benediction: "Sweet silver gray, the color your hair would have turned in our dotage. What do you think about this big guy in the middle, Deidre?"

The time had come.

Yes.

My answer was distinct. The breeze's murmur didn't keep it long, but long enough for Myron to be sure. No ringing in his head this time, no squealing freight car wheels or caterwauling birds.

"Deidre?"

Yes, the largest cedar will do nicely for the totem pole, Myron.

He rose from the yielding earth and faced the clump of trees. The seedling quivered in his hand like a sprig of lightning. "Deidre! It's really you!"

Together, we listened to the wind and the tree trunks groaning.

Chapter Seven

"I can cut the tree down, but getting it to camp's another matter." Alex wiped maple syrup from the corners of his mouth and sucked his thumb clean.

My husband's wide, unblinking eyes stared at his soggy flapjacks. "Let's cross that bridge when we come to it. Did you know the mortuary channels in Giza's great pyramids were made of granite slabs mined in Aswan over six hundred miles away? Each block weighed thousands of pounds." Myron unscrewed the salt shaker cap and poured a white mound onto his uneaten stack of pancakes. The sides of the cone cascaded in minute avalanches. Breakfast conversation rose and fell around them. Stainless steel ware rattled on plates, chairs screeched across the wooden floor.

Mye emptied the shaker. "They built a causeway from the Nile where boats unloaded the stones." He pinched some salt into a line. "Groups of men in two rows ramped each block up to sleds. They kept the sleds moving with log rollers underneath." Mye's gaze wandered over the rippled bangles in Alex's black and orange headband. "It took 100,000 men almost thirty years to build the largest pyramid."

"What's a totem pole compared to that?" Alex asked. "Right?"

Mye nodded, his eyes distant and stuck. "I wanted to use red cedar like the Nisga'a and Haida totem pole makers," he said, "but it doesn't grow here in the Adirondacks. We'll make do with white cedar." Myron left his flapjacks on the table, got up, and walked away.

Our handyman knew his chain saws. "A saw's real grit," he told me the summer before when he was clearing brush, "comes from the relationship of power to weight. Most week-enders use cheap, heavy clunkers with twenty inch bars that don't have the guts to rip willow. The sixteen inch, lighter weight Husqvarnas—Huskies for short—or the Poulins, can tear through ironwood or slice up black locust in a rain squall. You can tell when a chain is well sharpened," he said. "The engine sings like Roy Orbison's falsetto. A well-sharpened chain won't choke and labor through wood. It chews up the timber and spits it out." Alex kissed his fingertips in appreciation, "Bees streaming from the hive."

With a good saw in his hands, Alex said he felt 95% invulnerable, 5% naked as a ripe watermelon. He was good, but not perfect. Sloppy cuts happened. He was working through snagged, storm-damaged hackberry limbs soon after we hired him when the branches snapped and flung the saw at his face. Twenty-five hundred RPM sliced a ragged edge along the rim of his hard hat. A few inches to the left and the spinning chain would have burrowed to a stop in his brain.

"Chunks of flesh, fingers, bone, can fly back and stick to your shirt before you know it," he had said. During his first week at Tree Works, Inc., the other new guy in the cherry picker electrocuted himself on residential wires over a snarled sycamore. His Poulin lopped off two fingers on its way to the ground. The man was already dead, but that made no difference to the saw. "A good chain saw, like a vintage Harley, always demands respect," he told me and Myron.

Alex's working life began at 13. He caddied for 35 cents an hour, 6 days a week during two sweltering summers to earn enough for a battered '38 Plymouth five-window coup'. He wasn't old enough to drive, but Alex primped over the car and spent what little extra money he had on its internal and external resurrection. He nurtured the hulking, oil dripping possibility of it into erratic idling in his father's driveway.

In 1964, when he was 20, he joined the Army and served 2 years of duty in Vietnam—although Alex called it hell, not duty. Luckily, he returned from war with all his faculties unharmed—the visible ones, anyway. The Army had taught him that the best men died as unpredictably as the worst: in agony; in calm naiveté, "like hearing their mother's call for dinner," he once described it to me, "then turning and taking a round in the head." Some died in the last hour of enlistment. Death did not discriminate, or so it seemed to Alex.

In the service, Alex had also learned how to disarm and—if necessary—kill a man at close quarters. "Command thought I was efficient," he told me. They sent him stateside to Ft. Bragg in 1966 to train other recruits. He admitted to us that he wasn't that good, but he was fast. "Faster than thinking," as he put it.

When the work day was done preparing for camp's opening, Myron and I would sit with Alex on the veranda. It didn't take him long to loosen up, to pick at the trauma he had suffered, to pull the stitches out of healing wounds.

Alex had seen too much death to fear his own. Like mine, it would arrive on its own schedule.

But he feared dreams of death: the surprise on the Viet Cong's childish face as Alex stormed the hut and rammed the man's nose into his skull; the sound, like cocking a spring, as it broke through into the brain; his enemy's buckling legs as he crumpled onto his side; the old woman's terror and anguished wailing as she tore at her clothes that looked like the pajamas Alex wore as a kid. "The dream repeats itself over and over," he told us. "Over and over." Now at 25, he had a master tinkerer's permanently stained hands. After work in the owl light of our 20-foot Airstream camper that doubled as maintenance quarters, he'd open his pocket knife, cut away dead cuticles from the beds of his finger nails, and try to forget what happened to him in the war that America was losing.

After Alex finished his coffee and loaded Myron's dishes in a stack by the kitchen, he headed for the work shed. A good day for a takedown, he thought: not too hot, not much breeze—not yet, anyway. He unbolted the shed and swung the doors wide. His three-day stubble snagged a cobweb. The beaded leather headband plastered footloose hair to his temples. Two hanks cascaded over his ears.

With a gritty rag, he wiped spilled oil from the saw's filler hole and shined the Poulin's chartreuse enamel. He tugged the chain to check its tension on the three-foot bar. If my husband wanted a tree to come down, Alex would bring it down right. A saw that stalled or chattered through wood insulted its handler. A tree that twisted or fell off the intended mark was the result of simple incompetence. The notch slice and fall cut should be clean and true as a wedding cake's first, careful piece.

A gust of wind caught the machine shed door and banged it against the dented gas can. Alex fueled the heavy Poulin and the smaller Husky and filled the oil tanks that lubricated the chains. He capped the cans and sloshed them back onto the shelf. The shed smelled like wet woolen rugs and mushrooms. By the end of summer, the aroma would tang of gasoline and oil. Alex wondered what Myron would be like by summer's end.

"He'll be talking to you over coffee about the weather," he had said to Popeye, "and all the while his eyes just bulge. They don't blink." More than once, Alex had swiveled his head to follow Myron's gape. Nothing there. Nothing he could see, anyway. Since my death, pallor had settled into the flesh around Myron's eyes.

Word spread rapidly that the camp director had decided on a tree for the totem pole and that Alex would cut it down that afternoon. The gathering crowd grew into a throng.

I flitted among them like an invisible moth.

Maria Azavedo's lake-front assistant, Wally, worked the mob. His hawker's voice rose above the excitement. "Coconut oats," he called. "Get your coconut oats. Only a quarter a bag. Just the thing to gnaw when Alex starts to saw. Get your coconut oats here!"

Wally wore his lucky Stetson hat with the lining's trademark image of a horse drinking water from a cowhand's outstretched Stetson. The hats' miniature lining repeated itself: horse drinking water from the hat. The power of endlessly repeating and diminishing pictures of a drinking horse was Wally's voodoo: cowboy and colt standing side by side in smaller and smaller encores; thirst forever quenched in progressively diminutive hats. To bring the enchantment full circle, our CIT vowed one day to entice a chosen steed to drink from his lucky Stetson, and then—like funhouse mirrors curving into infinity—his kismet would align. West Point would accept him.

Wally slapped snacks into impatient hands, made change, and tucked the bills under the Stetson's brim. The crinkled dollars fringed his forehead in rumpled bangs and obscured the mop of straight brown hair. "Coconut oats here!"

The camp staff hung back chatting in a jagged crescent. Stanley lectured Popeye and Fanny on Einstein's theory of the space–time continuum.

I could have told them a few things about that.

"Consider Sonja's left-over bananas, the ones a-swarm with fruit flies," Stanley postulated.

"Uh, huh," Fanny answered.

"The banana's scent is not unlike gravity. If you're a fruit fly, you can't escape. You're trapped. Gravity bends you to its will." Stanley gazed at the coniferous mystery crowding the speckled afternoon. "Gravity can bend light, bend time. Believe it or not, my young friends, time—like thought—is multi-viscous!"

"Groovy," said Popeye.

"Yeah, groovy," Fanny said.

On the outskirts of the crowd, Kurt worked a square-framed puzzle which, when correctly manipulated, spelled out 'Happy New Year' in small, fading tiles. The Stone House bunch—Colleen, her friend, Betsy, and the twins, Megan and Thea—ambled through the mob in a loose pack, their glances wandering over the adolescent boys. As a group, they had decided Kurt might become something of a heart-throb in a few years. Even Angela, who trailed after her four roommates with Freddie, had fished for and caught Kurt's eye, then turned away, smiling.

Near the center of the cedar stand, Myron circled the largest tree whose branchless trunk rose 40 feet into a sparse crown. He patted the tree's thick girth, wrapped his arms around it, and flattened his ear against the bark. He mumbled words no one, but I, heard. The revelers quieted.

Scotty slapped his hand over his heart and silently mouthed the national anthem: "Oh, say can you see." Rope followed suit, snickering. Bags of coconut oats skipped through the crowd, passing quickly from hand to hand. Quarters cross-threaded back.

Myron released the tree's trunk, stepped back, and nodded to Jake.

"Stay back," Jake warned, making his way to the forefront. As head counselor, he reasoned his stature demanded a position at the fulcrum of power even if the campaign itself was flawed. Jake raised his arm and called to the man with the saw, "Alex, wait for my command."

"Yes sir, major, sir," Alex said under his breath. Jake swept his arm down and across his body. The throng peeled back. "Lock and load," Alex said. Expressionless, he stared at Jake. Our head counselor made chopping motions with his arm. Alex pointed to his chest. "Me?" he mimed, "Are you talking to me?" Jake scowled and chopped the air in agitation.

Alex hefted the saw's flat bar onto a shoulder and carried the 36 inch blade and its boxy engine to the tree's side. The spectators' arc widened. He circled the trunk, judged its angle and sighted the line where the giant would fall. Hemmed in by surrounding brush, the cedar's canopy crowded its neighbors. Alex grounded the saw, walked to Myron and conferred.

During the lull, Scotty and Rope took advantage of some low, wild cherry limbs—ideal perches. Others saw the logic and filled nearby branches. Rope bet an 8-year-old girl a dime her branch would snap, break both her legs, and squish somebody underneath.

"Won't either."

Rope leaned down and inspected the limb's crotch where it joined the trunk. "Bet a dime it will."

"Will not." She moved closer to the main trunk. "You're crazy."

Alex returned to the tree, looked off into the woods then back at the cedar. The fall line, narrow as a foot path, allowed no mistake. He knew Myron trusted him, but unless he notched the trunk precisely, the takedown would decapitate one of Sally Moffett's smaller cedar children— or unthinkably, one of Myron's human ones.

Most tree men start a large Poulin on the ground, boot snug in the handle. Not Alex. Starter cords got snapped that way. Setting the spring and rewrapping the pull line on a bull saw was "a royal pain in the keister," as he phrased it to Popeye.

He flicked the 'on' switch and pulled the black choke button out. Left-handed, he gripped the thick metal safety bar and let the heavy saw dip as he yanked the chord up with his right hand. The engine chugged and went dead. He stroked it again and the saw came to life. He tapped the choke in, fingered the trigger in two short snarls, and let the saw idle.

Alex sighted into the woods before angling the top notch cut in a high-pitched blast. The spinning chain pulled the saw's body against the rugged bark and ate down into the wood. With the notch cut the depth he wanted, he idled the machine and pulled the bar from the cedar's narrow gash. He looked again into the forest. Alex positioned the blade's tooth-studded chain parallel to the ground. He revved, sliced through to the notch cut, and when the wedge shrugged free, backed off leaving the saw in place. The chain grated to a halt, its engine sputtering in congested fits. With his boot, Alex kicked the triangle of freed wood onto the ground. Leaning into the sun-speckled forest the cedar's mouth gaped, its darker heartwood a puppet tongue in mid-sentence.

Alex gunned the machine and committed the Poulin to wood on the opposite side of the tree. He rocked the three-foot shank in its diagonal scar, encouraging the blade to burrow into pith. The saw's screaming head crept through the cambium. Sawdust, scented and warm as living flesh, illuminated slanting shafts of sunlight. Over the engine's full throttle, the cedar shuddered; its heartwood cracked.

Our handyman withdrew the blade, flicked the 'off' switch, and stepped back. The evergreen slipped from the notched butt, snapping the core's slender tether. The air—strangely quiet after the Poulin's keening—gathered the tree's collapsing length in creaks and moans. The cedar's crown whistled through a chute of blue sky. The ground accepted its body with a roar. Pine needles and dirt roiled out on either side. Scree curled above the trunk then settled, heavy particles first followed by a finer, misty rain.

The applause and hooted appreciation swelled like a second cloud of debris. "Three cheers for Alex," Jake bellowed. "Hip, hip."

Myron waited as the spectators straggled back to camp. When only he and Alex were alone in the brush, he crept to the fallen giant. The colossus appeared much smaller to him now. He plucked at the shaggy bark and ran his fingers along the narrow ridges.

"Your home, Deidre," he said to me. Mye patted the trunk remembering horses he and I had groomed after a hard ride. He wrapped his arms around the neck of our memory and kissed it. Alex stoked his smaller Husky and began winnowing the upper branches. The *Kyrie Eleison* of the saw chanted deep into the woods.

Seated on her cabin porch near the cove's tip a half-mile away, Shotgun Sally rocked and listened. "You owe me one, Mr. Cravitz."

Chapter Eight

Reginald Farrouk thought Cheryl Mariano's calves were smooth as the sand bars on New Jersey's Mullica River. Sometimes she wove her hair into plaits and pulled both hanks onto her shoulder—just as smooth—to stroke them.

But it was her ears that tugged Reginald's eyeballs as surely as the moon commands the tide. Was it sick, he wondered, to want to suck them, to nibble them like Fig Newtons? What would his psychiatrist father make of that? Just the thought of nuzzling into her hair—his mouth on her ear's florets—made his toes itch.

As the group dispersed after the tree crashed down and Jake Daryl's cheers for Alex petered-out, Reginald found himself walking toward the road with Cheryl.

"The water's getting warmer," he said. She murmured agreement. "Ever notice the cacophony of sound at night in these woods?" he said.

"You mean the noise? So, you come out here and listen?"

"Sometimes. I heard an owl last night. A barred owl, I think. Most people call it a hoot owl."

"I know what you mean," she said. "The other night I listened to the wind for a long time and thought about being on a boat in the lake with the waves splashing all around."

"Water is a universal symbol."

"For what?"

"Life, dreams."

"You talk about strange things, Reginald." She glanced down at him, two inches shorter, and smiled.

Cheryl's interest in the seemingly broad horizons of Reginald's knowledge encouraged the boy. He slowed his gait. Their footfalls creaked the pine needles. "The wind is symbolic, too."

"Mmmmmn."

"When Boreas kidnapped Orithyia, he couldn't help himself. I mean, everybody in Athens hated Boreas, but he was the North Wind. He could take whatever he wanted."

"What are you talking about?"

"Mythology."

Her eyes, lovely as pools, he thought, widened. "Oh."

Finally! Latin and classics were paying off. With his finger, he snuggled his stout frames against the bridge of his nose. "When you were daydreaming about the water and wind ..."

"I wasn't daydreaming. I was just—thinking."

"Wind and water are important symbols. Our feelings are part of nature's elemental forces. Just like with Boreas, everyone eventually acts on feelings too strong to hold back."

Cheryl gazed into Reginald's large and troubled eyes behind the thick glasses. "I wasn't trying to hold anything back. I was just thinking about the water and the boat and the wind ..."

Reginald unearthed a stone with his shoe. "Maybe. But you were really thinking about something else, weren't you?" This, he thought, was the sort of skillful questioning his father used with patients.

Cheryl stopped and parked five fingertips on Reginald's chest. "Wait a minute. You're telling me I wasn't really thinking about wind and water, that I was thinking about something completely different which I didn't want to *tell* myself I was thinking about, but I *had* to because I couldn't hold my feelings back any longer?"

"*¡Exactamente!*" he said, a five-syllable Spanish word he had practiced at the Friends of Mexico day camp until it assumed undeniable authority.

"Okay, doctor." Cheryl's daddy long-leg fingers scurried up his shirt. "I can no longer deny it. I must sail to Australia—with a midget." She snapped her hair.

Reginald removed his glasses, fogged them with his breath and swirled them clean with his T-shirt. He squinted up into her blurred and scowling face. "Sorry, didn't mean to make you mad."

"I'm not mad. Are you always this personal?" But before he could respond or replace his glasses, Cheryl's sputtering laugh parted his hair. "God, you look different without your glasses!"

"So do you." He replaced the nose guards which slipped, like puzzle pieces, into the indentations at the bridge of his nostrils. Cheryl's delicate ears were again distinct as the Calla Lilies in his mother's garden.

She touched his arm. "I didn't mean to laugh at you, Reginald. I just ..."

He could feel the heat from her fingers but feigned indifference, as Boreas would. "You just let your feelings out, honestly expressed yourself."

"Yeah. I guess that means we're compatible."

Victory flushed his cheeks. He didn't want the walk to end. He wanted 10 more miles for this odd feeling to finally assert itself, for the promises their words hinted at in conversation to materialize—in action.

"Maybe I'll see you after dinner?" Cheryl hurried onto the road to Stone House, rubbernecked a glance at him and, through a tangle of hair, flashed her self-conscious but inexplicably alluring, smile. A smile of collusion—Reginald was positive.

Dinner was torture. Cheryl sat at the next table over and glanced at him in teasing snippets. She chitchatted with her sniggering girlfriend. The food wasn't funny. The other girls at the table weren't funny, except maybe Megan who shot water from a straw into her twin sister's glass. Not really humorous, just Megan's infantile hunger for attention.

It's me, he sulked. Without my glasses, I'm a pitiable, mole-faced jerk. The custard's saccharine aroma turned his stomach.

I could see his morose thoughts: Cheryl flicking his glasses off his nose; Reginald groping for them in the dirt; Cheryl's belly-laughing entourage stomping his specs; their jeers as he tried to rescue the mangled frames and shattered glass.

It was too much for him. Reginald's anger rose up like a serpent, like Orithyia's sons seeking the Golden Fleece

112

and defending the Argonauts against the Harpies, swords wreaking revenge. Snicker-snack! Snicker-snack!

"Reginald?" Cheryl loomed over him.

"Oh, hi," his hand clipped his dinner cup. Kool-Aid vaulted onto the table.

"Are you going to the movie?" she asked.

"I thought I'd take a walk first." He hoped she could hear the invitation in his voice.

"Mind if I come along?"

"Sure! I mean, I don't mind." Reginald mopped the spill and bussed his dishes with deliberate poise. Another mind image—a more pleasant memory this time: throbbing drums; Tarzan vines; sweaty teenagers—a documentary film about the West African Nuba tribe. I observed its quaint, 16 millimeter flutter with him. His brain had branded the ritual into his ripening libido. Once a year, the tribe's unmarried adolescent men punished each other in stick fighting. The winners, sitting in a line on the acacia-swept ground, became eligible suitors for Nuba girls. During day-long dancing, the adolescent women picked their man by swinging a leg over his head.

Like the drums, Reginald throbbed with hope. Perhaps tonight Cheryl would choose him. Tonight at last, with the barred owl as a witness, the boy would unravel this summer's sexual mystery.

The sun had disappeared into the trees. Shadows entangled the woods. Cheryl slipped a cool hand into Reginald's. This was it. Finally, he would understand love's wonderful

and terrible forces on which the world pivoted: why
Medea killed her own children when Jason betrayed her;
why Romeo and Juliet died together rather than live apart.
Like the victorious Nuba men whose limbs quivered with
quiet expectation as they waited for their brides, Reginald
felt a trembling in his chest. His hand began to sweat.

"Cheryl?"

"Mmmmmn?"

"Do you know the story about the quest for the Golden
Fleece?"

"I think I've heard of it."

"It's mythology."

"You know a lot about the Greek and Roman Gods, huh?"

"It's fascinating. Cheryl?"

"Mmmmmn?"

"You are my Golden Fleece." It was not exactly what he
had wanted to say, but it summed up the proportion of his
longing.

Cheryl tilted her head and moved closer to him. "That's
sweet, Reginald. Would you like to ... ?"

Reginald felt her breath on his cheek. They nudged, and
with intermingling voices, Cheryl said, "kiss me?" and
Reginald said, "go all the way?"

Cheryl stepped back. "What did you say?"

"Cheryl, let's go all the way."

Cheryl's indignation dilated. "You little creep!" She flung Reginald's hand back at him. "You little pervert!"

"I thought that's what you wanted."

"Who do you think I am?"

"I thought that's why we took this walk!"

"Think again, pip-squeak." Cheryl caught the side of Reginald's shoe with a sweep of her foot and knocked him down. His glasses landed at her feet. "Mythology! Don't ever come near me again, you four-eyed runt."

"Don't worry. I won't." Reginald rubbed at the knot swelling his ankle. "Amazon!" he yelled at her retreating back. He decided to skip the after-dinner movie.

In his cabin, under the dangling light bulb whose glare threw the ballpoint's shadow across the page, Reginald composed "The Golden Fleece," a sequel to his first poem about Cheryl:

> Not only did you fail
> To invite me in,
> You failed to tell me why
> You kicked me so hard it hurts
> To think about it.
> You are the Golden Fleece
> And I am the ram
> That got sacrificed in the end.
> You said we were compatible.
> I say, maybe we're not.

Chapter Nine

"Keep kicking! Straighten your legs, Freddie." Maria popped the whistle into her mouth and popped it out again. "Shortstack, turn around." Maria drew a "C" in the air. "Turn around!" She paced the shore. "Girls, don't look at me, keep kicking."

Twenty feet out where the bottom still allowed the younger ones to stand, the placid lake boiled and foamed as they made slow progress in lines parallel with the shore. Each student lay on her stomach death-gripping the training board's edge. Maura, now universally known as Shortstack, pressed her left ear against the white polystyrene and shut her eyes in concentration. Freddie, a giant among her pale, fellow swimmers, plowed up an ineffectual froth.

"Kick," Maria urged them. "Kick, kick, kick!"

Jake's eyes were fixed on the life guard. On his way from the younger boys' cabin to the boathouse, he nearly tripped over the mattress Scotty and Rope had dragged into the woods for a makeshift camp out. "String bean," he muttered at the bedding and his mind's image of the lanky young counselor, "you're in charge of overnights, get your boney ass in gear and organize one."

At the meadow's periphery above the beach, Jake stopped to watch Maria call out encouragement. She grazed the shore keeping watch on the swimmers, her slender feet grinding pockets into the sand. Jake envied the Tank suit's fabric stretched taut across her nipples and grapefruit breasts. Wisps of pubic hair clung to the mocha skin at the border of the suit where dark cloth covered her Venus mound.

Earlier that morning, Stanley and Jake had left the dining hall together. Maria had gone to her cabin for her swim suit. A towel and the suit swung from her hand as she trudged to the boathouse cabana to change.

"At least I'm not the only one whose accent is" Stanley gestured toward the life guard, *"funny* as one of our pubescent campers put it."

"That walk's not funny." Jake's eyes were riveted. "If she were any riper, she'd split open."

"You are obsessed," Stanley said. "No good will come of it. Besides, you have Fanny."

"Want to trade?"

"What do you mean?"

"Fanny for Maria."

Stanley laughed. "Caution, my friend. You're a married man. Although the holy state has eluded me, from what I gather, it's a fulltime job."

They watched Maria open the cabana door. "Later," Jake said to Stanley. Our head counselor crossed the meadow toward the cabana near the beach. The life guard had pulled the door shut, but Jake knew the lock hadn't worked in years. When he reached the dressing room, he yanked the door open. The cubicle flooded with light. The black straps of Maria's suit dangled at her sides. She slapped her forearms over her naked breasts. "Out!" she ordered.

Jake lingered with the door knob in his hand. "Oh, didn't see you in there."

"You are seeing me now. Out!" she yelled. From then on, Maria changed into her suit in the safety of the girls' latrine.

Jake returned to the mattress and hugged the keeling drunkenness of it upright. He slapped the dirt off, dragged the pallet into the bunkhouse, and brushed the earth off his trousers. He looked at his watch: mid-morning.

"*¡Brava!*" Maria called. "Okay, let's take a break and practice the arm strokes." She waded out to them. "Up and across. See, my arm is curved, hand cupped." She stooped over the water while the children draped their rafts like ship-wreck survivors. "It's easy, watch me first. Up and across."

With the beginning of drier weather and the black flies' expected departure, summer was finally opening her legs (as Jake liked to phrase it). He had honeymooned with Fanny in the Adirondacks during August a few years after Myron and I hired him. He spent $40 an hour—more money than he should have—lake-hopping with his new wife. They made love in shallow water hidden under willow limbs overhanging the shore line while the bush pilot smoked French cigarettes on the dock, water slapping the sides of the plane's pontoons.

After sitting for 2 days in Schroon Lake's hotel bar drinking gin gimlets—lime wedges speared by trout-shaped pickets—Jake and Fanny left the moose head's glassy stare and went back to Jersey, the Pizza Palace and life with one another. Now he wondered, where had the years gone?

119

Fanny wasn't as tolerant of his sexual needs anymore. And he wouldn't beg for it. Yesterday, lust overwhelmed him in the infirmary. He insisted even though she wasn't willing. His violence permanently loosened the joints in one of our better cots. The bunk would bleat from now on with every 12-year old headache and 9-year old upset stomach. The episode had angered Fanny—which delighted Jake.

"Breathe and blow," Maria instructed. She dipped her face into the lake. Bubbles erupted into her thick hair spread on the water's surface like an oil dollop. She lifted her head, turned her face, took an exaggerated breath, and blew it back into the water.

From the Stone House veranda, Jake's wife also watched Maria. "You don't belong here," Fanny said to the far-away woman standing in the lake's sparkling shallows. Fanny's brooding appraisal had begun silently while sorting through commandments her mother pressed upon her when she became Mrs. Jake Daryl. Now, the irritable thoughts huffed out loud.

"Parading around camp in your bathing suit like a harlot. It's not proper. Maybe that's how women strut around in your country, but here in America, women know their places. They keep their clothes on. They take care of their husbands. They tidy the house. They mind the kids."

Fanny turned away. Jake didn't want children because they weren't practical. But he wanted Maria. Why else would he stand there gawking at her? She knew her husband. He was coming on to this temptress and Fanny didn't like it.

"Fanny, there you are." Myron closed the veranda's double doors. "Who are you talking to?"

"Myself. Just me and myself."

Fanny's mouth, pinched sourly at the corners, compelled Myron to get to the point. "Some of the children have been complaining to me about headaches and swollen necks. They said you gave them pills for it?"

"Headaches and swollen necks? Do you mean Bishop and that little slip, Valerie?"

"I don't remember their names, Fanny."

"Well, they said they itched like crazy so I gave them something called Valium. I found a bunch of it in the storage shed."

"Does Valium relieve itching?"

"That's what Wally thought. He's almost an Eagle Scout."

Myron pressed a palm to his forehead. "Fanny, you shouldn't be giving the children Valium. I think that's for something else. The problem is black flies. Hopefully, they'll be gone soon, but in the meantime, if the kids are out at night, tell them to wear long-sleeves and give them insect repellant. We have insect repellant, don't we?" She nodded. "Good. Have you seen your husband?"

Fanny slipped a cigarette and book of matches out of the white lab coat's breast pocket. She turned and pointed to the lake-front. "He's down there." She lit the cigarette, peeled a flake of tobacco from her lip, and rolled the slippery fleck between her fingers.

Myron set out for the beach down the terrace stairs and crossed the sloping, sun-spattered lawn in that awkward, urgent lope of his. He was wheezing when he caught up with Jake.

"She's good with them, isn't she?" Mye said.

Jake dragged his eyes from Maria. "Just on my way to see you."

"Likewise. What do you know about horses?"

Myron's manner needled Jake. Leadership meant listening to your troops didn't it, finding out what they had on *their* minds? Myron didn't seem to care about anything lately except that "damn totem pole," as Jake often spat it out.

"What do I know about horses?" Jake said. "Next to nothing."

Myron sighed. "I can ride them, that's about it."

Where the hell is Cravitz going with this, Jake wondered? "Why do you ask?"

"We need a small team to drag the cedar out of the woods."

Jake belched. Frigging breakfast sausages. Of course, the totem pole again. Why couldn't they rent a jeep or a tractor? Clear a road into the trees and just back up to the thing? "Well, I'm afraid I don't know much about horses."

"Ask Lila Mae. She's in-between piano lessons. I saw her at the goat pen feeding Mozart."

"Myron, why would Lila Mae know about horses?"

"She grew up in Oklahoma before her folks moved to New

York. Everybody from Oklahoma knows about horses. Tell her we need the kind that can pull wagons. You know, 'Over the river and through the woods.'"

Jake Daryl's memory of a horse pulling a wagon flung itself at me. The animal arched a matted tail and extruded excrement the size of cannonballs. "Maybe a tractor would be better," he said.

"No, I've thought of that. Wouldn't be able to move laterally in the woods."

Jake was grudgingly impressed. If weak-minded *savants* could multiply three and four digit numbers in their heads or correctly predict the day of the week from any date in history, maybe Myron had a point. Jake generally dismissed my husband as a poor, pussy-whipped sniveler. But I saw a glimmer of respect, a brief flash in the morass of Daryl's contempt. Yes, Goddamnit! He had to agree with the crazy son-of-a-bitch. Tight lateral movement.

"I'll talk to Lila Mae," Jake said.

He found her kneeling in the grass by the goat pen, her dashiki a blue cascade. Rose quartz earrings dangled in strands below a penumbra of frizzy hair. A necklace with a silver piano charm bounced in the dell between smooth collar bones as she ripped grass in quick strokes.

"So," Jake said to her as she fed the goat through the fence, "what do I look for in a team of work horses?" He leaned against the ash tree. The sign said: 'Mozart Lives Here.'

Lila Mae stood up. "What will they be doing Mr. Daryl?"

"Hauling a forty-foot tree close to a mile."

"Ah, the totem pole. What do you suppose the log will weigh?"

"I don't know. Two, maybe three tons. Do you have any suggestions?"

"Well, I have some thoughts, but why did you come to me with this question?"

"Cravitz said you grew up in Oklahoma."

"And why would that make me an expert on horses?" Lila Mae tried to rub Mozart's nose, but the goat shied away. He wanted food. She stooped to gather more grass.

"Oklahoma's horse country, isn't it?"

"A lot of it is, but I grew up in north Tulsa on Peoria Avenue."

"So you don't know anything about horses?"

"About as much as you know about North Tulsa," she smiled showing very straight teeth.

Jake appreciated candor, but Lila Mae's cheekiness made him testy. "You said you had some other thoughts?"

"Why don't you use a tractor?"

"I suggested as much to Cravitz, but, well, he's the director."

"People talk about a local named Sally who lives around here," Lila Mae said. "Maybe she can help? Sorry I can't."

"Don't be sorry. Be happy. Smile!" He roughly tapped her shoulder, "I'll handle it." He strutted off toward the main drive that bisected camp.

Alex, on his way to the pottery shed, was lugging a brown, paper-wrapped block of clay the size of a 10 gallon fish tank. The slab's dense weight crunched his boots into the road's gravel.

"Hey! Alex!"

Alex heaved the block onto his opposite shoulder. "What's up?" he said when Jake reached him.

"Nice takedown the other day. It fell perfect."

Alex squinted into the man's eager, stupid face. Jake Daryl wouldn't know a nice takedown from a botched one if the tree crashed through his living room. "Thanks, but it's not how it falls, it's where it lands."

"Same thing," Jake said, and then, "You know where Sally lives?"

"Sally Moffett? Shotgun Sally with the overalls and Bowie knife?"

"That's her." Jake had last seen Sally Moffett in the Match general store wearing work boots with stained, denim pant legs tucked into her boot tops. A bone-handled knife protruded over her boot's rim. "Lo," she had nodded to him in a loud monotone, her wicker provision basket swaying on her arm. She turned her back and lunged down another aisle, her meaty backside solid as sand bags.

"She's off the main road into town, quarter mile south of the deer crossing." Alex grunted the satchel to the other shoulder. "Don't expect a welcome mat."

Although the trip to Sally's was less than a mile, Jake took his car, found her driveway and parked. She stalled him on her porch. The large woman nestled her thigh against the front door's rough panel and snorted through Jake's unannounced visit. "They'd need to be strong horses, Miss Moffett. The tree's real heavy."

"Humh."

"A truck can't maneuver in the woods."

"Uh-huh."

"If you could just help me out here."

From the front path, her ramshackle cabin's rustic charm appeared picturesque. But when Jake eventually got through the doorway, he welcomed the conversation's brevity. He had never seen grimier living quarters. A musty odor from wood ash in the fireplace forced him into shallow breathing. The front room overflowed with a catastrophe of clutter. Near the kitchen sink, filled with leafy, potted plants, stacks of books threatened to topple onto the stove.

He'd never let Fanny keep house like this. Disgust twitched his mustache. Sally Moffett was one sorry, frazzle-haired broad with no man around to straighten her out. She knew, at any rate, where Jake could rent a team of horses. As he left, Sally warned him not to crush her maidenhair ferns that lined the path back to his car.

The next morning, Jake's dream—squirming and thrusting under Maria's drumming heels as they sprawled naked on the backs of two harnessed mares dragging a totem pole— was interrupted when Fanny groped across him for her robe's sash. He turned away from his wife.

The logistics of erecting the pole intrigued Jake. He had no idea how Myron would upend the thing. Forty feet. Two, possibly three, tons? As he dressed, he decided to see if my husband was in his office.

Amid a litter of sketches and half-filled coffee cups, two totem replicas spiked Myron's desk. Crowning the larger clay model, loon wings jutted below a flat beak at the bird's breast. Myron's stylized bear—stiff on hind legs, paws drawn up in front—anchored the bird above. A map of upstate New York and, under the chart, my portrait painted 10 years ago by one of Myron's high school students.

Despite the room's warmth, Myron clutched a shawl tight around his narrow shoulders. "Did you know the U.S. Constitution took four-hundred-year-old principles of government from the Iroquois Nation?" he said.

Jake lounged against the wall. "No kidding," he said, his inflection bored.

Myron peered up at my portrait. "We've got to make the totem permanent, Jake. We've got to do it right."

"Why?"

"For Deidre. For the children."

"Oh yeah. What were their names again?

In Mye's head, sudden ringing bloomed and receded. He swatted at his ear in annoyance, knowing his disease was no longer a necessary medium for communicating with me. "Devon and Caleb."

"Is that an eagle on top?" Jake asked.

Myron refocused on Jake's face. "It's a loon. The animals are called crests. Each crest tells a story."

Jake sat, legs straddling the seat back. "What's the loon's story?"

Mye ignored him and scooted his chair to the desk in several small advances. "Alex trimmed out the tree's upper branches and flattened the back to reduce the weight. The totem's forty-two feet long, three-and-a half feet in diameter at mid-point. If we sink the pole 12 feet into the ground and run an iron bar through a stainless steel collar 20 feet up the center, no one will ever cut it down."

Myron's fantasy. Jake knew Alex could do many things, but doubted he could bore 20 feet through a tree's marrow. Old man, he thought, if you want something permanent, bulldoze a chunk of granite next to Stone House.

"I suppose," Jake said, "we should start asking around for heavy machinery to put the pole up."

"We won't need to." Myron rifled through the sketches and selected one. "When they finish their totems, the Tlingit and Haida raise them by digging a hole under one end." He pointed to a skeletal framework of lumber and rigging. "They build a superstructure and use pulleys and ropes to haul the other end upright while the butt's in the hole."

"Where are we going to carve this thing?"

"Alex has already cleared the center aisle of the barn theater."

Jake pulled his chair up to the desk, "Well, that broad, Sally Moffett, told me where I could find some work horses to drag the log out of the woods."

Myron sat up from his slouch. "Wonderful!"

"The horses should be here sometime next week. But how do we get the tree from the barn to," Jake shrugged, "wherever it ends up?"

Myron fixed his eyes on the totem replica and squeezed Jake's forearm. "We'll use people, lots of willing hands, the whole town of Match if we have to."

I could see Jake's cynical thoughts as though projected above the map of New York and my portrait on the wall. He imagined a tree trunk on the barn floor in front of the proscenium we used for theatrical events. The beginning of crude sculpture riddled the pole's length. Smooth ripples, worn shiny over the decades by fidgeting children, buffed the surface. Closest to the stage, the unfinished totem pole would be the ultimate front-bench seat. Some as yet unknown camp administrator—perhaps Jake's successor—would follow tradition and invite the smaller children onto the totem. The future head counselor would make a big fuss about the log's importance and announce the spot as the Totem Seating Gallery. He would tell its history to the spectators of the season's opening play while the little ones clamored onto lumpy crevices, excited to wriggle in their special perches.

"Many years ago, our camp's first director tried to build a totem pole," the future administrator would say. "What you're sitting on is the result of his dream. Although the project was never finished, we should all remember that Myron Cravitz attempted something special."

So much for doing it right, Jake thought.

Chapter Ten

Barefooted and cross-legged, Brad Stringer dragged the nail of his little finger over the 11 sympathetic strings. His sitar, bottom gourd cradled in the arch of his left foot, sounded to the piano coach like water trickling over pebbles. Lila Mae listened with her eyes shut, back pressed against the porch railing.

Brad brushed the slender wires again and reached to thicker, melodic strings above. He began an afternoon raga tossing seven notes—like jacks—onto the veranda's deck. He plucked the top strings and stretched them across the bowed frets of the instrument, teasing it to murmur and sigh. One o'clock aspen shadows danced over Kurt Willington who sat next to Lila Mae and listened. Kurt had never heard music like this at the children's home.

Brad quickened the tempo. In Kurt's mind, a kite wheeled and dipped, swooped and dove then fluttered to the ground as the melody subsided and the sympathetic strings droned. Brad repeated the melodic core and the kite surged again above the playful shadows.

Then the veranda doors banged open.

From the entry, Jake leered at Kurt, and then barked at Brad, "String bean, follow me."

Jake had discovered the theft when he went to unlock the snack hut. The jimmied door stood open under the candy-striped awning. "Looks like he strong-armed the front door and climbed in over the counter," he said to Brad.

"How much is missing?"

"Eight dollars and some change, and all the Good 'n Plentys. Selective thief." With his foot, Jake swept the empty Good 'n Plenty display box into the corner. "I don't think you'll have far to look. Willington's done it before, you know. He stole a watch from a teacher at the children's home. Kurt's ward warned us about him. Nail him, Stringer. Somebody has to."

"Can't you talk to him first?"

"You're his counselor. Find out what you can. See if he admits having any money. The home wouldn't have given him much. He's probably already stashed the candy."

One of Jake's many loathsome habits was how he assumed his own infallibility. While I lived, I had witnessed it many times. Jake immediately went to Myron's empty office. He checked the master camper list for a phone number and dialed.

"This is Jake Daryl, head counselor at the Cravitz Fine Arts Camp," he said into the receiver. "One of your residents is attending our camp and there's a problem. Thank you." He waited and then said," Mr. Haskell? Jake Daryl, Associate Director at the Cravitz Camp. I'm afraid Kurt Willington has let us down. We've had a theft. Yes, we discovered it today. I see. Well, I know you're busy. Not until late this month? Can't you come sooner? Okay. No, that's fine. We'll see you two weeks from Wednesday. Yes, we're sorry too and disappointed. Alright. Goodbye."

To Brad's annoyance, when he returned to his cabin Kurt was eating Good 'n Plentys in his bunk. "Listen up," Brad said to the boys, "afternoon workshops begin in a couple of minutes. If you want to help Alex strip bark from the totem pole, meet in the oval near the flag pole." Several boys scrambled for the cabin door. Kurt waited for the others to leave and then languidly got up. "Come on out a minute, Kurt. We have to talk."

"What about?" The boy finished the box of candy.

"Come on out and I'll tell you." He and Brad ambled toward the barn. "Enjoying yourself?" Brad asked.

"It's an okay place." Kurt kept his eyes on his feet.

"I hear you're a good swimmer."

Kurt shrugged. "The lake's a lot better than a swimming pool."

"Maria tells me you might try for junior lifesaving."

"Is that what you wanted to talk to me about?" Kurt stopped and looked up at his counselor.

Brad watched a pair of ducks waddle into the moss-green pond in Ringer's Field. "No." The ducks' wake rippled against the muddy shore. "Kurt, let's get one thing straight. I'm your counselor. If you have a problem, anything you want to discuss, bring it to me first."

"Problems? Like what?"

"I don't know. Problems like needing extra spending money for snacks."

Kurt stepped back. "What does that mean?"

"Well, those Good 'n Plenty's."

133

"They gave me ten dollars allowance for the summer when I left. I've still got most of it." Kurt was coiled for accusation.

"How much is left?"

"Eight dollars." Brad was sorry he had asked. This wasn't his job.

"You think I stole some money, don't you? Oh great," Kurt sneered, "so, now I'm a thief. A couple weeks in this lousy place and already I'm a thief."

"Nobody said you were a thief, Kurt."

"Come on, that's what you think." The boy's face seethed. "Somebody's missing money. So, of course, you blame me."

"Look, the money is missing. We don't know who took it."

"But you think I did. Haskell told you didn't he?"

"Haskell? No."

"He told you about the watch, didn't he?"

"Kurt, nobody—okay, Jake mentioned something about a watch but that doesn't ..."

"I borrowed that watch. If Haskell hadn't come back early from chapel, no one would've missed it." The boy fought to control his voice. "After track I was gonna put it back."

Brad wished Kurt would cry so he could comfort him. "Let's just drop it, Kurt. Okay?"

"Sure. Everybody already knows anyway, right? There goes Kurt. Better not leave your wallet around, Willington's at it again." His anger swelled to a hoarse rage. "I borrowed that crappy watch. And I didn't take the money!"

Kurt spun around and ran up the road. He fell, scrambled up, and snatched a handful of stones. He threw them one after the other at the ducks. They flapped away across the pond. Then the boy hightailed it across the playing field into the woods. He ran until he overtook his rage and then kept going—past hurt, past feeling. Enduring humiliation wasn't hard. At the home, Haskell yelled at him for no good reason. He'd learned to sleep with the lights on. He'd taken punches without flinching. He'd had lots of practice swallowing crap.

Alone in her cabin, Sally Moffett glued the last violet leaf onto the black circle of velvet. She set the tweezers aside and cocked her head.

"Maybe some blue chicory stems around the skirt," she mused. Her thick hand went to her mouth. She absent-mindedly bit a strand of dead thumb skin, turned her head, and spat. "And a scrap or two of Joe-pye weed." She bent closer in the cabin's subdued light to admire the half circle of white daisy petals. Her eyes drifted to the window. Even before she heard the limbs crackling, she sensed the approach of something large outside.

Sally eased off her stool, swung the near-by gun up to her right hand, and stepped out onto the hewn-timber porch. She held the shotgun stock under her armpit, the double barrels pointed two paces beyond her boots. Could be a bear, she thought, wounded by some damn, trophy-hunting tourist from New York City. She scanned the woods.

Adirondack black bears appear sluggish when rummaging the preserve's illicit dumps. I had seen them lumber through trash many times. But wounded with small-caliber slugs, they're dangerous, mad, and fast enough with their claws to shuck a human face to cheek bone. Although she always kept her custom shotgun loaded—left breach with a 30.06 caliber bullet, right with 12 gauge buckshot—Sally checked each chamber. She clicked the gun shut and waited. The woman had killed rampaging and wounded bears before, and she hated it.

A figure, moving fast, darted into the slatted pines—not the black bear she'd expected but a boy snarled in the undergrowth and struggling to free himself. He thrashed at the immature witch hobble, pulled loose, and lunged toward the cabin. The sight of the gun barrels pointed his way stopped him. Kurt raised his hands.

"Where you goin'?" Sally called to him.

"No place!"

"You're goin' no place in an awful hurry. Fact is you're trespassin.'" She lowered her voice. "There's a lot of animals call this piece of woods home, and when somebody comes bargin' through like a Mack Truck, they get upset."

Kurt dropped to his knees. "Sorry," he wheezed. Red splotches from wrestling with the undergrowth tattered his arms and neck.

"You from the camp?"

"Maybe." He swallowed the knot in his throat. "Yeah, the arts camp. They think I'm a thief, but I'm not. I swear it!"

"A thief." Sally snorted. "What do they think you stole?"

"Money." His rasped breathing slowed. Kurt sat back on his calves, thighs spread. He squinted warily at the large, snaggletooth woman with blowtorched hair.

Sally set the shotgun stock on the porch and leaned the barrels against the railing, sorry she had scared him. He looked to be only 12 or so. She knew she was imposing and the gun didn't soften her image. She depended on the weapon for more than shooting injured bears.

Last fall, for instance, Gerald Ratchet, owner of the Match General Store and town gossip, had confided to some of his customers that Sally's claim to the inherited land was a lie. Ratchet maintained the real estate had been stolen in a card game three generations ago. Like most gossip, there was an ounce of truth in the telling. Sally's great-grand-father, Bernard Dubonnet, had won what was then con-sidered a small parcel—500 acres—in poker, but the hand had been honest. The loser, Ratchet's great-grandfather, Enrique Rochette, had swizzled too much rye and had too little regard for his opponent's skill at cards.

After the rumors circulated around town to the point of irritation, Sally and her shotgun paid Ratchet a visit. She kept her finger near the trigger guard as she laid the gun on the oak counter, barrels pointed at the proprietor's fake Tiffany lamp. The lamp's dragonfly motifs, separat-ed by leaded veins, encircled the bright geometry of col-ored glass. Its twelve hundred dollar price tag allowed Ratchet to barter tourists down from a ridiculous to an unreasonable sum. "I need vitamin B-complex," Sally told Ratchet as he stood pasty and sweating next to the cash register. "Your lies have riled up my nerves." Her finger had scratched at the trigger guard.

"How much money?" Sally asked Kurt. "A lot of money?"

"I don't know. A lot, I guess," the boy said.

"And you didn't take it?"

"No, but what does it matter. They think I did." Kurt got to his feet.

"It's the accusation that matters." She strolled to the top step. "If you didn't take the money, defend yourself. Fight for the truth." Sally looked him over and changed the subject. "You're kinda skinny."

"Better than being fat."

I liked Kurt's spunk. So did Sally. The woman's forearms were baseball bats, solid as a man's but hairless. Her fingers, curled along the seam of the denim overalls, seemed stout enough to shatter a bowling ball.

"Muscle weighs a lot more that fat," she said. "I'm large boned. You're small boned and there's nothin' wrong with that, I'm not sayin' that. You just look like you could use a week's worth of dinner. What do they feed you at the camp?"

"It's not the worst food I've ever had." Kurt remembered the salt-choked chip beef on toast at the home, what Haskell called shit-on-a-shingle.

Sally sniffed the fetid odor moving upslope from the lake. "Smell that?" she said. "That's July algae and a week of wet weather. I can smell food cookin' at the camp, too. It's less than a mile down shore." Sally's tongue sluiced the gap in her front teeth, "Some days when the wind's from the east, the Cravitz place smells like carp bait. Carp's a trash fish, not like the brookies. Used to be, you could catch brook trout in any stream or lake up here. They're mostly gone now on account of the acid rain. Nothin' better than fresh trout fried in butter 'n pepper."

Kurt eyed the six-inch handle of a knife protruding from Sally's mid-calf boot. He pointed to it. "Do you know how to use that thing, or do you just wear it for show?"

"What. This?" Sally pulled the blade from its sheath and pitched the Bowie knife overhand into the porch balustrade 20 feet away. The Bowie's speed penetrated wood— *tthup.* The porch vibrated. A blue jay, flushed from a scrubby cedar, flapped away in terror.

Kurt worked his jaw in admiration. "Bet you can't do that twice in a row."

"The Moors say doin' somethin' twice is bad luck." She strode across the porch which shook under her weight. "This knife's for cuttin' off carrot tops, peelin' onions and, a' course, skinnin' bears." Sally rocked the handle to release the wood's grip and re-sheathed the blade. "Aren't you gettin' hungry?" she asked. "I could sure use a meal." She hefted the gun and disappeared inside. Kurt stood at the foot of the porch stairs craning to see into the dark front window. "Well?" she called out to him, "are you comin' or goin'?"

Sally's bungalow reminded Kurt of the chapel at the home: somber light, restful. Most of the preacher's sermons stank—constant reminders of how *not* to behave. He liked the hymns, though. He liked to sing and could picture Jesus walking his lonesome valley in the cabin's soft haze.

Sally's voice boomed out from the kitchen. "I make the best goddamn sourdough bread from here to Watertown, excuse my language. You want bologna or ham?"

"Ham," Kurt called back.

"Mustard or mayo?"

"Both."

"Tomatoes?"

"Yeah," Kurt said and then added, "please."

"Provolone or Swiss cheese?

Kurt had never heard of provolone cheese. "Swiss."

On a shelf over the kitchen sink, a line of small flower pots hoarded the bright light from the window. Sally slid books stacked on the counter top to the wall and slapped two pieces of thick bread with mustard and two more with mayonnaise.

In the front room, Kurt wandered along a display of sea shells. He snuggled his fingers into the smooth, sunset colored underbelly of a whelk and pressed it to his ear listening for waves. At the end of the room, a thick fireplace mantle jutted from rounded stones with a clock in the plank's center and two furry objects on each end. Shrunken heads? Kurt wondered.

Sally tramped into the room with a serving tray filled with two glasses of milk and two plates heaped with sandwiches, pickles, and two orange halves. She cleared books from a table by the couch and set the plates down. "Dig in."

Kurt brought the sandwich to his mouth, but couldn't surround its girth. He put the bulge back on his plate and flattened it with his palm. Flour from the crust, fine as powdered sugar, stuck to his hand.

Sally chuckled. "It's called a Dagwood sandwich."

Kurt took a bite. "Ompffur."

Sally took a bite. "Urhupchroff," she nodded.

When they had finished, Kurt asked about the shrunken heads.

"Koala Bears," she said. "Too bad people think they have to stuff animals to teach us about 'em. My father got those in Melbourne."

"Melbourne." Kurt repeated.

"It's in Australia," Sally said.

"Right," Kurt said. He relieved the mantle of its clock. The timepiece, shaped like a bell curve, had a silver-spoked tire on top. A tarnished metal plaque said: 'To Sally from Delmore—VAROOM!'

"Are you Sally?" She nodded and watched the boy poke the glass casement. "Who's Delmore?" Kurt slid the clock back onto the ledge.

"Somebody from the past. I don't know why I keep that thing." She frowned at the clock. "It runs fast just like he did." Should have trashed that ages ago, Sally thought. Few people in Match knew Delmore existed. Her life with him while working at the Ford Plant (if you could call her thankless servitude and his drunken debauchery a life) was long over.

"What' your name?" Sally asked.

"Kurt."

"Just Kurt?"

"Kurt B. Willington."

"What's the 'B' stand for?"

"I don't know. It doesn't stand for anything. Just B. Do you have a middle initial?"

"C, for Charlemagne."

"Wasn't he a king or something?"

The boy's bright, Sally thought. Amid the freckles, Kurt's curious intelligence flecked the eyes. A bruised wariness lurked there, too.

"You need some iodine for that scrape on your arm?"

"Nah."

Sally's healing abilities were legendary. Remote neighbors brought wounded animals—birds mostly—to her doorstep all year long. Most folks handed them over without a word. They knew her cages, stacked behind the cabin, would hold and protect the critters while they mended. Most serious bird injuries—except broken wings—didn't show under the feathers. Kurt's injuries didn't show either, but Sally figured he'd been wounded more than once.

When Sally disappeared into the kitchen with the dishes, the boy opened a drawer to the six-sided table by the couch. A large knife sheathed in leather, its ivory shank fluted for gripping, nestled in the bottom. He caressed its length, lingered on the handle's smooth bone, and then closed the drawer.

Sally lumbered into the room. "Maybe you'd better be gettin' back. They'll be wonderin' where you are."

The boy sighed and turned to the door. "Yeah."

"Walk straight out to the lake shore. Camp's that way," she gestured. "If you go the other way you'll end up in Canada. Eventually."

"Okay. And thanks for lunch." Kurt smiled.

Wounded, she thought, but still able to smile. That's a good sign.

"Where have you been?" Brad said from the doorway.

"I met this lady."

The counselor followed Kurt into the cabin. "Kurt, you've been gone almost two hours. I was about to tell Mr. Cravitz you were missing." Brad steered him to his bunk. "Where have you been?"

"I told you. I met this lady. Her name's Sally. She lives in the woods."

"You took off in a pretty bad mood."

"I didn't steal the damn money!" Kurt tried to leave but Brad pressed a hand on his shoulder.

"Kurt, I've been thinking about this. Maybe you didn't take the money." Brad noticed a thin line of blood on Kurt's forearm. "What happened to you?"

"That's what I've been trying to tell you." The boy's indignant voice stifled a growl. "Nobody ever believes me! I had lunch with Sally."

"You already had lunch in the dining hall."

"No, I mean a real lunch. Homemade bread, ham, cheese, tomatoes, an orange."

"You've got a cut on your arm."

"Yeah, I got that at Sally's."

"Who's Sally?"

Kurt sighed in exasperation. People didn't listen to him. He spoke to Brad as though he were one of the littlest campers. "I ran into the woods, okay? I ran and ran until I came to Sally's place. She invited me in for lunch."

"Sally? You mean the lady with the missing front tooth? The one they call Shotgun Sally?"

Kurt tapped Brad's forehead. "Now you're getting it. Man," he scowled, "can she throw a knife!"

Brad gasped. "She cut you!"

"No! No!" Kurt slapped his hands to his face. Why were adults so stupid? "She didn't cut me. Some briars cut me. I got caught in some brush and tried to get free."

Brad eased off. "Okay, calm down. You're back now. But

144

promise me you won't run away like that again." The boy stared at the door and waited for the lecture to end. "There's a play starting soon. In the barn. Be there, okay?"

"Yeah, I know. Reginald told me about it." Kurt got up, walked to the door and didn't look back. "I didn't steal the money."

In the shuttered half-light, the barn theater's worn seats were filling fast. Impatient children drummed the chair backs with their feet and cat-called into the rafters. Thea's twin, Megan, paced behind the moldering blue curtain. She snapped the long John's elastic waist band that peeked above her borrowed, and too-long Guatemalan skirt.

"Ho, ho. What man did ever dream to play for you who are but as a handful of dust thrown into the air? Nowhere." She repeated the line until it lost coherence: "Hohohowhatmandideverdreamtoplayforyouwhoarebutasahandfulofdustthrownintotheairnowhere." As she paced, the skirt's tattered hem leapt out in front of her. On Megan's brow, jagged black lines simulated age and were repeated at the corners of her eyes.

Silently mouthing her lines, Cheryl Mariano trudged back and forth near Megan. She wore body tights and one of Fanny's lab coats open in the front and pinned in thick cuffs at the sleeves. Construction paper butterflies spotted the coat inside and out, and adorned her hair as though (Leon McAdam, had said) "alighting to drink nectar." Around her calves, a donated sweater's cut-off arms were already making her itch.

On the other side of the stage, Reginald contemplated Cheryl. He still thought she was beautiful—conceited, dangerous, but beautiful.

Leon McAdam bounded onto the creaking stage. "Ladies and gentlemen, camp Cravitz is proud to present the American Indian Legend, *Butterfly Girl and Mirage Boy*. Our masque today is a simple allegory of love's power to transcend the earthly sphere through unceasing devotion."

The house quieted and from the audience, a furtive fart ended with a slight *pop*. McAdam endured the sniggering. From working with him last year, I knew Leon considered our summer camp job beneath his usual employment with community theater. He considered himself a semi-professional. Leon waited for their attention and then swept to stage left.

"Because of a misunderstanding about dates between me and the printing shed, no programs are available." He glared into the audience at Robin, the creative writing counselor, who shrugged. "So, I will provide the credits." McAdam recited the names of the players and stage hands to scattered applause: Cheryl—Butterfly Girl; Megan—Burden Maiden; Reginald—Mirage Boy; Angela—incidental flute music; and Wally—props and technical advisor. He finished with a flourishing hand, "I am Leon McAdam, your theatrical director," and extended both arms toward the curtain and retreated backwards into the wings. "And now, *Butterfly Girl and Mirage Boy*."

As the house lights blinked out, Wally hauled the squeaking curtain apart and the stage lights came up on a dangling roll of brown butcher-paper painted to suggest a waterfall and consequent pool. Three meat ball-textured paper-mâché boulders flanked the waterfall. Angela's flute melody began backstage.

Cheryl glided out with a large jug on her shoulder. "Yea, but I do hear thee, O flute-musician mine. Clear with the breath of morning, fluting over the brim of the pool of day." She cupped her hands along an imaginary line to imitate the flute, bobbled, and nearly dropped the jug. "Answer. So I'll answer thee back." As the flute answered, Cheryl set the earthen ware on the stage. "So each rosy morn, each fragrant eve, when Butterfly Girl to the waters come, there is music, lovers music." She eased the pot sideways with her foot and furtively opened her jacket. "See my butterflies?"

In the wings, Leon shook his head. Was she proud of her magical butterflies or selling contraband?

"This white one is the east. The Spirit Dawn rises with fanning wings from night's dark chrysalis. And this one rises to the whiteness of a new day."

"And this one goes *wee, wee, wee* all the way home," Scotty called out.

"Like a soft waft of autumn petals," Cheryl continued, "a drift of saffron clouds hovering over the sun set." As Cheryl identified her butterflies, her saffron cloud dropped off. She scooted the cloud away with her foot. "Oh, I have butterflies that I caught from Earth's six regions." One of the six regions also fluttered to the floor. "Butterfly Girl they call me, girl of the Butterfly Spirit, all because the white winged ones hover about me with light." She frowned and began to pout. "But they make mock of me, the village maidens. They laugh. They touch their brows as if to say featherbrains and fancies. Senses flown away!"

Cheryl crossed the stage with her hands clasped before her. "But they do not know what Butterfly Girl can see over the edges of the morning. Nor what she hears beside the pool. For I *see* it!" She stamped her bare foot; it skidded in a wet patch Wally failed to mop dry. The legging slipped to her ankle, her moist heel tore off the pool's shoreline where it stuck to the bottom of her foot. She hopped one-legged and tried to thrash the scrap free. "I *hear* it!" But the brown paper stuck. With what Leon would later recount as theatrical poise, Cheryl peeled the torn prop from her sole and tossed it—a soggy keepsake—into her audience.

"I know it because I *am* Butterfly Girl and Mirage Boy is my lover." Cheryl blew a kiss stage right. Reginald, waiting backstage for his entrance, glared at her. He snatched the kiss from the air, threw it at the floor, and crushed it with a turn of his tennis shoe.

During the play, Jake knew the cabins, including Kurt's, would be empty. He pulled the boy's footlocker from under his bed, removed the top lid, and dumped the contents of its two shallow squares into a heap on the bunk. He rummaged through the pile: a beat-up harmonica; an unopened package of handkerchiefs; a handful of smooth stones; a deck of cards; a square puzzle with sliding tiles; 45 cents in change.

Jake picked up the coins and shook them in a loose fist. He dropped them on the bed and continued his search: shoelaces; three large pine cones; a tattered paperback book entitled *The Hobbit*. What the hell kind of weirdo book is this? Jake wondered.

Two Good n' Plenty boxes. Bingo.

Jake put the candy in his shirt pocket and began pulling clothes from the trunk. He yanked a single pair of worn dress slacks from the compression of clothing and checked the pockets for dollar bills. He felt inside the scuffed dress shoes, looked beneath the bed, groped under Kurt's mattress then stood up to check the honeycombed sag of rusting springs under the upper bunk.

Laughter welled up from the barn. Jake threw the clothes into the footlocker and swept the items from the bed into the chest. He covered the clothes with the tray, shut, and slid the trunk back under Kurt's cot. The boy would know someone had ransacked his footlocker. Let the kid stew, Jake thought. Thieves don't deserve any better.

Chapter Eleven

My totem pole will be carved in the barn. To transport it to its permanent home near the lodge, Alex needed 21 four-by-fours in 12 foot lengths. To build the scaffolding that would help erect the pole, he'd need two bundles each of two-by-fours, and two-by-sixes.

"You're in luck." The hardware store owner slapped an open manifest. "We just got a shipment of twelve-footers. The camp have enough paint, brushes, kerosene, sandpaper?"

"Just lumber and cinder block, right now," Alex said.

"Why the magic number twenty-one," his partner, Popeye, asked as they loaded the lumber.

"Trimmed out, the tree's forty-two feet long. We'll need a plank for every two feet of length—like trestles under train tracks."

"Whatever you say, boss."

Alex tumbled a squared pole into the truck's oversize bed. One end skidded into the front wall under the filthy back window, the other banged against the rim of the closed gate. "We'll have to come back for more cinder block before the horses show up. You drive a stick shift, right?"

"I can drive a camel through the eye of a hurricane," Popeye said.

Although Jake's responsibility included overseeing the camp project, he rarely showed up. His excuses for avoiding work were grist for the camp comedy mill. "Haven't you heard, old boy?" Stanley confided to Alex, "Jake bit a nasty piece of tongue off watching Maria change in the cabana. He'll be laid up, or wishing he was laid," Stanley paused for the beat, "up for weeks now."

Alex had spoken to Myron about Jake's absence and made a deal with him: our handyman would act as the project manager if, at summer's end, Myron gave him some of the carving tools Mye had purchased on his Syracuse trip.

"Thinking of a second career?" my husband asked.

"Actually I'm thinking about a woman I know in Albany who sculpts," Alex said. "I figure the way to her heart is through her hands. Some ladies appreciate flowers. She likes a good chisel."

"Done," Myron said.

This was Robin's, second year at camp. During our interview the year before, the poet had stressed her writing and editing skills. We hired her to teach creative writing and produce Summerbook—the season's assortment of camper-poems, stories, and drawings. She had other talents, too, and could assist Popeye with silk-screening. She was a mousy young woman with bangs of lusterless, brown hair, and often pursed her lips as though preparing to critique what had just been said.

She and my husband were in the art hut. Its usual tenant, Popeye, was gone. Robin's assistants' clothes-pinned sweat-shirts on a makeshift chord stretched across the room. Robin held up a sweat shirt. "What do you think?" she asked Myron.

"Looks like it's about my size, all right," he said.

"I mean about the silk-screening?"

"'Can Camp Cravitz Get It Up?'" Mye read to muffled tittering from the girls. "Well, I understand, but I wonder if the parents will when they come across it in the laundry. Let's at least mention the totem pole on the other side, okay?"

Robin tugged at her bangs. "How about 'Totem Or Bust' on the front?"

Myron regarded the 30-odd sweat shirts already silk screened on the back and drying on the cord stretched taut across the center of the art hut. The rich pigments and even application of ink on the cloth's bulkiness pleased him. But my husband wouldn't have chosen the slogan, nor would I, for that matter.

"The back's already printed, it's fine," he said, "but instead of 'Totem or Bust' on the front, how about: 'The Cravitz Totem Pole'?"

"Will do." Myron was unaware that Robin's older apprentices had unanimously demanded the back's suggestive wording. The girls ducked to and fro under the line of hanging sweatshirts and avoided Myron's eyes as he shuffled among them.

Near the pottery kiln's miniature fortress of ash trays and pinched figurines on pumice cones, Betsy sat silent, her face turned to the wall, knees splayed, and head bobbing between heaving shoulders.

"Is she sick?" Mye asked Robin. "I hear there's a stomach virus or something going around."

Robin steered him toward the door. "Betsy gets the giggles every now and then. She's a bit high-strung."

Myron glanced back at the girl. She had unfolded her legs and—palpitating—hugged her knees.

"Well, I'll let you get back to it," Mye said. "Keep up the good work." As Robin ushered Myron out the door and onto the stairs, the art hut sputtered with restrained whispers and Betsy's strangled laughter.

He hadn't visited the workshops in days. They all seemed to be functioning well enough. I had often reminded Myron that an administrator delegates authority. Now that I was gone, he saw the usefulness of my advice. He trusted Jake to compute the paychecks and signed them without review. He scratched his name onto unread documents reserved for the camp's owner. Occasionally, he talked on the phone with local authorities as he had that morning after the older Stone House girls, Betsy and Colleen, strutted into the Wild Cat Bar and Grill asking for beer.

"Mr. Cravitz, we're a small town." The cop's voice sounded weary. "Our force is stretched thin. You've got to police your own. If these girls are caught again trying to purchase alcohol, we have no choice but to contact their parents. You wouldn't want us to do that now, would you?"

Myron said, "certainly not," apologized, chatted with Fanny and let the incident go. He didn't want to spoil camp's final year for anyone.

154

Myron stopped next to the flagpole where lengths of two-by-fours and two-by-sixes, his future superstructure for raising the totem, were bound in steel ribbons. He had considered yanking the flagpole's metal rod out like a giant manioc root and replacing it with the totem pole. But the Haida erected poles at the corners of their dwellings. A better site, he thought, next to the northwest corner of Stone House with my loon on his bear's shoulders, both proctoring the camp grounds.

Mye opened his pocket watch. He had glued my oval picture to the casement. After a second glass of merlot, he said my Winston Churchill imitation was positively inspiring. It wasn't too bad: "Uhmm, give the little tykes impediments, let them struggle, then lead them to victory! Uhmm, struggle and victory forge iron spirits!"

And every year by the second or third week the campers seemed content with camp life. They whined about the food, about lights out, and the draconian enforcement of reveille played over our aging PA system at 7:00 every morning except Sunday. Yet, at camp's conclusion on the last Saturday in August, parents—who had received their children's complaining letters all summer—watched stunned and confused as their offspring wept. They wept in swoons of fondness and regrets. The summer before, a 14-year-old girl had fainted. When we revived her with an ammonia ampoule, she told her parents she was leaving every friend she had ever made in her whole life.

"Deidre," Mye said aloud, "I'm putting the totem pole at the corner of the lodge." He stopped and glanced at the puffs of cumulus stalled in the sky. He carefully closed the watch and pocketed it. The day was almost hot. "Deidre?"

Myron slowly turned in a full circle.

I could have answered him, but as he closed the watch, his mind retreated to the morgue when they unzipped me, my ashen face—mouth swollen into a sinister grin—tainted his memory. "You understand," the coroner had said, "there's no way of knowing for certain if she died immediately from the head injury or drowned after the fall. We'll do an autopsy if you request it." In the room's necrotic fluorescence, the doctor's fingertips pranced on one another. "Of course, there's an extra fee."

"Mr. Cravitz?" A small girl, whose name he thought was Lynn, peered up at him. "Mr. Cravitz, I pooped my pants." The girl's lower lip trembled.

Myron didn't remember how long he'd been standing in the center of the oval. Where had she come from? He bent and hugged the child, smelled her shame and felt her shoulder's small flat bone and delicate arms around his neck.

"I couldn't help it," she said. "My stomach hurts!" He caressed her hair, sprung from large plastic barrettes. Tears slipped down the soft cheeks in two lines.

"Okay, honey, let's get you cleaned up and feeling better." She abandoned herself to misery with a wail. Myron took her hand, "Fanny can give you something to help the hurt in your stomach." On the way to the infirmary, they passed a group of campers who had just left the dining hall.

"Yeeew. Another one!"

"God, I'm gonna be sick."

"Look! It's going into her socks."

The girl's diarrhea streamed down the insides of her legs. She whimpered and walked rocking from side to side, knees locked.

Up the road, white lab coat flapping and arms swinging as though boxing a strong wind, Fanny bore down on them.

"Mr. Cravitz, this is a crisis," she said when she reached him. Fanny brandished a plastic bottle, cap encrusted in a glazed pink ring. "I'm down to one bottle of Kaopectate." She fumbled with her cigarettes and violently rapped one of the black sticks against the bottle's side. "If the law comes in here, they'll blame me." She lit her cigarette with a flip of her lost-again, found-again Ronson, inhaled deeply, and expelled smoke in a vengeful stream. "Jake should've handled this. He's the one who insisted I pretend to be a nurse."

"Fanny, calm down. How many are sick?"

"There must be at least ten. Where am I going to put them? We're almost out of toilet paper." She sucked on her cigarette and glanced down at Lynn. The forlorn girl had waited between stomach spasms for the grown-ups to finish talking. "Cripes, another one!" Lynn's whine began like a soft siren. Fanny took the child's hand, leaned down, and urged her to walk. "Come on honey. Fanny'll make it better."

When Myron entered the dining hall, a lunch clean-up crew of three had worked their way down to the last tables. The boys hurried through their work, splattered the frog-green water onto the table tops, and plowed through brown applesauce spills. The residue would harden overnight into swirled circles. Half a hotdog rolled off the table edge onto a chair. Myron considered stopping them, making them change the water in the bucket, pointing out the half-eaten frankfurter and filthy table, but the boys finished in a rush and left.

He opened the Dutch doors to the kitchen. Sonja's territory; he felt intrusive. Black-bottomed pans and ladles the size of tennis rackets dangled from an iron carrousel above the grill's cooking surface. Blackened sludge, scraped into a trough at the stove's center, oozed toward a slop bucket on the floor. Across from the grill, stacked cooking pots airdried on the drain board. A few minutes before, Sonja had opened the automatic cup washer next to the sink. Mugs nestled in the steaming trays.

Myron called into the back room where he could see the cook's legs propped on the table. "Sonja?"

She rustled her newspaper. "You finished with the tables, boys? Put those buckets away. Rinse them first."

"Sonja, it's Myron Cravitz."

Her legs dropped. "Oh, it's you, Mr. Cravitz. I was just putting my feet up before I start dinner."

Sonja, thin and in her mid-50s, shambled into the kitchen with the torpid grace of a much larger woman. Her eyes roved, attentive in the copper secrecy of her face.

"I was reading about this terrible war over in Vietnam." She half closed her lids, lower lip protruding. "I just don't know. I worry about this war and all these young men my son's age. All these boys without training or a decent job.

158

Bernard, that's my son, quotes Lao Tzu. Are you familiar with Lao Tzu, Mr. Cravitz?"

"Chinese philosopher?"

"Yeah, that's him. Bernard says, 'The farther you go, the less you know. Thus the sage knows without traveling. He sees without looking. He works without doing.'" A wry smile puckered her mouth. "He writes me that and then studies fourteen hours a day to become a doctor. He also quotes Malcolm X, but I won't go into that."

"You must be proud of him."

"Oh, I am, but I try not to be. He's proud enough for the both of us." Sonja scooped up a large can of opened apple sauce and plunged the food into the blocky refrigerator's lowest shelf.

Myron and I hired Sonja the year before when her predecessor, Gladys, lost touch with her responsibilities. One day following breakfast, the former cook had filled a huge, copper-clad cooking pot with water, beans that had soaked overnight, carrots, onions, spam squares, a hefty mound of minced garlic—and a pair of ruptured work shoes.

The soup simmered all morning and by 11 o'clock it smelled pretty good. But during lunch, half a carrot-dolloped insole surfaced in the center of my meal. Next to me, Myron extracted a dribbling shoe lace and held the string up for examination. Within moments everyone in the dining hall knew lunch had been sabotaged. I stormed back to the kitchen to confront Gladys.

"What is this?" I demanded, dangling the dripping shoe lace inches from her face.

"Shoe lace," she said, feet propped on the edge of the grill. Her hand clutched an empty vodka bottle.

"And what is that?" I asked pointing to the bottle snuggled between her sprawled breasts.

"Smirnoff. Never touch that rot-gut McCormick's stuff." Gladys started to laugh—a derisive snorting and coughing. Myron got her to the bus depot in Tupper even before she sobered up.

We felt lucky to have found another cook so far into the camp season and planned a quick interview. Sonja, however, was bent on telling her life story and took her sweet time.

Her parents had brought her on a fishing trawler from Jamaica to New York City when she was 10. They moved to Rochester 2 years later after her father lost his job as a doorman at the Ambassador Arms Hotel. His replacement's English lilted less often and more delicately.

Sonja was once a licensed practical nurse but lost her renewal when she followed her future son's father to Buffalo. She worked there as a home health aide until her ballooning pregnancy interfered with her ability to haul the 180-pound woman she nursed into and out of bed. Her new son's father became infatuated with a Guyanese chanteuse from Toronto.

Alone, yet with high expectations, she reared Bernard. He grew into an inquisitive young man and graduated first in his class on a pre-med scholarship from the University of Alabama at Tuscaloosa. But Sonja thought most men were children at heart. Their avowed passion for specific members of the opposite sex often turned apathetic. A common male disease, she thought, its pox evident as their gender wrestled with articulating the agony of commitment. She loved her son but worried about his fiancé.

"My son's going to be married in the fall." Sonja sponged the counter.

"Congratulations!" Mye didn't know how to begin an inquiry about the diarrhea outbreak without making his concern sound inquisitional. Sonja relieved him of the task.

"Mr. Cravitz, I'm glad you came in. I hear some of the campers are getting sick."

"Yes, diarrhea, stomach pains."

Sonja shifted the sponge to her other hand. "Must have been that grease. Getting old. I really didn't want to use it. Some stomachs can't handle it." She clucked her tongue and shook her head obliquely, "Mr. Cravitz, that food budget you gave me only allows for a mixture of vegetable oils and lard. Gets stale faster than I can afford to replace it."

She wiped around a half-finished cup of apple sauce, its plastic spoon abandoned in the brown mush. "If I had the money, I'd have yogurt for every child here. What little I can buy is gone ten minutes into breakfast." Vexed, she finished the apple sauce's last inch in precise, circular flicks of her wrist.

"I'm sure you do the best you can," Myron said.

"I do the best I can with what I've got. Do you remember the memo I submitted before camp started? It called for almost double the food allowance I was given. If I could just have another $100 a week."

Myron backed into a hanging pot and reached up to steady it. "The campers seemed healthy enough before this rancid grease problem."

Sonja settled against the counter. "Mr. Cravitz, what did you have for lunch today?"

"Let's see," Mye pinched his Adam's apple, "a hotdog with relish and mustard, some green beans, custard and coffee."

"No potato chips?"

"No."

"No white bread? No Kool-Aid? No fried tater tots?" He shook his head.

Sonja's face hardened. "Here's what most of your campers ate for lunch. Potato chips, a hotdog or two on white bread or a cheese sandwich grilled in old grease, tater tots, two, maybe three helpings of starchy custard and Kool-Aid. That's why the corners of their mouths are purple. The more *discriminating* ones," she plucked each syllable from the word, "had peanut butter and apple sauce, cottage cheese—if there was any left—a banana, or, if they were gone, half a canned peach in sugar water thick as Karo. The late-comers had to settle for stewed tomatoes which, I am told, look like fish guts." Myron winced. "They need variety, Mr. Cravitz."

The mouth softened. Her eyes retreated from the flat plain of battle. "As far as a balanced meal goes, it could be worse. They have to eat something but, unfortunately, when the pickins' are slim, children aren't the best judges of what it should be. The scraps go into that bucket under there. The thin girl, Angela, comes in sometimes for something to feed the goat. Mr. Cravitz, that goat eats better than most of your campers."

"Maybe we should eat the goat."

"Maybe we should," Sonja shot back. "It's the frozen soy meal and fatty hamburger gunk, the canned beans, the peanut butter day after day. These kids are sick of white bread and cottage cheese. They want what I can't afford to buy—fresh, lean meat and fruit, ripe fruit, the kind you chew." Sonja bared and chomped her teeth. "Canned fruit cocktail's about as close to fruit as Spam to sirloin."

She fanned her face with her hand. "I apologize, but we can't keep having sick children on account of my kitchen. I can't do that, Mr. Cravitz. I'll quit first." She hadn't wanted to fly off the handle like that. Since my death, Myron rattled so easily. If she were fired, finding another job this late in the season would be next to impossible.

Sonja turned to the sink and began to sing "Stormy Weather" into the basin, her back to Myron. She filled a large pot with water; the tune's sultry lyrics were lost in the spigot's torrent. Gripping the heavy cauldron's steel bar with both hands, she faced Myron again. "Excuse me," she said, and glided past him to the stove. "Would you pass me that sack of noodles please and that big tin of mixed beans?"

"One of Deidre's favorite songs," Mye said.

"That lady's got the blues real bad." Sonja knifed the muslin bag and deftly filled another pot with a portion of the sack's contents. "It's a terrible thing to lose someone you love."

Myron smiled at the ingredients label which was too small for him to read. "I haven't lost Deidre."

"No, I suppose you never forget a spouse, even if he runs away."

Myron shook his head. "She's not dead, not really."

Sonja regarded him with gentle reproach. Still grieving, she thought. Poor man.

"When I lost my father," she said, "I thought the world would cave in on me. Crush me into a thousand, useless pieces. I couldn't sleep in the house that night. The walls closed in, the ceiling sank a little every breath I took. I slept outside. A grown woman sleeping in the yard. My mother played our beat-up piano all night like she was going over and over an old quarrel."

Myron watched the flames under the noodles.

"I could almost hear his voice calling to me like I was a child again," Sonja said. "'Sonja, honey, So-So,' the way he used to call." She stirred the pot.

Myron gaped at her. "You heard his voice?"

"I still do sometimes, when it's quiet. Meal times in this place, you can't hear yourself think."

He clutched both of her shoulders and held her at arm's length. "Have you ever seen him? Does he come to you in the flesh?"

"In the flesh?"

"When he talks to you, does he ever appear?"

"Lord, almighty," she breathed, "Mr. Cravitz, he's been dead for forty years."

"It's okay, Sonja. You can tell me. I've heard Deidre, too."

"It's your heart aching, Mr. Cravitz."

He shut his eyes against her denial. "You don't need to be afraid. I don't know why it happens, but it does. We're blessed with a miracle, Sonja."

"Mr. Cravitz, you are filled with grief and haven't accepted it yet. I have no right being the one to tell you this, but your wife is dead and gone. Gone forever. You've got to accept that."

Myron let her go. "Why are you so afraid to accept your father's death?"

"I was never afraid," Sonja's agitated fingers stroked her forehead. "I never thought to be afraid. When papa died, I was in shock, stunned. And then just—heartsick."

"I didn't believe it at first, either." Myron said. "I thought it was the Meniere's syndrome, the ringing in my ears. I doubted my senses." He stalked the room, eyes searching the floor, hands restless. "But you talked to your father, you saw him. Deidre will appear too, I'm sure she will. That's why I have to finish the totem pole before camp ends. If I don't, she'll never forgive me. I'll lose her forever." He scanned the sooty ceiling. "All of this could be gone soon. All but the totem pole. You're the only one I've told, Sonja. Deidre liked you. You're the first one who knows about her."

165

She touched his trembling hand, "Thank you for the confidence," and patted his fingers, "it will be our secret."

The water had just begun to boil in gauzy wafers of steam. Sonja turned the flame down. She thought of her son, Bernard. 'Without going outside,' his letter had quoted, 'you may know the whole world. Without looking through the window, you may see the ways of heaven. The farther you go, the less you know.' Mye's rapt attention to the circle of blue flame under the pot saddened her.

"Macaroni and cheese, right?" he said.

Sonja covered the pasta. The Jamaicans said when you couldn't cry for the dead, it rained. She had never cried for her father. Her teeth had chattered for an hour in the cool September night until she passed out in her bed roll. She had seldom cried for anyone except her son, and joy brought those tears as much as grief. Her temples thickened. Why, she thought, does this man love so hard?

"I've got a lot to do before dinner, Mr. Cravitz. Think about that extra $100 a week—for the children's sake."

"All right Sonja. Are you okay, you look upset?"

"Tired, bone tired."

"Me too. Deidre would want me to get some rest."

"You just take her advice."

"I will. I always have."

In their bedroom, Jake read to Fanny from the Kaopectate bottle. "It says two *teaspoons* for children, not two table-spoons. And the extra toilet paper is in the lodge, not the infirmary. You are one—stupid—bitch."

Fanny flapped the blanket and let if fall back onto the bed. She smacked the creases out.

"You're lucky nobody died," she said. "You know that? You're supposed to be the big-shot around here. Hot-shot head counselor." She wanted to tell him she'd seen him slinking around the boathouse when Maria was on duty. She knew what he was like, charm oozing out like tooth-paste when he wanted something. 'You stayed in there way too long,' she wanted to say. Instead, she said, "and you don't know anything about horses."

"I know how to direct your ass into a parking space. If you don't mind, let me handle it. I know what I'm doing."

Fanny punched the clammy pillows into shape on the bed. "This place is full of people, but it's always lonely."

"There's Lila Mae. She's new like you. Make friends with her." Jake scraped at his front teeth with a finger nail and sucked off the scum.

"She's hard to talk to. It's like she thinks she's superior to me."

Jake wanted to say: 'that wouldn't be hard to think.' I could hear it like an echo in an empty room. Instead, he grimaced, froze with his knees bent, and spread his but-tocks with his hands. He broke wind. "You're excused," he said.

Fanny tucked the blanket under the pillows. "For once, I'd like to spend the summer on the Jersey shore near a Safeway."

"How about Atlantic City? Lenny Bruce said that's where neon goes to die." Facing the mirror, he picked at the flaked dandruff in his mustache. "Gotcha, you little bastard."

Fanny's shoulders slumped under the cotton nightgown. "I'm glad Lynn is feeling better. She's sweet. I wonder if she'll come back next summer? She told me she misses riding camp."

"No, not Atlantic City. Miami Beach."

"Wouldn't it be fun to watch them grow year after year? Little people growing into big people?"

"Where'd you put my whistle?"

"You haven't heard a word I said."

"Little people growing into big people. Yes, I have. You're a little den mother at heart."

"I'm not any kind of mother."

"Where the hell is my whistle?" His face threatened total disregard. "You could help you know."

Unless his mood changed, Fanny knew he would blot her out of his mind. She wouldn't exist. "I'll check the dresser," she said.

"You could comb your hair or something," Jake said. Fanny dragged the comb off the dresser and pulled at her hair. "Smile," he said, smiling. "Come on, smile like you mean it. It's that time of month isn't it? Cramps. Am I right? Or am I right?"

"Why is it every time I get depressed you think I'm having my period? Menstruation follows the moon's cycle, remember? Once every twenty eight days."

"Oh, yeah. I forgot. Pardon me. I didn't mark it on my calendar."

"We could do something about it, you know. If I got pregnant."

Jake peered through her and blinked. "I saw it yesterday." He turned to the dresser and flipped through his T-shirt and underwear drawer.

Fanny tapped the floor with her bare foot. "What will you give me if I find your whistle?"

"A pinch on the butt."

"What else?"

"Aren't we greedy. You're my wife. For better or worse, remember?"

"You're one to talk about greed, having your cake and eating it too!" She batted the window curtain. Sunlight flashed the whistle's flat side. "Here," she scrabbled into the change tray on the nightstand, "your symbol of authority," and tossed the whistle across the bed.

Fanny pattered down the hall to the toilet. She urinated and, after blowing her nose, groped for the Chap Stick on the shelf above the John. She knocked the cylinder—*fflup*—into the commode's slowly spinning raft of tissue. It sank like a waterlogged maggot. I'm getting clumsier, she

169

thought. This place is making it worse. If I got pregnant maybe the clumsiness would stop. Pregnant women move differently. They don't smack into things or drop cosmetics into the toilet.

In the mirror, Fanny studied the lines around her eyes. They weren't pretty eyes. She poked at the splotchy skin. Nothing about her was pretty. If she could just pluck it out, reach up inside, and rip that IUD free. Didn't it get old? Didn't it rust or something—whatever worn-out plastic does? Why was it always up to men? Her doctor jammed the thing up so far inside her only he could remove it.

Fanny tore at the roll of tissue. "Momma," she said to her mother's faint reflection in the window pane, "you said he'd forsake all others, you lied to me!" She blotted her tears with toilet paper and walked back to the bedroom. "I want a baby."

Jake was tying a shoe lace through the hole in his whistle. "I think I might have a thing or two to say about that."

"You promised. You said after we were financially stable."

"What do you know about finances? You can't even balance a checkbook. You think it's easy raising a kid?" Jake rammed the dresser drawer shut with his knee. "Spare me your financial expertise. Anyway, when Cravitz kicks the bucket we'll be on easy street. As you've probably forgotten, I'm in his will." He tested the knot. "You'll get pregnant when I'm good and ready to knock you up."

"You're afraid."

"Of what?"

"Afraid you're not man enough." Fanny edged toward him, "that you're not potent."

"You're a joke, you know that."

"You and your high speed jack hammer. You're afraid you're sterile, half a man."

"Fanny, if you weren't so pitiful, I'd cram this down your throat." Jake flicked his whistle's small, dense mass into her nightgown—*whump*—where it slid to the bed.

"Takes a real man to threaten a lady, huh?"

"You think I like fucking you? Fucking you bores me. You fuck like an asthmatic nun. I could get a better lay in a nursing home."

Fanny shoved her feet into a pair of slippers and then kicked them off again. One landed on the dresser, the other hit Jake in the chest. She leapt at the bed like a frustrated child.

"Damn you! You know something? You know what?" She yanked her nightgown up to her waist and flapped her knees at him. Strands of flaxen curl glistened within the dark, pubic pelt.

Jake yawned. "Well, well. Frances Daryl plays the sex kitten, rated G, general audiences. Go ahead Fanny, show us what drives sterile men crazy."

"You can't last a week without it."

"You're the one in a rutting frenzy." Jake lifted his slender wooden shoe-horn from the door hook and tossed it at her. "Put yourself out of your misery. Screw this."

From the far end of the hall, girls' voices tumbled toward them and spilled down the stairs. "Fanny?" A tenuous knock rapped the door. "Fanny, it's Angela. I need a Band-Aid."

"I'll be there in a minute, Angela. Wait for me downstairs."

Fanny pulled the gown off over her head and threw it behind her at Jake. As he stood glowering at her, she tugged her clothes across the bed and wrestled into them. I'll screw you, Jake Daryl, she thought. But not in the way you think. Maria can have you. I don't want you anymore.

She brushed past him out the door and into the stairwell. The familiar clatter of her rubber soled pumps filled the wooden vestibule. Near the bottom she faltered, an extra *ka-thump* in the rhythm of her descent.

Chapter Twelve

Sonja first noticed the disappearances the day before as she re-filled the salt and pepper shakers. Two sets were missing from the dining hall tables in an area the campers called the pit. She assumed the cleaning crew moved them.

"We didn't take them," the chubby boy said after lunch.

"I'm not accusing you of taking them," Sonja said. "I'm asking if you moved them someplace else. We had ten sets and now there are only eight."

"Who would want salt and pepper shakers?" the other boy asked.

"So you didn't move them?"

"No, ma'am."

Sonja kept an eye out that morning. Sure enough, two syrup pitchers vanished sometime during breakfast. Could raccoons do that, she wondered?

Later that day, Lila Mae returned to her piano hut after a respite helping Angela feed the goat, Mozart. Her metronome was gone. She had used it just 20 minutes before with Shortstack as they plodded through Debussy's Arabesque Number Two. Lila Mae had recalibrated the metronome to progressively slower settings to keep her pupil within the beat. She finally arrived at a lethargic tempo Shortstack could handle. The girl's turtle-claw fingers crawled across the keys—suffocating the composition, Lila Mae thought, within the notes of its own arpeggios.

I had to agree. Murder by music.

Lila Mae caught up with Shortstack as she headed down to the lake. Her swim suit, fringed in netting, flounced at her waist.

"Pretty suit," the piano coach said shocked that anyone over 6 would wear such a thing.

"I got it for my tenth birthday. I'm in the double digits now."

Lila Mae acknowledged the girl's new status with an appreciative nod. "Did you, by any chance, take the metronome so you could practice with it in the lodge?"

Shortstack shook her head. "Was I supposed to?"

"No. I guess I just misplaced it. Have fun swimming."

"I'm taking lessons and Maria says I'm already an otter. There's beavers and then otters, then ducks and, when you'll really good, you're a porpoise." Shortstack turned to the lake, her tutu bouncing and flip-flops smacking in syncopation.

During staff meeting the night before, Jake Daryl had informed the other counselors about a theft in the snack hut. "Brad and I talked it over. We think we've identified the guilty party." Jake had hoped he sounded clever. Lila Mae avoided Mr. Daryl whenever she could and decided to ask Brad about the theft.

She found Brad on the waterfront scrubbing canoes in preparation for the overnight canoe trip. "So, who does Jake think the thief is?"

"There's no proof." Brad dipped the sponge into the boat's brown suds. "Jake Daryl's an idiot. You don't need soap to clean a canoe. All you need is a scrub brush, elbow grease, and three feet of water. But no! Gotta soap 'em down and pollute the lake." Brad rolled the canoe splashing dirty lather into the sand.

Jake was, as Lila Mae's brothers would say, jive turkey. He used his authority unnecessarily and too often. "Okay, who does Jake *want* the thief to be?"

"Yeah, you've got that right. Kurt Willington, the kid from the home."

"Why him?"

"The stolen Good n' Plentys. I shouldn't have mentioned to Jake that I found Kurt eating from a box right after the theft. And Kurt admitted having eight dollars, about what was taken ..."

"Good n' Plentys?" Lila Mae interrupted. "I sold Kurt four boxes of Good n' Plentys working the snack hut a couple days ago. I remember thinking—here's a kid who really likes licorice."

Brad threw his sponge into the canoe "I knew he didn't do it. For some reason, Jake's got it in for that kid."

"Well, I'm missing a metronome, and if it's one and the same person who's stealing things, we have a serial larcenist on our hands. Petty larcenist," Lila Mae corrected herself.

The next day, Kurt returned to his bunk wondering about Bilbo Baggins' next move against Gollum, a nasty new character he had just met in *The Hobbit*. He pulled his footlocker out from under his bed to retrieve the book and finish the chapter. The arm of a blue shirt was snagged in the closed lid. When he opened the trunk's top, the chest's jumbled storage box baffled him.

His Good n' Plentys were gone. At first, he thought the snack hut thief had raided his things. But nothing else had been taken, not even his change. And the bills from summer allowance were still hidden in the folds of his handkerchief. He peered down at the open trunk and realized he hadn't been robbed. He figured his counselor, Brad, had ransacked his things looking for evidence and taken the candy.

"Shit on him," Kurt said and then in a near scream, "shit on all of them!" He fled the cabin. Kurt headed for the only place he knew he would be welcomed.

Sally felt the tread of feet stamping up the porch stairs, probably Jake Daryl who had bothered her about horses. "He's screwed something up," she said to herself and yanked the door open to send him away. Kurt stood on the porch, wounded again by the look of it, Sally thought.

"Can I come in?"

"Entre vous."

Kurt hesitated.

"French. It means come on in. What happened?"

"My counselor went through my stuff."

"Why'd he do that?"

"Looking for evidence and money I never stole." The boy went straight to the couch and pounced on one end.

"I'm havin' tea, want some?"

"Sure," Kurt said, his tone flat.

Sally lit a kitchen match and ignited the butane fueled burner. She waited by the sink for the kettle to whistle. Kurt would need a few minutes to calm down. When the spout sang, she poured hot water over the shriveled berries at the bottom of her yellow tea pot. She left the pot on the counter and returned to the front room.

"I used to race motorcycles with Delmore." Sally sat on the opposite end of the couch. "Pretty exciting at first, until I saw what a cross-country course did to the land. Burned over woods one year strugglin' to come back, and a sand pit the next. Nothin' but criss-crossed trails."

Kurt felt her weight settle in. "You belong to a gang?"

"Sort of. Only we called it a club. Red and white leather jackets, Canadian colors, monthly dues. God knows where *that* money went. I had an orange wig then and both front teeth. Delmore knocked this one out when I called him a liar."

"I wish I could kick him in the balls."

"Kick who?"

"Haskell. He started the whole thing."

"Who's Haskell?"

The boy glowered at her and then turned away.

Sally grunted to her feet and headed for the kitchen. "Tea should be about ready, and I've got some Ritz Crackers around somewhere. You can do better than kick him in the *couilles,"* Sally called into the front room. "You can prove him wrong."

Kurt heard cupboards and drawers being opened and slammed shut. The boy eased from the couch and crept to the six-sided table. He coaxed the drawer open. The knife's allure pulled at him like Bilbo Baggins' ring. Kurt tucked its length, sheathed blade first, down his pants front, handle against his hip. He tugged his shirt tails out for cover.

"I guess I'll be heading out now," he called to the kitchen.

Sally came into the room with a cracker box and two steaming mugs of tea. She set the tray on the table by the couch and spied the drawer across the room, not quite shut.

"So soon?"

"I've got a lifesaving lesson this afternoon." Kurt went to the door, his back to Sally.

"What's the plan, Kurt?"

"If I get my junior lifesaving, maybe I can get a camp job that pays money."

"That's not the plan I'm talkin' about."

Kurt's hand covered his hip. He relaxed his shoulders and turned his head toward her.

"What do you mean?"

"That knife you got under your shirt. You got a fifty caliber bullet for a seventeen caliber gun. It's too big for you." Kurt's hand dropped to his side. Sally slurped her tea. "A knife like that'd leave you without a pointer the first time you slipped. You need one that'll fit your hand." She walked to a bureau next to the fireplace and rattled through the top drawer's contents. "I'll trade ya." She walked back to Kurt and extended a jackknife.

The boy hiked up his shirt and retrieved the knife. They exchanged hardware solemnly.

Hinged shut, the jackknife's three inch silver blade nestled in a curved wooden shank. Kurt ran his fingers over the handle, its four gold pins smooth within the wood. He tilted the shaft to catch the subdued light of the cabin in the polished brass that capped each end. The boy pulled on the groove near the blade's top flange. When he couldn't open it, he pressed his index finger—which fit perfectly— on the notch in the knife's spine.

"You got it," Sally said. "That releases the blade."

He opened the shank with a soft click, transforming its folded wing into curved grace. He tried to close the blade.

"Press the release."

Kurt turned the folded knife in his hands. "It's what they expect," he said. "Everybody thinks I steal things, so I might as well."

"So that's your plan? Do what they expect? What about your own expectations?" Sally sipped her tea. "What kind of tea did you expect me to make, Kurt?"

"Regular tea, I guess. They give us Lipton's at the home when we're sick."

"The home?"

Kurt hadn't wanted to mention the children's home to Sally, it just came out. "It's where I live."

"Well, in my home I'm particular about the tea I drink. There's nothin' wrong with Lipton's, it's just that most people don't realize there are other choices." For the first time since Kurt stumbled into her life, Sally felt as though a long-tensed muscle in her chest was beginning to relax.

"So, what kind of tea did you make?" Kurt asked.

"Elderberry. A health tonic, good for the immune system."

"Like a shot?"

Sally slid her tongue through the sluice in her teeth. "Kinda. Only it doesn't hurt and tastes good with honey."

"Are you going to send me back to the home?"

"Now why would I do that?"

"Because I stole your knife."

"What knife?"

Sally's sideswipe confused him. "The one in the drawer?"

"You didn't steal it. You chose the wrong one. We traded, remember?"

"So you won't tell?"

"Did you expect me to tell?"

"I wasn't sure."

Sally lifted her head and chuckled. The laugh fluttered in her throat like a moth in a bottle and then burst into the room.

Kirk giggled with her in self-conscious sputters. He held out the knife. "This is really mine to keep?"

Sally set her mug on the table. "But before you go flingin' it around, let's review a few things. First off, always keep the blade sharp. A dull knife's dangerous."

For most of an hour, Sally and Kurt focused on the knife. He learned how to sharpen the business end with oil, grinding the blade in circular motions on her whetstone. He oiled the release lever and practiced opening and closing the knife until he could do it with quick efficiency. They scavenged under her porch for wood to practice whittling—branches of oak, beech, white cedar, yellow pine.

Sally wrapped her huge hand around Kurt's to guide his thumb; her tongue flirted with her upper lip. "When the wood's soft like this pine, *press* the blade along the grain so you don't cut too deep. When you use the point like an auger, make sure the release is locked firm. Otherwise, there'll be lots of blood and pain."

"Can you show me how to throw it?"

Sally frowned. "I don't think this is the best knife for throwin'. It'd put too much strain on the blade lock. Single shank's a lot better. Besides, knives have a way of ricocheting, like bullets."

"I promise I'll throw it only once in a while, and when there's no people around." Kurt's right hand crossed his heart in two sweeps.

Sally knew he'd try it sooner or later.

"Grab the blade with the thumb and index finger," she said. "And when I say grab, I mean hard. The trick is learnin' when to let go."

They took a short walk into the forest. Sally's attempts with the smaller and lighter knife lacked her usual finesse. Kurt struggled with the rudiments of controlling its flight.

"Do the folks at the camp know where you are?" She finally asked him.

"No, I'd better be going."

"Plan what you're gonna do with the knife, Kurt. Get to know it. Whittle somethin'. Let it work for you. A good blade's like an extra finger."

After Kurt left, Sally shut her door against the bright afternoon. She sat for a moment as her eyes adjusted to the light, then went to the dresser by the fireplace. The second drawer stuck, so she worked her Bowie knife into the slots to free the bottom runners. In the middle of the large drawer the crumpled, tangerine-colored wig smelled like old linens. She left the drawer open, scooted the clock off the fireplace mantle, and tossed it on top of the wig. She began to close the hutch, but stopped.

"What's the plan, Moffett?" she muttered. She pulled hard on the metal handles and wrenched the drawer from the dresser. The wig and clock plummeted to the floor. She slammed the empty crib back into the cabinet, swept its former contents from the floorboards, and strode to the front entrance. Sally bounded down the steps toward the lake, and when she reached the water, hollered across to its distant side. "Get the hell out of my space, Delmore!" She flung the wig into the air. It caught the rising, off-shore breeze and tumbled on the water like a shaggy beach ball before sinking. She threw the clock even farther, its splash barely audible in the wind. "And stay out!"

Kurt, ambling back to camp along the lakefront, heard her muffled cry and stopped near the water's edge on a crescent of beach. He watched Sally turn from the lake and march toward the cabin through cedar outcropping. She was soon lost in the evergreens.

He opened his knife, sighted along his extended right arm as she had taught him, brought his hand back, and snapped the glittering blade 30 feet end-over-end into the woods. He nailed a chokecherry's slender center. The boy threw up his arms, tipped his head back, and hopped on both feet.

I had never seen such joyful footprints in wet sand, a whirligig of triumphant cuneiform. Kurt whistled most of the way back to camp.

In her cabin, Robin was finishing the first draft of a poem she called "Wilderness:"

> ... cabin bunks
> a war zone of snack wrappers,
> rank clothes
> and thieves.

To keep the cabins tidy, campers twice a week endured the paramilitary ritual of inspection Myron and I had mandated years ago. Each counselor was free to choose her method of scrutiny. Not surprisingly, the wordsmith, Robin, employed stencils: "Passed" on heavy green cardboard squares and "Failed" on red ones. She was distributing the indicators mid-morning when she found a metronome under the pillow of Star's bed.

While Robin sat on the bed's rumpled corner pondering the metronome, the plump, vacuous 13-year-old who slept there returned to her bunk. "My parents sent it to me, honest!" Star said, her eyes defiant and fixed on her counselor's.

"Why would they send you a metronome, Star? I thought you were a potter." Robin lifted a jumbled pair of trousers off the foot of the girl's cot to fold them. Under the pants, two pairs of salt and pepper shakers lay on their sides, black and white granules imbedding the brown blanket.

"Cat got your tongue?" Robin asked.

The girl's chin sank to her chest. She stared at the floor. "I can't help it. My parents said if I couldn't stop stealing, they'd get me help." Star's liquid whimper rose into her throat. "They promised, but they won't. They're too busy to help me with anything."

Robin found Myron in his office. Reluctantly, he called Star's parents. "Yes, it's unfortunate," Myron said into the phone. "Star was doing so well here. We're all going to miss her;" he rolled his eyes at Robin who sat on his desk top swinging her legs. "All right, we'll expect you Sunday at noon. I'm sorry, too. Goodbye." He cradled the receiver. "Have you told Jake?"

"Yeah. He didn't believe me until he talked to Lila Mae. I found the syrup bottles in Star's trunk, too, and at least ten boxes of Good n' Plentys along with a sweater that had Angela Twining's name sewn into the neckline."

"Did Kurt show up for lunch?"

"He came in late with Brad, a big smile on his face. I don't think I've ever seen Kurt smiling. He's a handsome kid. Word must have gotten around fast. When they walked into the dining hall, half the camp cheered. Jake was not happy being wrong about Kurt." Robin bobbed her head, "you'd think Mr. Daryl would be glad to get at the truth."

"Jake's truth is Jake's truth," Myron said. "It's sometimes hard to know what he appreciates." My husband hoped Jake's hostility for Kurt would dissipate, although he doubted it. During the last few years of my life, Jake's flammable temper ignited at increasingly modest provocations. And now he mocked our totem pole in alternate bursts of surliness and ridicule. Myron overheard him call it "Cravitz's folly" in a conversation with Stanley.

After Jake had completed his probation and community service years before, we hired him when no one else would. We treated him like a son. He lived with us at camp during his first summer of freedom. He drove our car. Later on, Myron included him in our estate plans as a beneficiary.

But I sensed an irritation in Jake's heart, a festering canker. And finally, the summer before I died, I convinced Myron to cut Jake from our will. "He may think he's the child we never raised," I said, "but I'm glad he was never ours to begin with."

Myron, fortunately, had not argued and now felt a bleak satisfaction in our decision. The estate (after New York seized its lion's share of taxes) would be divided between the Nature Conservancy and the State University in Montclair where Myron double majored in art and English. We never got around to telling Jake he was out of the will. He didn't know the environmentalists and academicians had replaced him.

Robin heaved the sweatshirt box onto Myron's desk and unfolded one to show him. "The Cravitz Totem" inscribed the front in letters resembling logs, the second "t" in "Totem" larger and emblematic of a totem pole.

"Kurt suggested the lettering style to give it a woodsy feeling," Robin said.

Mye was pleased circumstances had turned out well for Kurt. He liked the kid—rough and tumble, he thought, yet there was a scrappy courage about him, too. Whatever Sally Moffett did during their time together, Myron knew it nourished the boy. "Let him visit Sally anytime she'll see him," he had told Brad. And why not? As the camp song (which I wrote) pledged:

> When it's Adirondack summer,
> Camp Cravitz we will go,
> to get old friends together
> and to get new friends to know ...

Summer was half over. Depending on how you viewed the season—half full or half empty—time was either an old friend or a new enemy. The Adirondacks had offered up its log, stripped of bark now, and naked as a new born. But my future totem pole waited for life in a dry rill on the forest floor. Myron had beaten the odds and now the odds were pushing back. The days remaining to finish the Cravitz totem were ticking away.

PART II

Chapter Thirteen

Hunched inside his idling pick-up, Alex honked again for Popeye. "The Haida masters take months to carve their poles," he said when Popeye hopped in. "I hope we can pull this off in four weeks." He wheeled out of the drive's ruts into the meadow and headed for the barn.

"Hey, we got eighty slaves workin' this bale," Popeye said. The four-by-four trestles jostled in the back.

"And fifty of them are kids who think chiseling's a form of negotiation." Alex let the wheel slip through his fingers.

"The little kids can do the sanding. They can paint. They can bring us cold beer."

"Don't count on beer." The truck's front wheels, then the rear hiccoughed over a branch. Alex looked up at the mirror to check his load.

"Anyway," Popeye said, "the real crests will be the ones Cravitz and I carve. The birds and animals and shit on totem poles are called crests, you know." They pulled in next to the weathered building.

The two men hefted the posts from the bed of the truck, carried them into the barn, and dumped them in a corner with the others. Dust speckled the feeble light. Popeye slung the last two beams onto his shoulders, balanced them with a few shrugs, and carried the timbers to the front of the stage where he dropped them on end atop the ragged line of cinder block in the broad, center aisle.

"What are you doing?" Alex said.

"This is where the four-by-fours end up anyway, right?"

"Yeah, but we need to finish with the blocks first. We'll lay the four-by-fours on top of the blocks while the pole's suspended above them."

"You mean I have to drag these things under that monster while it's dangling over my head? What if the horses decide they don't like standing still?"

"Then you will be crushed like a worm and, even with your shirt off, the girls will look away in horror as your guts spurt out."

"Nah," Popeye slapped his turtle-shell stomach, "it would take more than that for the girls to turn away from *this* six-pack."

The carving process intrigued Alex. He didn't know much about it, but had watched his lady friend in Albany closely enough to know that sculpting took strict concentration. When Alex had dropped by the office one evening, Myron bragged about a bust of me he'd carved in cherry for our last anniversary. The pleasant recollection soon changed to trembling, pressed lips and Myron's morose attempt to smile.

"What do the numbers on the sketch mean," Alex asked hoping to snap Mye out of his funk.

"It's not like sculpting with clay," my husband said. "With clay you build the medium up. With wood you remove it. Once it's gone, you can't put it back." Myron tapped the line drawing of a bear on hind legs, front paws raised beside the oversized head. "This is the bear crest." The bear's upturned snout swirled into nostrils above a ferocious triangle of teeth. Its claws extended menacingly. A loon—my loon—straddled the bear's erect ears, its webbed feet fringing the brow.

The carving lines were numbered from one to nine. "The bear's nose is the highest point of relief," Mye said, "the eye sockets among the lowest. You carve the lower numbers first, the higher numbers last. It's like a topographical map. The nose is the mountain. The eye sockets and ear canals, the valleys." Myron poured Alex a tepid cup of coffee. "I need a favor."

"Shoot."

"Can you rough-out the two large bear and loon crests with a chain saw? It would be much faster than using a hand adz."

"I don't see why not, as long as I know where to cut and how deep to go."

"Popeye and I'll be right there with you." Mye had at last smiled, the flashing smile I remember when his life included me and our twin babies.

The draft horses arrived pulling an odor of manure with them in a battered trailer hauled by a hard-scrabble man who called himself Snake. Alex helped the man hammer out the chained pins that secured the trailer's dung-smeared gate, and then toppled it back on squealing hinges where it thudded to the ground. One at a time, Snake backed the snorting horses—hooves the size of dinner plates—down the ramp as they shimmied their hackled coats.

A small crowd gathered to hobnob while Snake worked with somnambulistic deliberation collaring each horse with a leather yoke, rocking the heavy wooden frame up the animal's neck and joining the yokes together with a wooden crosspiece and finger-thick iron rings.

"Easy, Dunce," he stroked the mottled, gray and brown coat. Snake shoved a stout pole into the collar's slot near Dunce's breast bone and did the same with the other animal. "Easy, Sadie. Easy, now." He coupled each stave with another crosspiece behind the horses' back legs and threw a leather strap across their rumps to link the shafts on either side.

Jake monitored the man's efforts, hands on his hips, whistle in his mouth, and Snake's $40 payment wadded in his pocket.

The old-timer turned to Jake. "Don't spook 'em with that tooter in your maw," he said. Snake unhitched the trailer from the back of his truck leaving the horses to thrash their tails and shake their enormous, bony heads. He restarted the truck into rough idling. The crate's fenders shuddered. Snake pulled forward and lurched to a stop. He and Alex hauled a steel ramp from under the truck's bed and thumped the gangplank to the ground. They wrestled the other end's curved, three-inch teeth into slots at the vehicle's back ledge.

Together, the two men guided a two-wheel cart down the ramp and rolled it behind the horses. Snake snapped the leather straps into the collars above the animals' withers and threaded the ends into the cart. When the beasts were hitched for work, they hung their heads, motionless as air before a storm.

Myron led the lumbering procession—horses, cart, counselors, and campers—through the meadow into the woods. Behind him, Snake swayed on his feet in the two-wheeler flicking the plodding horses' rumps with leather straps. When Myron stopped at the wood's edge, Snake dropped the reins, sat, and scooted off the cart's rear deck. He pulled the horses and cart around in a half-circle facing into the meadow, heading away from the cedar log.

The male counselors and older male campers kicked wedges of wood skimmed from the cedar's back under the tree. Popeye, Kurt, and the others heaved down on sharpened poles using their improvised fulcrums to nudge the tree's lighter crown high enough for Alex to wrap a chain around the trunk.

Snake yanked the hesitant team of horses back until the cedar's top hovered over the cart. Alex snapped carabineers onto the chain and into the rings anchored along the axel that crossed the cart's bed.

"Let her down real easy like," Snake said. The tree's mass made the wagon groan and nearly flattened the large rubber tires. The horses froze, turning their ears back against their heads as though facing into a gale.

"Sadie and Dunce ain't real happy 'bout this." Snake said to Myron as he stroked Sadie's shivering haunch. The man ambled to a small pine and urinated against its smooth bark. Colleen, at the edge of the milling crowd, watched the twisted yellow stream splash Snake's shoes.

"I don't believe he just did that!" she said to Betsy, who grimaced.

Snake returned to Myron. "Atsa big log," he said.

"It's for a totem pole," Mye said.

"Yeah, I heer'd about that totem pole idea, only I ain't sure Sadie and Dunce will budge it."

Myron was stunned. "They're work horses, aren't they? Isn't this what they do?"

"Yes, sir. And they can pull it okay once they get it started. But gettin' it started—well, let's just say they ain't got a paycheck to motivate 'em and you're on a bit of a hill here." Snake put a thumb to his nostril, turned his head, and blew a wad of snot from his other nostril. He wiped his nose with the back of his hand. "We're gonna need to coax 'em a little."

The downed tree, pegged between its neighbors, had no room for lateral movement. The horses would need to drag it, butt trailing—a straight shot out of a shallow rill.

In the distance, Maria's assistant, Wally, minced his steps across the meadow and bee-lined straight for Snake. He clutched his Stetson's brim, the crown bulging water.

"Do you mind if I give the horses a drink," he asked when he reached the man. "It'll bring us luck."

"Suit yourself," Snake said.

"What are their names?"

"Sadie on the right, Dunce on the left, only Sadie's a gelding and Dunce ain't stupid."

"Got it!" Wally winked at Snake whose head snapped back as though the young man had tried to kiss him. Wally carried the elixir to the animals. The horses whipped their tails as he approached. Sadie turned an inquiring head to Snake who spat on the ground. Wally held the hat under Dunce's bristled muzzle and quivering nostrils.

"No, sir," Wally whispered to the animal, "Dunce ain't stupid." The horse dipped its head and drank, snout pushing water onto and over the brim. At that moment, Wally knew he would finish his Eagle Scout and West Point would accept him. His career was set. Dunce had completed the lucky Stetson's voodoo by drinking from the young man's hat.

Maria and Lila Mae relaxed together on a moss-patched, granite berm. The lighter-skinned woman pulled a cashmere top on over her swim suit and watched Wally water Dunce.

"In this country," she said, "I think men are very different than in my country. Here, it is difficult to know what they are thinking. Although," she gestured with her right hand, nails filed to perfect red ovals, "men everywhere think mostly of one thing, no?"

"In America we say men have two brains: one here," Lila Mae pointed to her head, "and one here," she pointed to the gathered cloth's long valley between her legs.

"¡Madre de Dios!" Maria covered her mouth with her fingers. "This is so true. But the men here are indirect. They say one thing. They mean another. In my country, men may be pigs, but they're honest pigs."

"Are you speaking of someone in particular?"

Maria leaned toward her. "Can you keep a secret?"

"As long as it don't land me in jail, as the song says."

Maria's eyes widened. "I don't think what he's doing is normal. In Colombia, men touch women all the time. It's expected. But you are warned first. They tell you what a nice bottom you have before they pinch you."

Lila Mae waited.

"I was asking about my paycheck and he just reached up and grabbed my—" Maria covered her left bosom with her hand. *Pecho. ¿Como se dice?* Busts?"

"Breasts?" Lila Mae offered.

"Claro, Breasts. Not a word, just grabbed me. I said, 'please keep your hands to yourself,' and spanked his fingers. He would not stop and said, 'you know you want it.' How does he know such a thing? In my country, normal men would never say this."

"You're speaking, of course, about Mr. Jake Daryl."

"Is he like this with you, too?"

"Girl, you see Popeye over there? He's like most men, only with bigger muscles. I wasn't here forty-eight hours before he comes on to me. Tells me I'm a black beauty. And I say to him, 'sorry for being opinionated. It's not that I dislike you and your muscles. I just dislike what white folks like y'all did to my three brothers, my parents, my grandparents and great-grandparents. You dig? So don't be spreadin' your mayo on my wheat bread. You're cute in a honky sort of way, but my eye's on a bigger prize, unh, huh.' He never bothered me again."

"Honky?"

"That's what us black beauties call uppity white folks."

Maria grinned. "And did Popeye understand about the bigger prize?"

"He understood it wasn't him."

Maria brought her knees to her chest and encircled them with her arms. "Okay, I won't tell Mr. Cravitz. But if Mr. Daryl tries something like that again, I'll poke him in the stomach with a paddle."

"That'll get his attention. Welcome to the U S of A."

With her hands, Maria loosened her damp hair. "Oh, I've known about the United States for a long time. In Colombia, we have oil. And emeralds." She flashed her ring's beryl opulence—surrounded by tiny diamonds. "We export oil to America, but your corporations pay us whatever suits them. I would not call it stealing, but it's not really commerce either. Are you upset that I talk like this?"

Lila Mae sang softly. "'When Pharaoh was in Egypt land, let my people go! Oppressed so hard they could not stand, let my people go!' It's an old spiritual," she said. "Oppression is everywhere. American corporations oppress nations like yours. Jim Crowe justice oppresses Bobby Seale, George Wallace oppresses students trying to get an education."

"When I graduate from Amherst and then medical school, I'm going back to Colombia to help my people."

"That the bigger prize you got your eye on?"

"*¡Claro que si!* And your eye's on fame, no?"

"I got into Julliard on a full piano scholarship. That's supposed to be a first step." Lila Mae looked out at the men and boys milling in the meadow. "Sometimes, though, I think it just comes down to men oppressing women. Doesn't matter what color you are or where you're from. If you got a penis, you got a union card for all good 'ol boy functions."

"My parents worry that I won't find work as a woman doctor in Colombia. They say, your men patients won't let you touch them or tell them what to do."

Lila Mae said, "Listen, I got three brothers," she paused and dropped her eyes, "two brothers now. If they're in enough pain and you can make it go away, they'll let you touch them wherever you want." She resettled herself on the rock and eyed Maria's ring. "Quite a jewel."

"My mother's. It's a ..." Maria hedged, "decoy, yes?"

"What every beautiful, unmarried woman wears among the wolves, yeah. Removable for Mr. Right, though."

"*¡Por supuesto!* Of course! After medical school."

Neither animal had budged since the workers had lowered the pole into the horses' cart. While Snake stood by sucking and then spitting out tamarack needles, Alex had tied each end of a 40 foot chord onto the horses' stout collars. He dragged the slack to its midpoint 20 feet in front of the animals. With a bowline that couldn't slip, he attached a longer rope to the middle of his improvised tether and walked it straight out in front of the horses.

Lila Mae stood up on their boulder and squinted at a line

forming in front of the horses. "Maria, are they about to do what I think they're about to do?"

"It looks like, how do you say it in English, a pull-of-war?"

"Tug-of-war. Uh, huh. Between Camp Cravitz and those two horses. Get your guitar and meet me out there. Let's get this mob organized." The two women scurried off their rock.

Alex held up the line's end. He slapped his chest at the dozen or so men and older boys. "Come on guys, show the girls what you're made of. These horses won't budge without a little help from us."

A half-hearted battle: thirty-two hundred pounds of downhill horse flesh against complaining musicians, actors, and artists. They strained at the rope while the horses leaned back in stubborn counterbalance. Men and boys entangled each other, their angles at the rope either too steep or too shallow. Stanley stumbled into Leon who fell into Jake who gave up and left.

Alex worked the line while the women, girls, and smaller campers watched with flagging interest. "Keep your arms bent at the elbow, Leon. Use your weight to pull, Kurt. Lean back like Wally and Popeye."

Lila Mae, regal in her flowing robes, strode into the forefront. Maria, smaller but comfortably in charge, walked next to her. A strap around Maria's neck supported the guitar, its fingerboard at an angle.

"I have a suggestion," Lila Mae called to them. "Everyone!" she shouted. The weary group let the rope sag. "I have a suggestion. In Africa, people sing while they work. The music helps them pull together. I think what we need is a work song."

"Precisely," Stanley called. "What do you suggest, Lila Mae?"

Lila Mae bent down to Maria. "It's two alternating chords: E-minor and B-7 major. You'll pick it up right away." She turned back to the group.

"This is called 'Many Thousands Gone.'" She nodded to Maria who strummed an E-minor chord. "No more auction block for me," Lila Mae sang, "no more," and gestured to Maria who strummed B-7. "No more." Maria returned to E-minor. "No more auction block for me. Many," E-minor, "thousands," B-7 "gone," E-minor.

Lila Mae's earnest alto floated on the afternoon air and quieted the men. "Many thousands gone," she sang again while Maria alternated chords.

"Two chords. Easy," Maria said. Much of her country's folk music was also simple, haunting, and beautiful like Lila Mae's work song, but lighter: young love and loss; regret and reunion—or melodramatic self-banishment. The American's lyrics, on the other hand, were written by the sick at heart who shared fatigue and the common yoke of human bondage. Maria felt the distance between their two shades of brown skin lengthen across an ocean. Her ancestors had arrived as conquerors in Spanish galleons. Lila Mae's had arrived shackled and crammed into slave ships.

"Now you try it," Lila Mae called to the group. The two women paced the workers' line, the rope limp at their feet. Maria's measured *rasgueado* rattled the guitar strings like a snare drum.

"No more auction block for me." The tentative, shy voices soon captured the song's straightforward melody and rhythm. "No more. No more." The lyrics repetition rolled into the meadow. "No more auction block for me—" extemporaneous harmony colored the chorus bridge "—many thousands gone—" Stanley's tenor voice led a descending descant "—many thousands gone."

"I'll call out each verse's first line," Lila Mae told them. "The chorus is always the same. And when I say 'pull,' *pull* on the rope. *Yank* the stubbornness out of those mules." Lila Mae chanted the next line for them to follow. "No more driver's lash for me."

They picked up the rope and sang with her, "no more driver's lash for me."

"Pull!" Lila Mae shouted.

They weren't ready for the order but kept singing. "No more," and prepared for the next command. "No more."

"Pull!" The line snapped taut.

"No more driver's lash for me."

"Pull!" They grunted the word with her, and then sang, "many thousands gone."

"Pull!" The rope, tight in their hands, quivered.

"Many thousands gone."

"Pull!" Colleen and Betsy moved in to grab the cord. Lila Mae cued the next verse in a quick chant to maintain the down beat. "No more mistress call for me."

"No more mistress call for me," they sang digging into the

dirt and making room on the cable for more volunteers.

"Pull!" Lila Mae urged them. Bodies synchronized into a slanted line.

"No more," the line swayed toward the woods, "no more," and pulsed toward the meadow. "Pull!" Maria drummed the chords, her beat a hesitating walk.

"No more mistress call for me," they sang.

"Pull!" Like ants on a sugar trail, the once reluctant by-standers swarmed the rope. The horses' huge hooves began to slip on the pine needle floor. They threw their heads back in defiance.

"Many thousands gone."

"Puuuuull!" Lila Mae screamed. The animals' trembling knees buckled and the cart lurched forward.

As Snake had predicted, once the horses were in motion they submitted to their heavy load, lowered their heads, and leaned into the shoulder harnesses. The cart creaked up the small hill. Sadie and Dunce scored a shallow furrow with the tree's trunk all the way across the meadow into the barn.

Later that evening, Snake and his wife, Clarice, were just starting dinner. "That crazy Cravitz and his camp." Snake speared a limp scallop of cabbage along with a meatloaf slice and dragged them onto his dinner plate. Clarice stuffed the already greenback-filled coffee can with two more $20 bills. Jake had kept the money folded in his back pocket and only surrendered it after the tree trunk was resting on the plank-stacked cinder blocks in the aisle between the barn theater seats.

Chapter Fourteen

2:16 a.m.

I think our cook's son had it right when he quoted Lao Tzu in a letter to his mother, Sonja: 'the sage knows without traveling ... the farther you go, the less you know ....'

Hundreds of millions of galaxies exist, millions of parsecs apart. Time is merely one dimension of conveyance. Death is another. Our story requires this odd rabbit hole, and its telling necessitates the linear observance of *time*. I am not a stranger to it; I am a stranger in it. It was, and is, July 20, 1969.

9:30 a.m.

The camp's three aluminum, Grumman canoes limited the camping trip to nine people. Brad decided our other quaint, wood-slatted boats weren't strong enough to withstand ramming the inevitable rocks and boulders that lurked in the shallow water. He needed a counselor in each canoe and had asked Lila Mae and Wally to assist him. Wally was delighted.

Lila Mae had misgivings. "About the only time I've ever been in a canoe was at Spring Lake Amusement Park in Oklahoma City right after it was integrated. I think a pulley system guided the boats."

"You can swim though?"

"I can side-stroke with the best of them."

"The food will be ... better than usual, and I'll give you two good oarsmen to command."

A smile crept onto Lila Mae's face. "No more driver's lash for me," she sang.

Brad cracked a phantom whip. "Pull!" Their eyes met and lingered longer than either had intended.

11:03 a.m.

The sign-up sheet had languished for hours on the Stone House bulletin board. Only the three counselors had written their names on the nine available lines. The slots filled quickly when Brad added a menu at the bottom. Freddie and Angela were the first to discover the food list.

"Angie, listen to this. Lunch, day one: ham and Swiss cheese hoagies on whole wheat buns."

"Wow, that's a change. I love hoagies. Since when did they start posting a menu?"

"Naw, this is what they're having on the canoe trip."

"You're kidding!" Angela squeezed in next to her friend for a closer look. "Spinach salad," she read, "with artichoke hearts and ranch dressing, whole milk, fresh strawberries."

Freddie swallowed hard and moaned. "Strawberries!"

Kurt and Reginald, on their way to the lakefront, saw the girls huddled near the bulletin board. Freddie's cotton stretch pants, tight across the ample buttocks, quivered with excitement. Kurt motioned for Reginald to follow him.

"What's going on?" Reginald wedged next to Freddie, Kurt by Angela.

"Hi Kurt," Angela said. "Listen to this. Dinner, day one: barbecue shish-kabobs made with real steak."

"*Steak!* Let me see that." Reginald pushed past Freddie and adjusted his glasses. "Barbecue shish-kabobs made with real steak, fresh onions, green peppers and cherry tomatoes. This is the canoe trip menu."

"Let's sign up," Kurt said.

"We haven't finished dinner," Angela said. "Fresh, not canned, peaches, graham crackers with chocolate marshmallow melt."

"Oh, Oh! S'mores, that's s'mores!" Freddie rocked on her heels.

"What's s'mores?" Reginald asked.

"Roasted marshmallows on graham crackers with chocolate on the top. It's all melty and gooey!" Freddie's fingers fondled the air. She bit her lower lip.

"And spiced tea," Kurt read imitating Stanley's English accent. "Brrrrreakfast, day two, western omelets—"

Angela mimed cracking an egg on a frying pan's edge, pulling the shell apart at the bottom, and releasing the raw glob. She tossed the shell halves over her shoulder.

"—with ham," Kurt read, "cheese, onions, green peppers, spinach, toh-ma-toes, and olives."

"One mustn't forget the olives," Reginald said.

"Quite," Kurt said. "Toast of the whole wheat variety, home-made hash browns with bar-bay-que sauce," Kurt peered at the menu like Stanley squinting over his reading glasses, "coffee and whole milk."

"So much better than half-milk," Freddie said.

"Quite," Reginald said.

"Lunch, day two," they read as a chorus, "left over steak," and tittered in amusement, "unlikely," said Reginald, "ridiculous," Angela said. "Ham," they continued, "and olive roll-ups on crackers, dried apricots, nut medley—"

"Tra-la, la-la-laaaah," Freddie trilled.

"—with almonds, walnuts, pecans, raisins."

"And soda," Kurt added.

"Soda? Well," Angela sniffed, "I'm not at all sure soda is appropriate considering the nature of the accompanying cuisine."

They paused to consider her remark, and then Freddie took the pencil dangling from the thumb-tacked string. She signed the fourth line and dotted the "i" in her name with a small heart. The others followed suit saying, "after you," and "no, no old chap, after you."

1:22 p.m.

Myron had planned for the bear and loon to crown the totem, but the wider surface area near the trunk's base provided the additional room he needed for sculpting. Without reluctance, he released the top for smaller carvings and the children's paintings. He'd given them free reign for their work with only two restrictions: no dirty language and no dirty pictures. The work was going surprisingly well, he thought—a few splinters, a few bloodied fingers but no need for more than Band-Aids.

The older carvers had chosen their themes with maturity and restraint, although Colleen's helmeted toadstool seemed suspiciously phallic to Myron. And he wasn't sure what Megan and Thea's yin-yang flying saucer collaboration was all about. He had stressed the importance of using sketches to work from and asked that the images be related to their experiences at camp.

The younger children were delighted with the prospect of working alongside the big kids.

The older campers—particularly the boys—had been harder to inspire. But that changed when the chisels, gouges, adzes, V tools, cabinet scrapers, and assorted implements with sharp edges and slashing curves were displayed on the Stone House registration desk. Rope grabbed a six-inch chisel and would have dug a canal across the table if our head counselor hadn't interceded.

"Put it back," Jake ordered, "now! And don't even think about it Willington. I still have my eye on you."

"I'm just looking," Kurt said.

Megan and Thea snatched two D hand adzes to smooth and iron a pretend table cloth. Mye demanded them back. "Not without proper orientation," he said. The girls' indignation quickly turned to abject boredom.

"We have wood to practice on," Myron said. "When you're

ready, show Popeye your sketch and we'll go from there. If you don't want to work on the totem pole, that's okay. We'll need people to help with the party."

"The party?" Reginald asked.

"The Haida threw potlatches when they finished their totem poles," Robin said. "I just wrote a poem using the potlatch as a symbol of capitalist decadence."

"What's a potlatch?" Kurt asked.

"It's a party," Myron explained, "where the hosts give away gifts to impress the guests." Myron pinched a coppice of nose hairs. "But since we're the hosts *and* the guests, a pot-latch doesn't make much sense, does it?"

"Not really," Freddie said.

"Okay. So, we're having a pot-*luck,*" Mye said. "We'll invite people from Match who've helped with the totem. Sally Moffett, who gave us the tree. Mr. Snake who hauled it for us. Mr. Ratchet from the general store, the fire chief. They can each bring their favorite dishes. Once we have a date, Jake will send out the invitations."

Jake scowled. Another hair-brained idea, he thought.

"My parents have a Christmas potluck every year on the first Saturday morning in December," Colleen said. "People bring all kinds of great stuff. Cinnamon rolls, fruit, soufflés. My parents supply the Mimosas."

"Aren't Mimosas trees?" Reginald said.

"Actually, Reginald," Colleen stroked him from Adam's apple to the tip of his chin with her finger. "Mimosas are orange juice and champagne."

208

2:28 p.m.

"I'm tellin' ya," Alex said to Leon, "Sally Moffett's a piece of work." Even though he labored with a light-weight, electric chainsaw his hands were weary from fighting the bar's skittering tip. Groaning, he flung the chord aside and set the tool down. Alex repositioned his body in the saddle between the bear's jutting chin and its nappy chest—scooped in small gouges like wind-tossed water. He snapped the clear goggles onto his forehead. "It's a lot faster this way, but I'll be glad when I'm done with the rough-in." He opened and closed stiff fingers.

"What do you mean a piece of work?" Leon dropped his chisel next to Alex's electric saw.

"She lives like a hermit," Alex said. "Wintertime up here, people can freeze solid in hours. Nobody'd know it for days. Built that cabin all by her lonesome." He lifted an eyebrow, "I'd be hard pressed to do that, and she's gotta be close to fifty." Alex's face contorted. He shifted his weight. "Sally's got a real feud going with Gerald Ratchet. He owns the general store. Scuttlebutt is he once sold her a clunker outboard motor. He wouldn't replace it and she never forgot the insult. It's the town melodrama."

"An Adirondack tale of the Hatfields and McCoys," Leon said. "Might make a pretty good one-act."

"I lived up here one winter," Alex said.

"Why would you do that?"

"If Ginny hadn't kept my bed warm, I'd have left by Thanksgiving." Alex's nostalgia accumulated in a faint smile.

"Ah! The lusty plot thickens."

"Ginny was one of the few who could knock on Sally's door and be invited in. Moffett tolerated me. There wasn't much Sally couldn't do, but she had trouble doing some of it by herself. I swear, riled up she can bench-press three hundred."

"Where did she pick up the charming nickname of Shotgun-Sally?" Leon asked.

"I think she got yoked with that when poachers trespassed on her land trying to steal exotic ferns. She packed her shotgun with rock salt and pelted the fern poachers right off their horses. I'd like to have seen that. Didn't do much harm to the horses, but scared the crap out of the poachers. That talk about her sleeping with the shotgun? Unlikely." Alex snapped his goggles into place. He reached for his saw and went back to work. Tiny chips sprayed up around him.

Disgruntled at the usurpation of his theatrical space, Leon regarded the pole and the campers hunched over it. Flies on rotten fruit. I could feel his bitterness rising like a stench. Three yards away, Popeye chopped wood sparks into the muted light. To Leon, Popeye's hand adz seemed better suited for ritual suicide. They were automatons invading his theater. Forced labor. Mind control. Leon was supposed to be working on a musical with Stanley and instead had to settle for a ridiculous Cole Porter *homage* that didn't sound anything like Cole Porter. The rehearsal space in the barn was *restricted*. Hey! It was his theatre. Why couldn't Myron restrict it to theatrics, instead of manufacturing totem poles?

"I wasn't hired to chisel," Leon said to Alex who wasn't listening. The drama coach picked up his tool and pushed laggard strokes along a red line painted on the wood. Thin curls white-capped and rolled onto the floor.

My husband came up behind him. "You're doing a great job, Leon." He clapped him on the shoulder. "Just keep rounding it off. Cedar's easy to carve, isn't it? And I love the smell!" Myron moved down the totem and congratulated some younger campers who were sanding a long, flat surface with blocks wrapped in gritty paper.

Serfs, Leon thought, children on their knees scrubbing a façade that would never come clean. He made sure Mye was beyond hearing and tapped Alex on the back. The younger man stopped his saw and pushed the goggles up into his hair.

"What is it now, Leon?"

"What are those kids doing? It'll take forever to sand that down."

Alex brushed cedar dust from his chin. "Each kid has a spot on the totem's upper part. See the initials? That's why the top's parceled up into all those segments. Once their section is smooth, they can paint something. They gotta smooth their section before they paint it, though." Alex held a finger to his temple. "Motivation and reward. Cravitz may be odd, but he isn't stupid."

"If you ask me, he's both," Leon said.

"Where's your sense of drama, Leon? Who else on the east coast is carving totem poles these days?"

Scraping and muttering, Leon went back to work with the chisel.

4:10 p.m.

The week after Cheryl Mariano whacked him down with her foot at the indelicate conclusion of their stroll, Reginald started a letter to his brother. He wanted to tell him what Cheryl was *really* like and show him his Golden Fleece poem but thought better of it now that the bruise and swelling had disappeared. He corrected the letter:

> ~~7/14/1969~~ 7/20/1969 (In Farroukian numerical code, that's: Playful / Burp, Peanut butter / Fart, Idiot, Amazon, Idiot—I've changed the number "6" from "Cheryl" to "Amazon.")
>
> ~~Boy was I wrong about Cheryl!!! I wrote a poem that~~ The totem pole (our camp project) is in the barn and we've already started carving and painting it. Mr. Cravitz really likes my drawings and asked me to carve something near the top of the pole. He lent me a book about the Haida, Tlingit, and Nuxalk totem pole carvers on the west coast. They don't have a written language, so the totem poles are like history books that tell the tribe's story. When our pole is done, we'll raise it Indian-style and have a celebration, called a Potlatch, only ours will be a pot<u>luck</u>. The words are similar, aren't they? Maybe that's where our English word comes from!
>
> My favorite crest (that's a symbol or animal carved on the totem that tells the tribe's history) is Sisiutl, the two-headed sea serpent. So, I'm carving it—reptile eyes, long fangs—above the other kids' drawings. The Haida say the shiny mica pieces you find on the beach are the serpent's scales he's

lost in battle. Sisiutl can guard your house and bring wealth, but he's dangerous too. Just looking at him can kill you. Just like looking at Medusa can turn you to stone! Isn't that far out?!

Cheryl didn't much like my acting in *Butterfly Girl and Mirage Boy*. Anyway, I've made friends with a guy named Kurt. He's teaching me to throw a knife so it will stick into a tree and I don't mean from three or four feet away. It's more like twenty or thirty feet and it's SO GROOVY when it lands right.

In a few days, I'll be going on a canoe trip with my counselor, Brad, and we'll be eating REAL FOOD. I'm having a great time! It's probably not a good idea to show this letter to Mom and Dad (on account of the knife). But if they want to send goodies, I wouldn't mind some of Mom's banana bread and that beef jerky she gets at Angustinos.

It's time for before-dinner workshops, so I'll sign off (Popeye's helping me with the Sisiutl design). You say "adieu," I say "a don't." If you recall, that's Farroukian for "so long for now."

REGINALD

5:05 p.m.

In the Stone House commons room, Brad turned the TV on. The local weather report flickered within the 19-inch screen. Campers needed approval before watching television, but its lure always faded from collective memory after the first week or so. The rain for the season was down,

Brad noted, which meant the river would be down for the canoe trip. A good sign. The water would be slow moving but deep enough to canoe in and shallow enough, for the most part, to stand in. Brad was concerned about Freddie who admitted, "on a scale of one to ten, my swimming's maybe a two-and-a-half, but I'm about to be promoted from beaver to otter. *Please* can I go?"

How could he say no to such an eager canoeist? Maria assured him Freddie could now "paddle the dog" and keep herself afloat. "Kurt's an excellent swimmer, almost as good as Wally," she told him. Rope and Scotty were both porpoises, apt since they always swam and frolicked together. The rest were proficient. Maria suggested to Brad that Wally go along for everyone's safety. "Maybe he can keep Scotty and Rope out of trouble. Nitro and glycerin, yes?"

Brad was pleased that Kurt had signed up with his new friend, Reginald Farrouk. He didn't know Angela Twining, but Fanny, her counselor, described her as "sweet." Fanny's discriminatory faculties were limited. She was, as Brad once remarked to Alex, the camp's sad sack, married to the camp's prick.

I couldn't have put it better.

Brad hadn't watched TV in weeks. The national news, he thought, was surreal. Walter Cronkite estimated 75% of college students felt disassociated from politics because of the war in Southeast Asia. Brad figured disenchantment at about 99% and the term "disassociated" seemed to him anemic considering the police brutality his college friends endured in Chicago at the Democratic National Convention the summer before. His roommate took 15 stitches in the head and spent 3 days in the hospital with a concussion. Brad remembered an older student who had come to school on the G.I. Bill after service in Vietnam. One day after class, Brad asked the quiet, six-foot bull of a man with short blond hair and nails chewed to the quick if he had ever killed an enemy soldier in 'Nam.'

"God, I hope not," he had said.

Brad grunted in disbelief at the closing segment of the news. Cronkite removed his glasses and said into the camera, "by this day's end, America will have landed human beings on the moon and, with God's grace, will return them safely to earth thus fulfilling President Kennedy's challenge to the nation made nearly a decade ago. And that's the way it is. This is Walter Cronkite. Goodnight."

Holy shit, Brad thought. We're going to land people on the moon and bring them back again smiling for the cameras. We send them to Vietnam, their brains get scrambled. They return to an empty tarmac at a small airport someplace in central Indiana. A week later, one of them takes his wife hostage in the barn, holds off the local police and finally swallows the barrel on the farm 20-gauge. His wife doesn't need to divorce him. He's splattered himself all over the horse stall.

10:12 p.m.

Growing up in Maryland during the 1950s, Brad collected outer-space trading cards, five to a pack, stacked on a powdery square of pink bubble gum. The cards featured eerie paintings of the solar system's planets and artists' interpretations of other worlds in space: alien worlds with icicle-cragged mountains and methane waterfalls; worlds circling unknown suns—places where serrated vegetation spiked menacing blooms that propagated in dismal swamps. Each card had an intriguing caption: *'Some worlds within our own galaxy are so distant that a space ship traveling at the speed of light would take 70,000 years to reach them!'*

Brad watched the grainy television transmission from across the lodge commons and remembered his treasured moon card. Gray craters pocked the lunar surface below a black, star-pricked sky. The cloudless blue earth hung like a portrait in the upper right corner. The caption said: *'When man finally sets foot on the moon, scientists predict the experience will so overwhelm the astronaut, paralysis will momentarily seize him!'*

The entire camp squinted with Brad at the iridescent TV monitor. All, that is, but Myron who was carving in the barn. The glaring klieg lights threw his hands' shadows down the totem pole's crevices.

Past 10 o'clock, and even the youngest ones were still awake. Transfixed, they watched Neil Armstrong's boots stumble from the lunar module's ladder and then glide the last few feet to the lunar surface. He didn't hesitate and tested the moon's dust with a probing footstep. His voice, distorted from its quarter-million mile transmission, was, nonetheless, heard world-wide: "That's one small step for man, one giant leap for mankind."

Despite Brad's trading card prediction of paralysis, the astronaut went straight to work for science in the harsh contrasts of lunar light and shade. And, as it turned out, the intense static from Houston's Mission Control had corrupted the first part of his brief, historic speech by omitting the article, "a." What the astronaut actually said was: "That's one small step for a man, one giant leap for mankind." Distorted by a hundred-millionth of a parsec, Armstrong's personal modesty was usurped by the grandeur of his new status, not as a man, but as mankind's cosmic representative for the technological prowess of the United States.

An hour into the broadcast—after Armstrong and Aldrin stamped a confusion of crisp tracks into the powdery mantle at the feet of the space craft—some of Armstrong's younger humanoids (whom he now represented) began to nod off. Shuffling and groggy, their counselors steered them to bed.

11:44 p.m.

At the northwest corner of the camp in ecstatic but breathable air, the klieg lights blast a Halleluiah chorus through cracks in the walls of Leon's erstwhile theater. Inside, three praying mantis tripods focus their white brilliance on a totem pole and grub-worm man. He taps his mallet and is so close to the object of his obsession he seems to gnaw and eat the wood. Powdered cedar dusts the remnants of a grilled cheese sandwich. My husband—and everything he is and isn't—revolves around Orion's Arm near the Milky Way's rim in a tiny solar system containing a unique and fragile planet.

Chapter Fifteen

Brad speckled the halved roll with *Grey Poupon* mustard and presented the plastic butter knife to Kurt who licked each side, played his tongue over the gritty texture, and burst the tangy, pinhead granules with his teeth. "I thought mustard was bright yellow, like raincoats," the boy said. "But this stuff isn't really gray either."

"Grey was one of the guys who invented it," Reginald said. "Poupon was the other guy. The mustard comes from Dijon, in France."

Freddie chewed a strawberry. "How do you know stuff like that, Reginald?" She licked her fingers.

"Expensive mustard comes in a box. The story's on the side."

Rope wanted lunch. "Let's stop talking," he said.

After Brad and Lila Mae finished making the hoagies, Wally cracked his bread apart and stuffed extra spinach between the layers of Swiss cheese and ham. He dribbled ranch salad dressing over the greens and then attacked the sandwich, the creamy spread tipping his nose. Lila Mae nibbled hers open-faced without spinach. With her teeth, she pinched the bread's crust in snippets, paused, and then chomped off a quarter of her meal in a single bite. Angela rotated her sandwich in delicate turns and pared off the edges in small swallows. The *Grey Poupon* oozed between the bread. Her tongue speared pygmy mustard pillars.

"I'll just take a few more of those strawberries," Scotty said reaching.

Wally, lucky Stetson low on his brow, stopped chewing, and aimed his plastic fork at Scotty's fingers. "Slow down!" he said with his mouth full. The boy drew his hand back and stuck his tongue out.

Brad needed both hands to hold his loaded hoagie. "This is what I call a canoe trip," he said.

They had taken the bus late that morning to the end of the road where the Upper Salmon River bubbled over rocks. Salmon don't exist in the Adirondacks, neither do Grizzly bears even though they would pass into Grizzly Bear Lake on their way to the Lower Salmon, all part of the Salmon River Chain. Brad and Wally had planned the trip by consulting a topographical map and the state foresters in Glen Falls.

"Store your grub tight at night or, sure as spit, the coons'll have at it," the clerk in Match's cramped, overpriced food market had said.

After lunch, Freddie dangled from her arm the life vest's straps, pads, and buckles. "Do I really have to wear this thing? I'm an otter now. Wally, tell him. I'm an otter."

"She'll be fine in the river's shallows, but when we get to Grizzly Bear Lake, she'll need the vest," he told Brad.

Rope and Scotty, who were cramming their mouths with the last of the strawberries, glanced at Brad. Rope spit a large berry into his hand. "Grizzly Bear Lake?"

Behind the two boys, Wally clamped his teeth in a grin and flapped his Stetson at them.

Brad bent to retrieve a paddle from the beach. He stabbed the blade into the coarse sand and leaned on the handle.

"Do you think we can cross the lake before dark?" he asked Wally.

Rope turned his tense face to Wally who scratched his eyebrow and slipped his hat on. He pulled the brim down. "We'll have to push. I'm in no mood to spend the night on the east shore of Grizzly Bear Lake."

Scotty finished his strawberry leaving a nubbed, green star. "How come?"

"I thought you knew about Grizzly Bear Lake, Scotty," Brad said. "Didn't Wally tell you before you shipped aboard?"

"He didn't tell us," Rope said.

"Well, I considered borrowing Sally's shotgun." Brad gazed down river where it's ruffled eddies flattened into the silken lake. "But I'm not sure it would have done much good."

Sitting on a small boulder next to Angela, Kurt wondered how the grizzly bombshell would play out with the two little pests. He pried a smooth, driftwood limb from the rock's crevice where it met the beach and snapped his knife open to whittle.

Freddie bowed her head and mumbled what sounded to Scotty like prayers. Angela made the sign of the cross in a delicate flourish. Lila Mae crossed her arms over her chest. "Humph!" The boy's uneasy glances skittered among them.

Reginald licked his thumb and flipped a page from his *Pocket Guide to the Adirondacks*. "Black bears are occasionally seen ..." he read.

221

"Grizzly's are tough," Wally interrupted, "no doubt about it. Wasn't it last summer they found those canoes on the east shore? Sheriff said it was homicide, blood everywhere and all those bullet holes in the sides." Wally's glance whipped from boy to boy. "They weren't bullet holes, though. The forester in Glen Falls knew better. Grizzlies. Four-inch claws. They can shred a car's hood like paper."

Reginald pocketed his book and curled his hands into talons behind the backs of the boys' heads.

Kurt whittled. "Sally told me a shotgun gives you almost a fifty-fifty chance against a grizzly. Of course, you've got to use slugs, not buckshot. And if there's more than one bear, you'd never have time to reload."

"They're mean as hornets protecting their turf," Wally said. "It takes one powerful critter to punch holes in something like this." He banged the side of the beached Grumman.

They packed up lunch, the quiet a relief to the others weary of the boys' taunts about 'Freddie the blimp' and 'elbows Angela.' Even Brad had been a target. Within a quarter mile of their put-in, he became Mad Captain Brad. Separating the boys only encouraged the water fights. With his paddle, Scotty had drenched Lila Mae in arching waves meant for Rope.

"Once is okay, I can dry off," she told Brad before lunch. "But I'm not puttin' up with this all afternoon."

"I guess we'd better be going," Rope said after Wally wedged the lunch left-overs into the cooler.

"Yeah, no use getting a late start and spending the night next to Grizzly Bear Lake," Scotty said.

"No rush." Angela stretched the kinks out of her arms and sat on the pebble beach next to Kurt. She inspected the ragged "K" he was carving into the branch.

Reginald and Freddie started up the embankment to the woods, "We're going for a hike," she said. "Helps digestion."

"It's a little late for morel mushrooms, according to this." Reginald peered into his guidebook. "But you never know."

Seven against two and all seven remembered how pleasant silence could be.

The three counselors wandered up the beach and left Scotty and Rope standing next to the canoes, paddles upright. Wally straddled a white birch's trunk leaning out into the lake, his legs limp over the water. Next to him on shore, Lila Mae raised her face to the cloud-gathering sun and picked at her drying shirt.

Brad watched the small waves break on the beach. They swirled through pebbles, receded, broke, and swirled up again. His mind churned. According to Jake, a Mr. Haskell from the Upstate New York Children's Home would arrive tomorrow to take Kurt back.

"Have him ready to leave as soon as you return," was all Jake had said.

"The boot heel of oppression has kicked another little breach into the cozy wall of our summer camp," Brad said to Jake.

"Get a life, String bean."

Brad had spent 4 years of his life getting a liberal arts degree to come up with quips like that.

The remaining run on the Upper Salmon was uneventful, the conversation perfunctory. They drifted into Grizzly Bear Lake whose breadth opened into miles of water and shore. Scotty and Rope spoke to each other in cranky, hushed tones. Brad's idea of putting them in the same canoe with Wally sitting in the middle worked. Brad knew the boys had in mind to sleep on the distant, Lower Salmon River shore. Their imaginations had erected restraining walls that kept grizzlies from escaping the banks of the lake named for them. Grizzlies, after all, stayed close to home protecting their turf. Wally had said so, and Wally was working on his Eagle Scout.

"A little longer," Rope said, after paddling sluggishly for 2 hours "Please?"

"There's a lean-to up ahead on the lake. We'll have dinner and bed down there," Wally said.

Brad, in the lead canoe, looked back at Wally and pointed his paddle at the thickening nimbus clouds. Wally nodded. They had hoped against rain.

"I thought we weren't going to sleep next to Grizzly Bear Lake," Scotty said.

"Look's like we'll have to." The wind had died and the gray afternoon lake mirrored the sky. They glided into a bulge of beach, the bows of the canoes furrowing pebbles.

Freddie lunged from her canoe, rocking it, and stepped over gunwales into six inches of water. She pawed at her life jacket. "I hate this thing!"

Brad and Wally dragged the boats onto the beach near the lean-to. Surrounding the hard dirt floor on three sides, its log walls and tar-papered roof would keep them dry if a thunderstorm threatened. Blackened rocks surrounded a fire pit near the opening of the shack.

"Home sweet home," Brad said. Before they could scatter to explore, he added, "We'll need lots of fire wood to keep the bears away. Nobody strays out of calling distance. Try to find dead, not rotten wood."

Pouting, Rope and Scotty gathered kindling. "I thought this was going to be a lot more fun." Rope dragged a branch to the fire pit.

"I hope it doesn't rain," Scotty said.

"Do grizzly bears like rain?"

"How should I know, bubble-head." Scotty smacked the branch from the younger boy's hands and stamped back to the trees for more wood.

Reginald and Kurt collected two armfuls of dead limbs. They staggered to a clearing near the fire ring and spilled the branches into a spiked heap. Reginald leaned against a white pine's trunk and studied his guidebook.

"That's gotta be a Mountain Ash," he pointed at a small tree. "Pinnately compound leaves. Yep, just like the picture."

Kurt compared the drawing to the tree. "The bark's a match, too."

"You ever had poison ivy?" Reginald asked.

"Sure, itches like crazy."

Reginald tapped Kurt's chest. "It doesn't exist in the Adirondacks!"

"Just like grizzly bears," Kurt pushed his friend's shoulder.

"They got black bears, though," Reginald said.

"Yeah, Sally told me about the black bears. They come out mostly sniffing for garbage. Sally said the tourists shoot 'em and that makes them dangerous."

"If it doesn't kill them," Reginald said. The boys considered dead bears and wounded bears for a moment.

"Reginald, do you think Angela's pretty?"

"I guess so. Do you think she's pretty?"

"I guess so." Kurt snapped his knife open and flipped it a foot in the air above his palm. It spun twice. He caught the handle.

Reginald stuffed his guidebook into his breast pocket next to the ball point pen clipped over the fabric's seam. "I used to think Cheryl Mariano was pretty."

"You don't think she's pretty anymore?"

Reginald pulled the pen from his shirt and tapped it on the frame of his glasses. "Well, it's just she's really touchy."

"There's a girl at the home who won't let anyone touch her shoes. She'll walk through mud in them, but put your little finger on her shoe lace, she gets hysterical. That's called a fetish, right?"

"Cheryl got hysterical at me."

Kurt sniggered "What'd you do, touch her shoes?"

Reginald shrugged. "I just asked her a question."

"What was the question?"

Reginald picked at his ear lobe. "Do you know what 'going all the way' means?"

Kurt pushed the release to close his knife. "Well, yeah. It's when, you know, a guy and a girl, you know, do it."

"What's it like?"

"How should I know."

"It's never happened to you?"

"Well, not exactly. I mean, there was this girl I messed around with. She asked me to feel her titties." Kurt peered into Reginald's large, black-framed eyes. "What made Cheryl hysterical?"

"I thought it was what she wanted. I asked her to go all the way."

"Cheryl Mariano? Miss Priss with the sneakers and white socks? Butterfly Girl?" Kurt started to laugh. "I don't think so!"

"It's not funny. She hit me. It hurt!"

Kurt couldn't conceal his delight at Reginald's ignorance, "Reginald, don't you know that's how girls get pregnant? For a brainy kid, you sure are dumb when it comes to girls."

Kurt's revelation staggered him. Reginald collapsed onto his bottom, flung his arms over his head, and fell back on the pine needles. Of course! When you went all the way, the girl got pregnant. Suddenly it all made sense to him. Cheryl didn't want to get pregnant. She was thirteen, for God's sake. Why was he so stupid!

"Kurt, Reginald!" Wally shouted from the lean-to. "Wood! We gotta have wood if you want to eat."

Reginald scrambled to his feet. "We got a whole stack right here," he called back.

"Bring it over!"

Lila Mae and Brad set up supper just inside the lean-to's drip line. Alex had given Brad a squat board for a table top and a folded, rusting camping stand. Brad unfolded the metal base, pulling it apart like an unwilling accordion, and lashed the plank's ends to the stand with nylon chord.

"Ingenious." Lila Mae said.

They stacked the food on the makeshift table. Lila Mae dragged limp meat slabs from the cooler and handed them to Brad. He accidentally dropped one in the dirt. "Shit!"

"Don't worry about it," Lila Mae said. "It'll wash off. Make mine out of this one, seasoned in mother earth." She rinsed the sirloin under the red spigot of the bulging, two-and-a-half gallon collapsible plastic jug. "It's been too long since I had steak shish-ka-bobs." Lila Mae's large, graceful hands began to cut the green peppers. She wished the knife were sharper.

"You seem a bit preoccupied, Brad."

He sliced into the meat. "They're sending Kurt back."

Lila Mae stopped cutting. "Why?" She glanced over at Kurt and Reginald. The two boys were obvious friends. Angela had joined them to snap branches to fit the fire ring.

"I wish I knew," Brad said. "Jake told me right before we left. Gave no reason. Just said, 'have him ready when you return.'"

Lila Mae brought her knife down hard on a halved green pepper; it jumped apart. "I've heard Mr. Daryl's communication skills can be Neolithic."

"Maybe it's something positive. Maybe Kurt's being adopted. That would piss Jake off. He never liked the kid."

"Does Jake like anybody but Jake?"

Brad pared the top and tendril ends from an onion then cut it length-wise. With the knife, he peeled each half's outer layer into the plastic trash bag hanging from the table's corner. He repeated the preparations with another onion. When the four halves were skinless, he pried apart the remaining scalloped and translucent layers with his fingers and set them next to Lila Mae's chopped green peppers.

"I have to leave, too. But don't tell anyone."

She laid her knife on the table. "What are you talking about Brad Stringer?"

"I've graduated, I'm eligible. The letter from Selective Service came day before yesterday. I didn't open it. I didn't need to. They're drafting me. I'll have to leave the country."

"You're gonna throw away a college education and run? Where you runnin'?"

"Canada."

Lila Mae picked up Brad's sharper cleaver. She slammed through another green pepper and suddenly tossed the knife onto the plank.

"Are you crazy? Do you know what they do to deserters?"

Brad grabbed Lila Mae's arm and pulled her farther inside the lean-to. "If I left before I'm drafted, it's evasion not desertion, and you can't tell anyone."

Lila Mae straightened her frame the way they taught her at Julliard before going onstage to perform: head up, arms relaxed. Show them you're in command. "You white boys," she said. "This war chews up black boys and spits them out. But you're white. You run off to Canada, slap down your college education and escape."

Brad glanced up at the lean-to's slanted underside.

"You know the singer, Eartha Kitt?" Lila Mae asked him.

"Yes, I know who Eartha Kitt is."

"Lady Bird Johnson had one of those first-lady luncheons to honor black artists a few years back," Lila Mae said. "One of my professors was invited. Know what Eartha Kitt said to the President's wife? 'You sent the best of this country to be snatched from their mothers, shot and maimed in Vietnam.' Mrs. Johnson wept. I liked her husband. He's the one who finally heard what Dr. King was preachin' and got a Civil Rights Bill passed. But y'all just keep sendin' my black brothers to die in this war. You go to Canada to your new life. He goes to Vietnam and comes back in a body bag." Lila Mae gripped her face and sobbed. She jerked her head back up, shook the grief from her throat and exhaled evenly.

"Henry Lee was two years younger than me."

"I'm so sorry, Lila Mae. I didn't know."

"You're not sorry enough to stay and fight, though, are you Brad?"

"I'm a conscientious objector to war."

"Oh, you object to war. And you think my brother didn't object to killing other brown-skinned people half-way 'round the world?"

Brad raked both hands through his hair. "I have no choice, Lila Mae. I was born on February 14t^h, Valentine's Day. You know what that means? I'm number *four* in the lottery. I can't get an exemption and I won't be a part of their killing machine."

Thunder rumbled—low, lengthy and far away. Lila Mae brushed past him to the table. "We'd better get supper ready, Wally," and then louder, "Wally! Start the fire."

Since when is she the boss, Brad thought.

In the evening's darkening opalescence, everyone agreed that the shish-ka-bobs were delicious, worth the trip, best I ever had! Freddie's marshmallow caught fire on the end of her slender hackberry limb and lit her face in a brief glimmer of pleasure before she blew it out. The chocolate and graham crackers were gone but she didn't care. The marshmallow bag was still half full.

"You've had enough, girl." Lila Mae took the bag from her and dropped it in the cooler.

"Just one more," Freddie begged.

"I said you've had enough."

Kurt and Angela slipped from their log by the fire pit and walked together to the beach. Scotty and Rope were tossing pebbles into the water and scanning the dark horizon. Their heads roamed left and right like beacons.

"Would you guys mind going down the beach a little?" Angela asked.

"What for?" Rope said.

"Kurt and I want to talk."

"Go ahead and talk," Scotty said.

Kurt stepped toward Scotty. "Beat it."

Scotty dropped his handful of stones—*whoosh*—into the lake's still shallows. "Come on, Rope. The love birds wanna be alone."

Together, the couple watched the lightning—intense and silent, its erratic flashes dodged the clouds' rounded shoals. They waited for the thunder that finally growled.

"The storm's really far away," Angela said. "Maybe it'll miss us."

"You know how to tell how far away a lightning strike is?"

Angela knew it had something to do with the speed of sound. "Not really," she said.

"Sound travels at about a thousand feet a second. There's 5,280 feet in a mile, so if you hear the thunder five seconds after the lightning strikes, it's about a mile away. Light travels at 670 million miles an hour, that's 186,000 miles a *second*."

"You sound like Reginald."

"That's where I learned this stuff," Kurt said.

Lightning flashed again and they counted together, "thousand one, thousand two," Angela closed her eyes, "thousand three, thousand four," up to "thousand sixteen." When the thunder sounded far away and faint, Angela opened her eyes. Kurt's gaze followed the parting lashes. He reached out to stroke her cheek.

"Don't," she said.

Kurt dropped his arm. "You're pretty, Angela."

"Don't." She said again, her voice cold.

"What's wrong?"

The girl turned away from him. "I don't like to be touched."

"Why not?"

"Touching is dirty."

"Dirty?"

"My older brother does it before he makes me—" She didn't finish.

"Before he makes you do what, Angela?"

"Never mind."

"You can tell me."

"No, I can't. I can't tell anyone." Angela's breathing changed. Sometimes Kurt woke up from nightmares panting like that, inhaling fear's short bursts then driving the breath back out.

"Why can't you tell anyone, Angela?"

She looked at him, eyes glistening. "He makes me do dirty things. I never want to." Angela laced her hands on the back of her lowered head and squeezed her elbows together to cover her face. She bolted to her feet scrambling the beach pebbles and ran back toward the lean-to.

Her own brother? If I had a sister, Kurt thought, I'd never make her do something she didn't want to do. Not those kinds of things. Kurt got to his feet to follow Angela and comfort her, tell her he'd never hurt her, never force her to do anything she didn't want to do. But he couldn't. She had fled like the lightning. He figured it would take a while before they could sit together again and just talk.

Wally ordered Scotty and Rope to overturn the canoes against the impending weather. Brad instructed the others to drag firewood into the lean-to. They stored the food in the cooler and Wally lashed it shut. Each camper laid out a bedroll near the back wall of the shelter. When the chores were done, Brad built a fire and blew gray smoke into flames. Wally added wood to the fire ring. The popping blaze released bright specs into the overcast and starless sky. Huddled within the circle of nine, each contemplated embers brooding at the center of the ring—a pulsing language for all seasons, all questions, all hurts.

Reginald broke the spell. "Here's a poem about bears," he opened his Adirondack guide. "This is from 'Allen's Bear

Fight up in Keene.'" Reginald lowered the book, "This guy, Allen, is about to be," he paused, "eaten, I guess, by a grizzly." He adjusted the book again to catch the flames' light.

"As through the woods he trudged his way, his mind unruffled as the day." The boy lilted into iambic rhythm. "He heard a deep convulsive sound which shook the earth and trees around." His recently acquired baritone voice quieted in the crackling dark. "And looking up with dread amaze, an old she-bear there met his gaze." Reginald's large eyes loomed up to Rope and Scotty who were hunched on their log seat. "The bear with threatening aspect stood to prove her title to the wood. This Allen saw with darkening frown, he reached and pulled a young tree down." Reginald bent the illusion of a slender sapling from his line of sight. "Then on his guard, with cautious care, he watched the movements of the bear."

Scotty and Rope scooted closer together.

"Against the rock with giant strength," Reginald extended a quaking right arm to repel the bear's snarling snout and frothing teeth, "he held her out at his arm's length. 'Oh God!'" Reginald shrieked; the boys jumped, "he cried in deep despair, 'If you won't help me, don't help the bear!'"

Wally threw his head back and slapped his knee. "That's a good one, Reginald." Even Angela smiled.

Scotty and Rope examined the faces illuminated by the fire. "What's so funny about it?" Scotty asked.

"What's funny," Brad said, "is that the poem's a folk tale and grizzly bears don't live in the Adirondacks." Everyone peered at the boys.

"What about Grizzly Bear Lake?" Rope's disbelief hovered over the disappointment.

"It's just the name of a lake," Freddie said, "like ... hotdog is the name of lunch meat made out of pork and fat."

Scotty punched Rope's shoulder. "I knew it! I told you, Rope. Didn't I tell you it was all a joke?"

"You never told me that," Rope rubbed the sore spot.

"I knew it all along. There's no bears around here."

"Actually," Reginald corrected him, "there are no grizzly bears." He flipped the pages, then turned his guidebook to the boys, and pointed at a line drawing. "But the Adirondacks do have their share of American black bears like the one up in Keene."

"Is that true?" Scotty asked Brad.

"Well, yes, but the black bears are usually very bashful."

"Unless they're wounded by stupid tourists," Kurt said.

They all listened to the fire snap and sigh. The boys' shoulders relaxed, but their eyes wandered to the fire's shadows fidgeting in the trees. Lila Mae glanced at Brad. The flame's grotesque imps danced across his face.

"How about a song?" she said. "I know a good one called The Drinking Gourd."

"I know that song," Brad said. "It's a beer drinking song I learned in college."

"You don't know this version," Lila Mae said. "And I bet you don't know what the song is really about."

"It's about drinking beer from a gourd, a mug. The Germans call it a stein."

"Wrong," Lila Mae said.

"What's it about, Lila Mae?" Angela asked.

"It's a song from slavery times."

"Like the one you taught us when we yanked the stubbornness out of those mules? No more auction block for me," Freddy sang, "no more mistress call for me."

"That's right, my sister. But this song's in code. It's from a time in the south when abolitionists—white people who didn't believe in slavery—helped slaves travel north to freedom, sometimes as far as Canada, on what was called the Underground Railroad. That's also code." Lila Mae searched the sky. "Too bad there are no stars tonight. Otherwise, we could all see the drinking gourd."

Brad looked hard at her. Please don't tell them, he thought. Not here. Not now. When she lowered her eyes, they caught his.

"I'm sorry," she said to him.

Wally glanced at her and shrugged. "Cloud cover's not your fault."

"What does the drinking gourd have to do with the stars?" Scotty asked.

Lila Mae picked up her hackberry branch. The singed remnants of a marshmallow still collared the tip. "This is the Big Dipper," she pricked points in the dirt next to the fire. "Connect all the stars and it's shaped like a tilted cup. See the cup? Wide at the top, narrow at the bottom. And this," she poked three more holes, "is the handle. Polaris, the north star, is up here above the cup's lip." Lila Mae tapped the branch tip on a stone cradling the fire. "Polaris always points north. By following the big dipper—the drinking gourd—the slaves knew they were headed to freedom."

"Teach us the song," Kurt said. Angela nodded agreement.

"The chorus goes like this," Lila Mae pitched her voice high, "For the old man is 'awaitin'," and descended, "for to carry you to freedom, if you follow the drinkin' gourd." They sang the chorus together and then Lila Mae said, "The verses were code, too, like this one: the river bank makes a very good road, the dead trees show you the way."

"Follow the dead trees on the river bank," Angela said.

"And keep the drinkin' gourd in sight," said Kurt.

"I'll say the verses," Lila Mae said, "you follow by singing them and then we'll sing the chorus together." She taught them the song and when the verses she knew gave out, she made up verses: "Where Grizzly Bear Lake meets the Lower Salmon, follow the drinkin' gourd."

The first splatters hissed on the fire. The campers scattered for the lean-to in a sudden and convivial burst of conversation.

"Here it comes!" and "Glad I'm not in a tent tonight!" Everyone but Brad soon fell asleep. As he listened to the spattered pounding on the roof's drumhead, he thought of his mother and father in Maryland and the house with the silly fringed awnings he might never see again.

Chapter Sixteen

"What do you mean he isn't here?" David Haskell's jaw scar twitched. He glowered at Fanny through the car door's open window above the great seal of New York. "Mr. Daryl said he'd be ready to go when I arrived."

"Kurt's on a canoe trip," Fanny said. "But they're coming back today. I think." She nudged the drive's crushed rocks with her shoe. "You could wait inside." She brightened and pointed to the dining hall, "I could get some coffee."

"I need a drink," Haskell said. "Is there a tavern or something in Match?"

"There's the Wild Cat Bar and Grill. Straight down the road then left when the street ends. It's on the left." Fanny faced town; her hands, juggled options, "wait, no, it's on the right side of the street."

"When are they're getting back?"

"Sometime today after lunch. I think."

"That's a big help." Haskell backed onto the oval. He pulled forward into the wet road leaving tire marks in the thin grass.

Fanny watched him barrel up the drive. "You're welcome," she said.

The large woman in the dim tavern was the sole customer. Haskell figured she was a local. A tourist wouldn't dress in overalls and a work shirt. She ate a late breakfast with a deliberateness he found annoying: a bite of toast; a long pause before chewing; a forkful of egg; another pause; a sip of coffee (when would the dame swallow?); and, finally a throat-pulsing gulp. Then she'd repeat the process.

From behind the bar, Hal, the Wild Cat Bar and Grill's owner, peered at his television's small screen. His two young daughters read from a stack of *My Bookhouse Books* at the counter. They were the only other people in the café.

Haskell took his beer to the woman's booth. "Kind of quiet in here, mind if I join you?" He now saw she was a bit younger than he thought. And homelier.

"Suit yourself," she said.

"Thank you. Are you from around here?"

"What if I am?"

Haskell smiled, "Just trying to make conversation, miss."

"So am I," Sally fixed her countenance on him—an owl watching prey.

He started again. "I'm visiting the camp," and took a long drink.

"That so?"

"Cravitz Fine Arts Camp up the road."

"You have a child at the camp?" Sally sipped her coffee.

"He's not my child. I'm from the Upstate Children's Home. It's an orphanage that's ..."

240

"I know what it is." Sally carefully slid the sweating water glass from between them. "You're not Haskell by any chance?"

"Why, yes, I am. How did you know?"

"Kurt's told me about you."

"Don't believe a word of it," Haskell blurted. "Kurt's a very troubled young man. Where's the waiter? They're never around when you want them." Haskell slugged his beer, turned in his seat and called to Hal, "Hey, buddy, how about another beer?"

"Why shouldn't I believe it?"

"Because Kurt's a thief and a liar."

"That your official, state-endorsed opinion?"

"Madam, Kurt's behavior is why I'm here. He stole money and candy at the camp. He had money to buy candy and trinkets when he left. He's a thief by nature. The home pays for his attendance and this is the thanks we get?" Haskell sucked his beer's last suds. "The boy can't help himself. If juvy doesn't get him first, we'll have to release him at eighteen. Then who knows where he'll end up. I'm afraid Kurt is what we call problematic."

Hal brought Haskell another beer. Ruby, the barkeep's younger daughter filled Sally's coffee cup and set his empty bottle and her dishes on a small serving tray with the care an 8-year-old reserves for important duties.

"Would you like something else, Miss Moffett?"

"Not now, Ruby, thanks."

"I have a sister-in-law named Moffett," Haskell mused. "Never met her though."

Sally let his comment pass. "How did you find out about the theft?"

"A camp administrator, Jake Daryl, called two weeks ago. It seems he found some of the stolen candy in Kurt's footlocker."

"You talk with Myron Cravitz?"

"No, but Mr. Daryl ..."

"Jake Daryl's a peckerwood."

Haskell formed a tight smile. "Be that as it may, Miss Moffett, Kurt's a thief and I've come to take him back to the home."

Sally placed her hand's calloused blade—thumb up—on the table and with its back eased the salt and pepper shakers, the napkins' stainless steel obelisk, and the Tabasco sauce to one side.

"Mr. Haskell, I don't want to rain on your parade, but the real thief confessed last week. I know 'cause her parents had lunch in that booth over there and didn't mind yammerin' on about it. Girl's name was Star. As in movie."

Haskell stared at Sally and finished a slow drink of beer. "But Mr. Daryl said ..."

"Daryl has to pee sittin' down. Talk to Cravitz."

Haskell left the table and went to the pay phone next to the tavern door. Sally watched his back until he hung up. He returned and sat down.

"I came all this way for nothing."

"Yeah, Kurt'll be real disappointed." She finished her coffee.

Haskell drummed the table. "Mr. Cravitz said Mr. Daryl forgot to call and tell me the actual thief had been sent home. That's very unprofessional."

Sally plunked an elbow on the table. "I did a little checkin' up on Jake Daryl. You should too. He was once a resident of yours. Kurt and Peckerwood," Sally held up two fingers and crossed them, "they're cut from the same gunny sack. Familiarity breeds contempt, Mr. Haskell."

The man closed his eyes. "Why am I always the one to get stuck with the problems?"

"Give the boy a little slack," Sally said. "I don't think you have any idea how smart he is, what a good kid he is."

Haskell regarded the woman's calloused hands, the ragged shirt collar, and faded overall straps, her throat's tanned-to-pitch valley and the thin, wind-blown frenzy of salt and pepper hair. She's poor as dirt, he thought. For someone without resources, she seemed rather perceptive.

"Who was that sister-in-law you mentioned?" Sally asked.

"It was a long time ago. Maiden name was Moffett, first name Sally. She was from around here, actually."

Sally's broad smile crinkled her cheeks. She leaned toward him and worked her tongue through snaggle-gap.

"No!" he said.

"Small world," she said. "Sally's my first name. What's your first name?"

"David. But Delmore was my half-brother. His last name was ..."

"Bennett, right?"

"No!" Haskell said again.

"See, you didn't come all this way for nothin'. You came to say hello to your half-sister-in-law. How is that piece of crap, Delmore? Still beatin' up women and cheatin' on wives?"

"Delmore's dead."

Sally sat back in her seat. "Well then," she said softly, "God rest his sorry, moth-eaten soul."

"I didn't like him much either."

"When did he die?"

"Killed himself three days ago."

"You gotta be pretty lonely to do something like that," Sally said.

An older couple shambled into the tavern and sat in a near-by booth. They brought with them the fresh smell of dirt.

"When's the funeral?" Sally asked.

"Soon," Haskell said. "I suspect they'll be contacting you in a few days. Don't get me wrong, Sally, I'm relieved the boy didn't do it. How's he doing up here at the camp, any-way?"

"David, you ever seen a prickly pear cactus bloom?"

Kurt had been happy on the Salmon River Chain. He and Reginald swore abiding friendship. Each blotted the other on the forehead with a drop of blood teased from their palms at the tip of Kurt's knife. He and Angela talked together about themselves, about the parts that didn't hurt—the simple, happy parts. She put her head on his shoulder. He'd never felt this way before.

But when Brad told him Haskell was coming for him, the old feelings returned like a sickness. He didn't want to be sick anymore. He wanted to stay. He wanted to sit with Angela and watch the lake. He wanted to visit Reginald in his big house in Huntington. He wanted to ram his knife between Haskell's stinking ribs. He didn't know what he wanted.

"I'm sorry," Brad said. "Jake didn't say what it was about."

"It doesn't matter."

They headed back the way they came, upstream against a mild current. In the canoe's stern, Brad paddled on the opposite side and in unison with Angela in the bow. Her stroke had become stronger during the trip. Brad was proud of her.

From the center seat, Kurt watched the shore slip past. 'The river bank makes a very good road, the dead trees show you the way.' He could split to Canada. No one would find him. He could take a new name, become someone else, someone lucky, someone with rich parents who'd take him to far-off places like Australia or California.

"Could you drop me off at Sally's on the way back?" he asked Brad.

"Haskell's waiting for you."

"I just want to say goodbye, thank her for the knife."

Angela gripped the paddle and pulled the water toward her in desperate swirls. "I'll write you, Angela," Kurt said. "We can be pen pals, okay?" The girl slowed her strokes and relinquished her anger to tears.

They loaded the three canoes onto the bed of the trailer, two below, one above. Word of Kurt's departure hadn't taken long to circulate among the small group, and the ride back to camp was strained. Even Scotty and Rope kept quiet. Brad stopped the bus and the loaded trailer by Sally's nearly hidden drive. "Don't stay long, Kurt."

Sally met him on the porch. "Heard you comin'."

"You could hear a pin drop in a thunderstorm, Sally," and then in a sullen voice, "I came to say goodbye."

"That so?"

"Haskell's come to get me."

"That so?" She leaned against the porch post. "Did he say why?"

"That's just it, I don't know." The boy fought back tears. "It isn't fair. That damn Haskell!"

Sally hadn't hugged anyone in ages. She hardly knew how

to go about it. Best to just walk up and do it, she thought. When she opened her capacious arms, she hadn't expected the lightness of him as he rushed into her, limbs wrapping strong and thin around her back. She returned his embrace cautiously.

"Haskell's not takin' you anywhere."

Her words trickled through his mind. She released her grip like a gate opening when he backed away from her. "I don't have to leave?" he said.

"Not unless you want to."

"Swear you're sure!"

"He and I just had a conversation, Kurt. I'm sure as I'm standin' here. Haskell's already on his way back to the home."

"I don't have to go!" Kurt flew down the steps, skidded to a halt, and bolted back up the wooden treads. He hugged Sally hard, let go and in a leap that made her laugh, sailed over the steps onto the wet moss and pine needles. He stumbled forward but kept running. "I'm staying," he whooped.

Myron was pacing his office when Jake entered. "You wanted to see me," Jake said.

"Close the door."

Jake shut the door just as Leon McAdam reached the hall stair's summit. Leon was on his way to see my husband about the Cole Porter review he and Stanley were rehearsing for the totem-pole-raising ceremony. He hurried to the closed office door and was about to knock, but arguing voices from inside the room made him wait and listen.

"What the hell were you thinking?" Myron said.

Jake pared dirt from under his thumb nail and blew its thin line to the floor. "You mean about Kurt?"

"Yes, about Kurt. Who made you judge and jury?"

"I forgot to return Mr. Haskell's call."

"Like hell you did! Haskell called me this morning. He told me you called him twice, the second time on Friday. *Friday,* Jake. That was the day after the Star girl confessed. You could have told him, but you let him drive up here anyway?" Myron's face flushed. "What have you got against that boy?"

"Kurt's a trouble-maker." Jake sauntered to the filing cabinet. "Someone needs to make the hard decisions, Myron." He opened the top drawer, delved in, and snatched a handful of jumbled letters. "Look at this mess!" Jake threw the documents back into the drawer. "Look at your desk, look at this room! You have no idea how to run a camp. Now that Deidre's gone—"

"Leave my wife out of this."

"How can I leave her out?" Jake banged the drawer shut. "She's everywhere like the wood chips from your damn totem pole!" Jake throttled a scarred oak side chair by its arms and slammed it down next to Myron's desk. He tramped his foot into the seat and smacked a hand on my husband's shoulder. Jake squeezed Mye's tense muscle hard before he let go.

"You've lost your grip, old man." Our head counselor dragged his foot from the seat of the chair and sat. "Kurt Willington doesn't matter." He reached across the desk and rotated the totem pole's clay model a half-turn. "Camp's almost over. When you sell this place, you'll retire. I'll take over your business interests. You've always wanted to just paint. Just sculpt. Am I right, or am I right?"

Myron brushed his ear and shut his eyes at the sudden roar in his skull.

"We're a team now, daddy-o. Just you and me. Don't worry. I'll take good care of you. And neither of us will have to put up with these snot-nosed kids anymore. You won't have to teach English to tenth-graders who don't give a shit. That's not what you want. You want to be an artist. Am I right, or am I right?"

The shrieking birds swooped and parried in Myron's head.

"Look at it this way," Jake said, "you'll get yours, I'll get mine. Everybody's happy." Jake heard footsteps outside the office. He darted to the entrance and yanked the brass knob. The door swung wide. He stepped into the hall. Leon was scurrying away toward the stairs.

"What?" Jake barked at his retreating back.

Leon spun around, a hand at his throat. "Nothing! I didn't hear anything!" He backed up, pivoted, and clattered down the stairs. Jake stalked back to the office. He left the door open.

Slumped in his chair with the model in his lap, Myron tightened his grip on the totem pole.

"This place would fall apart without me," Jake said. He pried the model from his boss's fingers and returned it to the center of the desk. "You know I'm right."

Myron stood up. Weariness weighed on him like a penalty. "I've got more carving to do." He shuffled to the door. "Have you mailed the invitations?"

"Popeye and Robin will mail them this week."

Myron's slouch silhouetted the door frame. "I'll be working late. Would you ask Sonja to bring my dinner to the barn?"

"Certainly, sir."

Brad stared at the envelope in the center of his bed. The Selective Service return address was a dead give-away. He might as well tear it up. It didn't matter where or when they wanted him. He wasn't showing.

But his young life had been full of official notices—college rejection letters, college acceptance letters, car insurance documents, apartment leases. Brad couldn't bring himself to throw the summons out unread. He lingered with the envelope, turned it over, wriggled his thumbnail under the back fold, and carelessly ripped the sealed flap. He snapped the document open.

The letter had the official look of bureaucracy: the great seal of the United States; eagle facing right (for bravery) never left (cowardice). And in elegant print just below that: 'The President of the United States ...' and Brad's full name, in the largest lettering on the document (in case I forget who I am, he mocked). His local draft board's address, rubber stamped in an upper right square, collided with the missive's mailing date: 'July 19, 1969.' Under it, the digits of his selective service number. 'Greetings:' the letter began.

"Greetings to you, killing machine," Brad said aloud and continued reading silently: 'you are hereby ordered into induction for the Armed Services of the United States and to report at—' below the typed, upper case address, Brad's stamped appointment time and date jumped up at him: 'August 12, 1969, 7 A.M.' Brad dropped the letter on his bed and then snatched it up again to be sure.

August 12th? Too early! Camp wasn't over until August 24th. After August 12th, how would the United States of America officially classify Mr. Braddock L. Stringer? In the fine print, under 'IMPORTANT NOTICE—Read Each Paragraph Carefully,' he scanned through reminders to bring his selective service card, other 'valid documents,' glasses. He skimmed to the bottom: 'Willful failure to report at the place and hour of the day named in this Order subjects the violator to fine and imprisonment.'

Everyone knew his summer address—no secret there. But he hadn't expected to be called up before September. By then he'd have crossed into Canada. Could he get across the Canadian border after August 12th? On August 13th would he be a fugitive? Would he need fake I.D.? Would he be compelled to follow the drinking gourd at night on foot like the escaping slaves his Maryland forefathers had owned and whipped into seething obedience?

Brad pocketed the letter and walked out of his cabin into the brilliant sunlight. The rain-cleared air had sucked in cool, bright weather. He'd have to leave camp early, slink away like a thief.

Loping along the main drive, oblivious to puddles, Kurt headed straight for him. "Brad!" Kurt called and waved. "I don't have to go!" The boy reached him panting and smiling. "It was a mistake," he huffed. "Haskell isn't taking me back. I can go to Huntington with Reginald after camp! I can get my Junior Lifesaving."

The boy's ruddy, transcendent face beamed. Before he realized it, Brad was laughing: the perfect irony; great news on an otherwise fateful summer day.

Kurt and Thea's twin, Megan, were Maria's only Junior Lifesaving students. They stood together on the dock at lax attention. Megan sucked food particles from her braces. Her "Gidget Goes Hawaiian" bath towel still corrugated the beach with a dimpling of elbows and knees. Kurt felt ready for the final test, ready to prove himself. Not even Haskell could stop him now.

Wally dangled his feet at the pier's edge. Broad metatarsals slapped the lake's surface in alternating plumes of water. In Wally's mind, they were depth-charged geysers from the patrolling USS Wally Van Dusen.

The life-saving ring and its line hung on a nearby nail. Maria paced the dock, whistle bumping her stomach. "You've both passed the written exam and the first half of the swimming exam. *¡Bravo!* Now it's time for the swimming test's second half. Only this time your victims will resist."

Megan bobbled her knees and sucked at her braces.

"So," Maria said, "if you think your victim is too big for you to handle, or too excited, what do you do?"

"Swim away and wait until the victim tires," Kurt said.

"Exactamente. Megan, I am your victim. *¿Esta listo?* Ready?"

With a finger nail at her gums, the girl flicked a nugget of lunch into the lake. "Ready," she said.

Maria dropped her whistle, walked to the pier's planked edge, and dove in without breaking stride. She swam from the dock, turned, and called to Megan, *"Okay, Megita."*

Megan unhooked the ring's fringed collar, clamped her foot on the end of its coiled tether, and threw the lifesaver to Maria—a required first assist attempt. The throw expended the line but fell short.

"Nice throw, anyway," Kurt said.

Megan tied the end of the rope to the wharf's pole and jumped, feet first and spread, into the water. As trained, the girl kept her eyes on Maria and swam toward her with a frog-kicking breast stroke.

Maria began her bogus struggle when Megan was close enough to touch. Marie pushed Megan's head under. The girl came up a few feet away. Maria slapped and roiled the water.

"Help me! I can't swim. *¡Ayuda me!* Help!" Megan came at her again. The counselor grabbed her around the neck.

They went down together. Maria surfaced first smacking and churning.

Megan bobbed up, cranky. "God, take it easy, Maria!" she shouted.

Maria ignored her, *"¡Ayuda me!"* and flailed the lake.

"Okay, victim," Megan worked her cupped hands and arms under the murky water, "I'm here to help you, but you've got to help me, too. Try to stay calm so I can bring you to shore." Maria thrashed for a full minute and then relaxed. Megan swam to her victim's back and, with her hand, cupped Maria's chin. Working a one-armed side stroke, Megan brought her in to the shallows.

"¡Bien!" the lifeguard said. "You waited for me to tire, kept my head above water. *Esta bien.* But don't forget the chest carry. It's snugger. More snug?"

Megan snapped her suit's fabric at the stomach and sucked her braces in satisfaction. Maria recovered the lifesaving ring and re-coiled the rope. "Okay, Kurt it's your turn. Wally is your victim."

Wally sprang up from the dock, saluted Maria, and dove into the water. Kurt watched him swim out well beyond where Maria had stopped. The boy trusted Wally, but he knew the 12th-grader wouldn't give him any slack.

"If this was real life, I'd get in that canoe over there—"

"—and take the lifesaving ring with you. Yes, *bien,* Kurt. But let's pretend there is no canoe. He's out there and you're here and the ring won't reach. What do you do?"

"I go get him." As Megan had done, Kurt jumped in feet first, legs spread, cinnamon hair suspended above his foaming entry. He swam, face raised, eyes on his destination. Wally began thrashing when Kurt was within spitting distance. The younger boy stopped and coasted on the lake's surface. "I'm here to help you," he said to his victim. Wally screamed, his plea exaggerated. Kurt treaded water until Wally's cries seemed to slog, then he circled to Wally's back.

Moments before Kurt could grab him in a chest carry, Wally spun around and pounced on Kurt's head. The older boy engulfed the younger, dug his toes into spongy ribs, and grappled onto his shoulders. With his legs, Wally plunged Kurt chest first toward the lake bottom.

Kurt's cheek rammed the silt bed. He tumbled slow-motion onto his back. Veils of mud clouded the water. The bottom's quagmire spurted between his groping fingers. He sucked his hands free and planted both feet to impel upward, but the ooze inhaled his effort. Kurt's chest heaved for air—nine feet above him and distant as the moon. He wrenched his foot from the slime and stubbed a rock. Solid footing. Kurt forced himself upward driving the stone into the muck with his legs.

On the pier, Maria twirled her whistle around her wrist in a blurred circle and then unwrapped it. "*¡Madre de Dios!* Where is he?"

Kurt's gasp for air exploded the calm surface.

Wally's face bobbed a few feet away. "How you doin'?"

The older boy's grin irked him. "Great," Kurt wheezed, "no problem." He stayed out of reach.

Wally began to thrash again. "Ahhhhyeeee, heeeeelp!"

"Calm down," Kurt told his victim. "I'll be right back." The boy splashed around and returned to the pier. He threw his leg over the planking and stood up dripping on the dock.

"We thought maybe you'd drowned," Megan said.

"So, you are okay?" Maria asked.

"I'm fine." Kurt untied the life ring's tether and flipped a circle in the line, then another next to it.

"What are you doing?" Maria asked. "Your victim is drowning out there!"

"You'll see." He crossed the right loop over the left and stepped into the clove hitch. Kurt cinched the knot tight below his knee and nudged the ring into the water. He jumped in after it and dragged the buoy on the surface behind him.

Kurt upended near Wally and disappeared. Submerged, he watched his victim's legs slowly churn the lake. The boy quickly pushed his palm into Wally's left knee cap and, with his other hand behind the right knee, pulled. Wally corkscrewed in the water. Kurt pawed up the larger boy's back and surfaced next to the floating ring, then clamped his right arm across Wally's chest. He slapped the ring under his other arm. As Wally began to struggle, Kurt heaved the older boy's head under water with his upper body and clung to the buoy.

Wally came up sputtering, "Hey, you can't—"

The boy dunked him again and held him under. Wally

flogged. Kurt brought him up for air. "The victim should remain calm."

Wally spewed lake water from his nose. "Understood," he gasped.

With his legs, Kurt feather-kicked to shore, his right arm secure across Wally's chest, and the life ring snuggled under his other arm.

"*¡Chuleta, hombre!* Very effective," Maria clucked at Kurt. She turned to Wally, her eyebrows arched, "How do you say it in English: two ways to skin a cat? Or is it three ways?"

"Thanks for teaching me the clove hitch on the camping trip." Kurt shook Wally's hand.

"Remind me to call you if I'm drowning," Wally said.

Chapter Seventeen

Robin thought the invitations to the totem-pole-raising-ceremony were provocative enough to generate attendance. The glittered lettering on the front—*Homage to Cole*—would dress up the mimeographed message on the inside. Popeye had suggested glitter and cleaned out all of the Tupper hardware store's three-ounce glue bottles so campers could personalize their invites. "Make each card your own," he told them throwing his arms out in an expansive gesture of possibilities.

"Where do we sign our name?" an 8-year-old girl asked.

"Yeah, if we're the artists, we need to sign our art," a boy said.

Popeye remembered childhood get well cards, mumps, and orange-flavored aspirin. "On the back, like Hallmark."

My own recollection from a generation before hadn't included Hallmark cards, just cautious visitors, itchy chicken pox, and my mother's flat ginger-ale.

"Can we use glitter there, too?"

"There's feathers and string and stuff in the glamour box," another girl said. "Robin told us we could use stuff from the glamour box on our art projects."

"Is this an art project?" The boy asked. They began to bicker.

Popeye calmed them. "The card's message inside is already done, okay? *Homage to Cole* on the front in glitter, your

259

name on the back. Use whatever you want from the glamour box." Popeye paused for questions, but the switch to their young brains had engaged. They scattered in the art hut like penned mice whose walls had suddenly disappeared.

America: Love It or Leave It. Brad had scoffed at the ubiquitous bumper stickers plastered on cars parked in the smug streets of his provincial college town. Now, the childish slogan angered him. I have other options, he reasoned. I can report for induction, mangle my trigger finger in one of Uncle Sam's clunky filing cabinets.

But they could still manipulate his mind. They could station him at a table with a magnifying screen to interpret photographs the reconnaissance jets clicked at 300 miles an hour over Southeast Asia. With a black marker, he'd circle transport trucks hidden along the roads, tick off startled bicycle riders dashing for cover, their bulging saddlebags filled with small arms.

"Nice work, Stringer," they'd say. And by dinner, the B-52s would have unloaded their heavy bellies, taken a dump on target. Why waste napalm or wing-mounted missiles when you could blow the gooks to smithereens with bombs? He'd be rewarded with promotions, a Lieutenant's .45 caliber pistol, and non-combatant service medals to display like spilled salad above the breast pocket of his snappy uniform. His father, a retired Colonel, would be proud. His mother would fret and boast about him with friends over her breakfast coffee klatch. They'd send him home for some R & R.

He'd blow his brains out in the sunroom.

He wanted no part of this immoral war. They'd given him only one option: to split.

Brad found Myron stretched out on the totem pole tapping the wooden handle of his mallet, his face so close to the bear's mouth that the animal seemed ready to swallow him headfirst.

"Mr. Cravitz, I'm sorry to bother you."

"Grab the number five chisel over there, Brad. You can help texture the shoulder." Mye pointed to an array of chisels scattered on a canvas tarp next to the pole.

Brad peered down at the implements. "Which is which?"

"Take the number five. It's on the handle." Brad found the gouge, a hefty and slightly curved blade three inches wide. "Popeye's mallet is over there," Myron said.

Even in the half-light, the finely scalloped slope of the bear's shoulder resembled fur. The upper arms were semi-human, bent at the elbows. At the tip of each paw— held in stiff supplication on either side of its mouth—five claws curved in a flat distortion of perspective.

"Mr. Cravitz, I need to tell you something."

"If it's about your check, see Jake."

"No, it's not that."

"Hand me the number seven."

"I have to leave camp."

"Okay, but check with Jake first." Myron tapped into the deep recesses of the bear's upswept nostrils. The glaring, lidless eyes made the animal's face terrifying.

"Hand me that small D adze too, would you? No, that one that looks like an iron. Beautiful, isn't it?" Myron stroked cedar chips from the bear's grimace.

Brad put his palm on the center of Myron's spine-rippled back and held it there. "I have to leave camp permanently. Tomorrow."

Myron set his mallet and chisel in the valley between the loon's webbed feet. "Tomorrow? Why?" His eyes searched the outstretched wings pegged into the trunk, feathers overlapping like artichoke petals.

"It's the draft," Brad began.

"Right, but it's okay, I'm not finished with the wings yet." Myron picked up a V tool.

"Mr. Cravitz, I've been inducted. I'm going to Canada instead." Brad waited for Myron to face him, to see his anger and regret.

"The bear's ears aren't right. Not quite right."

"I can't fight in a war that's morally wrong," Brad said to the man, to the aromatic wood he had transformed into beasts and pookas.

"A war?"

"The war in Vietnam."

"Oh. That war. I don't understand why we're there."

"Neither do I, so I'm leaving."

"But check with Jake first. How do the ears seem to you?" For the first time, Myron looked into Brad's face. His intense, questioning gaze held the counselor speechless for a moment.

"They look like they can hear everything," Brad said.

Myron's eyes glistened. "Exactly. That's what's important. They hear me. And they'll hear Deidre. Now you understand."

"Sure," Brad said. "I'll say hello to Canada for you, Mr. Cravitz."

My poor Myron drove the sharp blade into a groove at the corner of the bear's staring orb. "Deidre didn't return from her Montreal fling, but someday she will."

Brad left him tapping in the twilight, legs dangling from each side of the bear's jaws.

Snake had already spent the $40 Jake Daryl gave him on new leather straps for the horses. When he opened the envelope, he was hoping for a tip and wasn't prepared for the glitter that spilled into his hands and onto the kitchen's chrome-trimmed Formica table.

His wife, Clarice, said, "Whatcha' got there?"

"It's a notice about somethin' or other."

Clarice took the card and unfolded it. "Friends of Match,"

she read, "Director Myron Cravitz invites all Match residents to the Cravitz Fine Arts Camp on Pine Cone Road ..."

"Up street," Snake said.

"I know where it is," she said, "... to help celebrate our eighteenth annual camp project."

Snake brushed at the glitter speckling his skin. "It's that totem pole thing he's carvin'." He poured coffee into a porcelain cup. His knobby fingers overwhelmed the delicate handle. "Been at it all summer."

"Lemme finish. The camp has been working all summer on the Dee-dray Cravitz memorial totem pole."

"I told ya."

"It's time to raise it," Clarice read, "and we can't get it up by ourselves."

Snake sniggered—a sound like a flat-blade shovel scrapping concrete. "I know what he means." He reached for his wife's buttocks splayed in the vinyl seat.

She slapped his hand away. "It ain't Saturday, yet. Lemme finish! We need you, people of Match—"

"Uh, oh, here it comes."

"—Join us Friday, August 22nd."

"Join 'em for what? Is he thinkin' of puttin' Sadie and Dunce back in the yoke?"

"Damn it, Snake!" she scolded. "Let me finish. It's got times and everything. Pole bearing from the Barn Theater at three-thirty—"

"I gotta see this! That thing weighs a couple tons."

"Pole erection in front of Stone House at four-thirty—"

"Hope they got a hole dug big enough to stick that erection in." Snake sipped coffee to hide his smile.

She ignored him. "Potluck dinner at six-thirty. Well, that'll be nice! I can make tongue, turnip, and leeks. Everybody likes my tongue, turnip, and leeks, even Gerald Ratchet who don't counter much of nothin'. And Snake, listen to this. Enjoy a musical revue, *Homage to Cole,* with the Camp Cravitz Matchettes at eight o'clock. They're doin' a show! We gotta go to this shindig, Snake."

"What in thunder is an *homage?*"

"It says Stanley Throckmorton—"

"Throckwhaddi? Sounds like a disease."

"He's the musical coordinator and Leon McAdam is the cho-re-o-grapher. What's that?"

"Must work with graphs or somethin'."

"It says these two, Stanley and Leon, have arranged a musical extravaganza to honor Cole Porter. I know Cole Porter!" she chirped. "He sang about ta-*mah*-toes and pa-*tah*-toes."

"Yeah, I heer'd 'a that."

"It says to bring your favorite dish for eight and that the camp will provide drinks, desert and hotdogs for all. I'll wager my tongue, turnip, and leeks will be a lot better than their hotdogs." She clamped the invitation on the refrigerator with an apple-shaped magnet. Glitter fluttered to the floor. "I'll have to go into Tupper for the tongue. Enough for eight, I'd say three pounds will do it."

"Make it two pounds and load up on the turnips 'n leeks," Snake said.

Laundry day. Lila Mae pulled at her bottom bed sheet. The puckered curves of white elastic at the form-fitted corners resisted. She yanked harder until it snapped loose from underneath the mattress in a mist of dust. Her pillow rolled to the cabin floor. His note landed beside it. She wondered where Brad had been during breakfast. She read it through twice:

> Dear Lila Mae,
>
> Please rescue my "see-tah" from Stanley—it's waiting for you in the commons room. And tell Kurt to stick to his dreams, no matter where they lead. Lila Mae I hardly knew 'ya. Perhaps in another life.
>
> Brad

"I'll give Kurt the message," she said to her empty cabin. "Follow the drinking gourd, Brad Stringer, and God speed."

Sally Moffett lifted the playing card's corner with a thick finger and snapped it down. She eyed her three poker partners. "I'm in." She tossed a white chip into the center of the tavern table where it whirled and dropped.

"I'll see you and raise you a nickel," Hal pushed a red and a white chip into the pile. He set his mouth, expression neutral, and looked at Emile Barr.

Emile was in Match on possible business. Sally had invited the lawyer to join her twice-a-month game with the fire chief and the barkeep at the Wild Cat.

The attorney tapped the rim of his red chip on the table top. His blue stack, next to the red, was the smallest of all the players. He squinted again at his two, face down cards. The lawyer sighed and snuggled the chip back onto his red cylinder. "Too rich for me."

Hal turned to Chief McIntyre, "Up to you, Bruce."

Bruce McIntyre pulled his two face-down cards from the stack of three facing up: a jack of hearts; an eight of clubs; and a nine of diamonds. He aligned the hidden cards next to one another, bent the edges, and furtively tilted his head to view them.

"The kid's got a possible straight," Hal said.

The fire chief gently returned the cards to the table. "I'll see your nickel and raise you a dime."

Sally grunted and sat back in her chair. "I'm out." She snatched her three cards and slapped them face down on the two still hidden.

Hal said, "Since Sally's out, I suppose I'll have to call your dime and raise you a quarter." He counted out 10 white chips and topped the stack with one red and two blues. Hal slid the pile with deliberate care into the middle of the table.

Bruce's face crinkled into a grin. "You're bluffing, Hal."

"You'll have to call my bet to find out." Hal plaited his fingers on the worn mahogany and rested his right thumb over his left.

"I don't think he's bluffing," Sally said.

"Or he's bluffing that he isn't bluffing," Emile said.

Bruce consulted his cards again and then glanced at the tavern owner's intense, close-set eyes and thin lips. Hal's sparse hair, combed over a cap of chalky scalp, hung in tufts above the side burn shaved in a severe line at his ear-lobe.

Bruce turned his three up-cards over on top of his hidden pair of fives. "I guess we'll never know."

They had been playing since breakfast. After a third round of coffee, Bruce laughingly suggested strip poker which immediately intrigued Sally.

"Say, I haven't played that since high school," she said.

"Things may be slow in here," Hal said. "But not that slow. Sorry, no strip poker."

"Let's play for truth, then." Sally said.

"What do you mean by that?" Emile asked.

"We all got our little secrets, right?" She glanced at the

268

men around her. "I've got somethin' I'm dyin' to tell somebody."

Bruce settled back into his chair slats. "Mr. Cravitz cut down the wrong tree?"

"I heard it went without a hitch—after they sang to the horses," Emile said.

"No, I'm talkin' about things no one knows. Things like, well, for example, I use to wear an orange wig. Things like that."

Bruce arched an eyebrow. "An orange wig?"

"Orange as a baboon's ass. See, you don't need to know why I wore a wig. All you need to know is the fact of it."

"So the hand's winner gets to hear a dirty little secret from each of the other three?" Emile said. "Is that it?"

"Doesn't have to be sinister, I'm not sayin' that. Just a hitherto unknown is all."

"That's innocent enough," Hal said. "Lemme wait on Bernie, first. I'll be right back." Hal left and greeted the old man quietly. Bernie ordered his usual: a banana and coffee.

Emile gathered the cards into a heap, face down. He jostled them into a prickled circle, thumped them lengthwise then widthwise on the table top. When he had a rectangular pack, he shuffled the deck twice. The cards purred in his hands as they overlapped. He set the stack next to Bruce. "Your deal."

When Hal returned, Bruce said, "Same game, five-card

stud, first and last down, red deuces wild. And this time," he acknowledged Sally with a nod, "we play for facts hitherto unknown." Bruce pivoted a wrist to glance at his watch. "It's ten o'clock, we'll play truth until eleven and then I've got places to go and people to meet."

Sally won the first hand with a flush. "How about that," she said glumly, and turned over all diamonds. The news wriggled inside her like a brookie frantic to throw the hook. Disappointed at winning, she had wagered as though her visible cards would never produce a decent hand on the last down card dealt.

"So," Emile said. "Who's first?" They all looked at him. "Okay, well, let's see." He gazed at the dirty tavern windows framed in tongue and groove pine. "I like trains, always have, ever since I was a little boy. I've got an entire O gauge village in the basement. Two F-3 engines—a '53 New York Central and '51 Santa Fe—24 cars, a 100 yards of track, all Lionel O gauge mind you." Emile wagged his finger at them. "None of that American Flyer S gauge junk they sell in department stores."

Bruce shrugged. "The corporate real estate lawyer plays with trains. My brother in Connecticut has a kite collection, all kinds, all shapes."

"I collect Nazi memorabilia," Hal said.

Sally jutted her chin in disbelief. "No!"

"Lemme guess," Bruce interlaced his fingers and slid them behind his neck. "You also work for the CIA. Undercover, right?"

"It's a decent collection," Hal said. "I just got a Waffen-SS concentration camp guard collar tab from a collector in Rochester. I traded it for a duplicate photo I had of Hitler with three of his field officers. One of the men in the picture is Werner von Blomberg, Hitler's first General Field Marshall."

"Don't you find that a bit morose?" Emile asked.

"History is history, Emile. We can't change it. And we shouldn't forget it." Hal looked over at the bar where Bernie was chewing his banana thoughtfully. "Mr. Bernstein encountered Hitler's *Schutz Staffel* first hand in Poland. He doesn't mind showing the tattoo if you ask him." They watched Bernie finish his banana. The old man folded the peel like a silk sash and laid it on the table.

"My collection's gem, though," Hal's comment brought their faces back to his, "is an early SS silver NCO panther-head sword with obsidian eyes. The Germans were wonderful craftsmen."

Bruce cleared his throat. "You're a hard act to follow, Hal, but here goes. And once I tell you this, you cannot ask me to demonstrate. Agreed?" Bruce put his hands flat on the table. "I'm teaching myself to yodel –"

"Ahhh, that's nothin'," Sally interrupted. "I'm gonna' make an offer on the Cravitz place!"

"I'm using those new cassette tapes—" Bruce stopped. "You're buying the camp?"

"And if New York finds me fit for motherhood, I'm gonna adopt a kid with red hair."

Sally's eyes darted from one astonished face to the other.

Her tongue squirmed like angler's bait at the gap in her teeth. "His name's Kurt, from the state children's home. Goes to the Cravitz camp."

Emile rose and extended his hand to her. "Congratulations Sally—I suspected the offer, but I didn't know about the adoption! I'll drop by this afternoon." At that moment, the tavern phone rang. Hal strode to the entrance hall.

"It's for you, Sally. Upstate Children's Home."

"That's the news I've been waitin' for," she said. "And none of you can breathe a word of this to anybody. Kurt's waitin' on tenterhooks. I want him to hear it from me—nobody else."

Chapter Eighteen

Calm and overcast, it's a late August morning, camp's next to last day. By 3 o'clock, the air is crystalline and perfect for pageantry. The villagers deliver their potluck delicacies to our cook, Sonja's, serving table and stroll the grounds. For the hotdogs, Sonja had purchased whole wheat buns with a sesame seed coating and sautéed 10 pounds of minced, red onions. The buns and onions were expensive but since mid-July, Myron had increased her food budget by $100 a week. Casseroles covered in aluminum foil, and salads, opaque under waxed paper, dapple the long table leaning dangerously downhill at the intersection of the beach-head and the meadow. Our cook juxtaposes the potluck dips—one plaster of Paris gray with what Sonja fears are imbedded insect parts—along the table's shorter edge. She sets the potato chips, most still in their bags, among the jiggling *hors d' oeuvres.*

Snake's wife, Clarice—gray hair pulled into a bun, lipstick, and rouge spackling a bread-dough face—wears a blue, begonia-festooned dress tied at the solar plexus with a wilting, foot-long bow.

"Jaunty!" Snake affirms.

Clarice sets an oval tureen on the table—what looks to Sonja like a huge slug surrounded by mop water. The woman announces her dish as: "ton, turn, an' it leaks." Rather than asking Clarice the nature of its leaky fluids, Sonja accepts the stew with a curt smile and carries it to the table's outfield away from the other food telling Clarice her entree should have its own place of honor. Snake closes his eyes in grave agreement. He wears a severely starched, white shirt three sizes too big for him, and buttoned at the Adam's apple. Under a shaved face, the man has left his neck to stubble which straggles into the gap around his collar.

When Sally Moffett plunks down a small boulder of baked beans and ham, the table shudders and threatens to collapse onto the downhill beach.

Sonja gasps. Sally sweeps the pot up again and with her thigh shoves the table's end onto firmer ground. Dishes clack and skirmish. "Never liked cookin' for one," Sally says. Sonja releases her held breath.

To me, the beans look like geothermal mud Myron and I had once seen simmering in Yellowstone Park. They smell wonderful.

Sally reaches into the sisal basket on her arm and slams down one, two loaves of bread the size of dachshunds. "Sourdough. You got any butter for this bread?"

"We have margarine," Sonja says.

"Butter'd be a whole sight better."

"So would caviar."

"I don't know what people see in *that* stuff," Sally clamps massive hands on her hips. "I've supposedly had the best there is, and it still ain't as good as an Adirondack brookie."

"A matter of taste, I suppose."

"Yes 'Ma'am you got that right. No accountin' for taste in food, fashion, or love."

Alex inserts new batteries into the amplified megaphone. From the barn door, he points the horn toward Stone House. "Campers, counselors, parents, ladies and gentlemen of Match," the megaphone crackles, "your attention, please. The pole bearing will begin in twenty minutes. Please assemble in the barn. The pole bearing begins shortly."

My totem pole, a leviathan on its back, reeks of fresh paint. Curled cedar chips litter the cinderblock footings. The camp has gone through nine rainbow-colored gallons of paint and five gallons of kerosene. Thick blobs and smears speckle the barn floor and spatter the aisle seats.

Scotty and Rope had gleefully dripped colors and snapped their brushes at Shortstack's daintily stemmed and flagged black notes dotting the pole. Even so, Miss Thurley's musical statement survived. "You told us Jackson Pollack paints like this!" Scotty's two-fisted grip was no match for Popeye's fingers as they pried the brush loose.

Robin had turned to Popeye. "I think the boys' extemporaneous colors enhance the primitivism of Shortstack's charmingly naive opus. Don't you agree?" Popeye flicked her bangs.

They had finished the project—despite still tacky paint—before the end of camp and in time for the celebration.

"I didn't think we'd do it, but we did it. Yes, we did it!" Stanley borrowed his tune from *My Fair Lady,* augmenting the words to fit their accomplishment. He and Leon sang his ditty at the staff's final meeting last night. Myron expressed his thanks, particularly to Alex, in rambling, sweet gratitude.

Lila Mae, on edge but never losing control of her emotions, explained that Brad Stringer wanted her to say goodbye for him, and thank them for a great summer. "His early departure has nothing to do with camp. It's personal," she had said, fearing a more detailed explanation would fuel Jake's self-righteousness. For his part, Jake kept his eyes on the table as Myron announced the camp's for-sale status, no longer a well-guarded secret among the staff. The meeting had ended quietly with Myron and Alex discussing final arrangements for raising the totem pole.

Alex now stands in the barn's somnolence and wonders if whoever plans on buying the place will need a handyman for the coming seasons.

Sally Moffett wanders through the open double doors. "Quite a conversation piece," she says scanning the totem pole's length.

"I don't think anybody but Myron expected to finish it before camp was over," Alex says to her.

"When is camp over?" Sally asks.

"Tomorrow's the last day. We usually have a counselor's night out at the Wild Cat on the last evening. Want to join us?"

Sally cackles. "These bones are a little too old for cavortin'. Appreciate the thought, though. When I was younger, I did a lot of cavortin'. It's how I met Delmore." She scrubs her cheek with the back of her hand. "When Delmore drank, he smacked me around. Then he got to smackin' me around when he was sober. I smacked him back one day, smacked him good, and he left." Sally eases her tongue into the light and pulls it back. "My cookin' may not have been up to Betty Crocker's standards, but Delmore made an Edsel look like a Caddie with diamond-studded mud flaps."

"Have any kids?"

Sally's chin lifts; her eyes soften and lose their squint. "Not with him," she says. "Probably a good thing, too. He would have made a rotten father." She glances back at Alex and smiles. "You and that pretty thing, what was her name? You have kids?"

"Ginny. No kids." Alex is enjoying Sally's relaxed manner. "No marriage. We broke up after she started talking about commitment."

"Commitment ain't always a bad thing."

"I wasn't ready for marriage."

"Who is?"

"Someday I might be," he says.

Sally regards the man with the azure, crows-feet eyes. "When you are, I'm available." She stares deadpan at him and then throws her head back in a heaving guffaw.

Alex scratches his neck in embarrassment. "Thanks, I'll keep that in mind, but don't you still have a husband?"

"Recently deceased."

"Sorry."

"We never got a divorce. Why give him the satisfaction of marryin' somebody else to smack around?" Her eyes narrow. "One time he came slinkin' back after money. I had two shells packed with rock salt. His name on both of 'em."

Gerald Ratchet strides into the barn. Sally catches his scowl and frowns at him. "When does this bash start?" she asks Alex.

"Momentarily," Alex says and excuses himself.

A wave of humanity follows Ratchet. Mr. and Mrs. Thurley have come all the way from Rhode Island to see their daughter Maura's mural on the totem pole. "I'm Shortstack up here," the girl corrects her parents.

Mrs. Thurley removes her cotton jacket and hands it to her husband. "What's that smell?" she asks Myron, who stands with them.

"That's paint!" Snake strolls in behind them with his wife. Clarice's blue begonias startle Mrs. Thurley who puts a hand to her cheek.

Hal comes in with his daughters, Charlotte and Ruby. The two sisters, dressed in smocks and Sunday pinafores, hold hands. Hal had closed the Wild Cat Bar and Grill for the day and hung a sign on the locked door: 'Sorry for the unavoidable inconvenience to my patrons.' He sports solemn, slicked-down hair and a five-inch-wide paisley tie.

Myron mounts the steps to the stage. "Ladies and gentlemen, thank you all for being here today." He pauses in the dusty clamor for quiet. "I have an announcement. Some may already know, but at the end of the season, the Cravitz Fine Arts Camps will be sold." Gasps and scattered babble confirm that many are unaware of Myron's decision. Mye holds up his hands. "Deidre and I spent eighteen years together here, and now a new chapter in our life together begins." This odd statement invokes additional whispering.

Hadn't I died in an accident? What does he mean by 'a new chapter in our life together?'

"We're here today," Myron continues, "to honor my wife's entrance into the other realm. Together, as a town and a community, we will bear the Cravitz totem pole from this place and raise it on Deidre's ancestral land. I want to publically thank Sally Moffett for making the Cravitz pole possible by donating the magnificent tree you see before you. The Deidre Cravitz Memorial Totem Pole tells the story of our camp's last year. When we raise it today, it will become the new home for my wife, Deidre, and our two beautiful babies."

Hal and his two daughters bow their heads and together say, "Amen." A few others follow suit in otherwise muted and bewildered silence.

As Myron descends the stage stairs, Alex ascends. They exchange brief, hushed comments. Mye pats Alex's arm. Our handyman needs 84 people to carry the totem from the barn to the prepared site at the corner of Stone House. He sizes up the crowd—enough and then some. "Okay, folks," he begins. "What we're going to do is simple. We've spaced 21, eight foot four-by-fours on top of cinder blocks. As you can see, the totem pole rests on the squared timbers. I want four people manning each timber, two side-by-side on the right side of the pole and two on the left. We'll raise the tree off the blocks and move it out of the barn like a human centipede. Remember to use your legs, not your back when you lift the pole. All right, smaller children at the top where it's lighter, older kids and adults at the heavier bottom."

Alex comes into the crowd as they began to arrange themselves between the timbers. He moves Scotty and Rope from the totem's bottom to its top and separates them on opposite sides of the pole.

"Aw, come on! We're strong," Scotty complains.

"Yeah, I can do ten chin-ups!"

Alex stares them down. They stamp and hiss, but stay where he puts them.

When Ratchet shuffles into place, Sally moves in behind him; her girth brushes my loon's wing tips. Reginald and Kurt choose a spot in the pole's center, Maria and Lila Mae just behind them. Snake and Clarice slide in across from Sally as though entering church pews.

Mr. Thurley tells his daughter Maura ("Sorry!" he says when she scowles, "I mean Shortstack") to join her mother near the lighter end. He moves in just behind them, a squat sumo wrestler among children and his four-foot-eleven wife.

The poet, Robin, and water-front Wally, looking unsettled as a bridesmaid and best man thrown together at a wedding, find a place together at the foot of the log.

Hal finds a spot next to Jake who wears his talisman whistle. The tavern owner sends his daughters to the top of the pole. The slots fill up like coveted seats in a railway car. Stanley stops next to Sally. "Is this seat taken, madam?" She tilts her head in invitation. He steps in beside her, "Jolly good. Such a spectacle!"

Leon edges in beside Ratchet who stays on the outside aisle. "Leon McAdam, sir. Theatrics." He extends his hand.

Ratchet regards Leon's greeting as though he were delivering an invoice. "Gerald," he says and turns away.

From behind Ratchet, Sally says, "Don't forget to use your *back,* Gerald."

Ratchet turns to Leon. "Did somebody fart?"

Colleen settles in beside her Stone House lieutenant, Betsy. "Let's go, let's go," Betsy chants.

Pretending they are rowers on a Roman galley, Megan and Thea pull together on a phantom oar with smooth, coordinated strokes. "Ramming speed!" Thea orders and quickens the pace. Megan tries to match her twin, but their synchronization falls apart into good-natured, open-handed slapping. Thea musses Megan's hair.

Megan cuffs Thea's cheeks with her palms and rocks her twin sister's head from side to side. "Wasa madder, Tee-Tee, can't keep you woodda head still?"

The fire chief, wearing jeans and a western shirt with pearl buttons, hails Maria four stations forward then sidles in next to Fanny who smiles at him—eyes lopsided and anxious. Fanny's lab coat, streaked with blue paint from the pole, grazes his jeans. She stoops to blot the hem with a disintegrating tissue and smears paint on her fingers.

"It's still a little wet! I'm Fanny," she offers her paint-smudged hand.

McIntyre uproots from his back pocket a rumpled handkerchief. "Bruce," he smiles. "Keep it."

Angela and Freddie wait together across from Reginald and Kurt. The slender girl looks over the totem at the red-haired boy and waves her willowy arm as though the carving between them is wide as a river.

My totem pole has brought this unlikely community of hopefuls, wise guys, schemers, innocents, curmudgeons, and dreamers together. And, although I am here with them, no one knows it—except Myron.

Alex stands up on the arms of a chair, his feet straddling the seat, and clicks the bullhorn's button. "Ready?" His voice blasts into the barn. Mrs. Thurley shrieks; Fanny jumps. Thea and Megan cover their ears. Alex raises an apologetic hand and drops the horn onto the seat's cracked vinyl. "Can you hear me at that end?" The totem's apex compliantly stirs. He turns to the pole's nadir closest to the barn doors, wide open on old hinges. "How about this end?"

"We hear you," comes back.

Alex takes a deep breath. His nerves jangle. If raising the totem off the cinder blocks isn't done with precision .... He pictures the children's end sinking, kids stumbling to their knees, the pole sliding into delicate ribs, pinning, and crushing their trusting faces against the chairs.

"We've got to do this right," Alex says. "We've got the manpower."

"And womanpower," Freddie shoots back.

"Yeah, we have the muscle," Alex responds, "but we've got to coordinate lifting the pole off the blocks. You'll need to get a good grip on your four-by-fours and lift exactly when I tell you."

Although a simple statement, consternation ripples

among the pole bearers. "What if we don't all lift together?" someone calls.

"What if we drop this thing?"

"Shouldn't we be wearing gloves?"

Alex whistles for attention. "Believe me, if we all lift at the same time, it will be a breeze." He hopes he's right.

"We need a work song!" Stanley shouts. "Where's Lila Mae?" This suggestion causes another flurry of conversation.

Lila Mae leaves her place next to Maria, her long dress swaying. "Why don't we sing something everyone knows," she suggests to Alex, "and use a key word in the song as a cue to lift?"

"Good idea. What's a song everyone knows?"

Lila Mae shrugs. "America the Beautiful?"

"Oh, beautiful for spacious skies," Alex mumbles under his breath, "for amber waves of grain. Even I know that one. We can all lift on 'grain.'"

"I'll start and keep the rhythm steady." Lila Mae walks back to her place on the pole.

Alex whistles again. "We're all going to sing 'America the Beautiful.' Everybody should know this one. It starts 'Oh, beautiful for spacious skies—'" The group joins his slow sing-song, "—for amber waves of grain.' That's it! Now, on *grain* we're lifting together. Lila Mae will start. Everybody get a hold of your four-by-four and remember to use your *legs,* not your back."

Alex waits for them to squat and adjust their grips. "Okay, Lila Mae whenever you're ready."

"Oh, beautiful," Lila Mae begins. Stanley joins her, "for spacious skies," and then the others, "for amber waves of—" Everyone shouts *"grain"* and the centipede straightens its legs. My pole's massive, earthbound hulk levitates between the couples. The feat stuns them into silence, and then the war hoops, congratulatory exclamations, and a few jovial obscenities burst forth.

"Now what?" Ratchet shouts.

Alex jogs to the heavier end. "Start with small steps in place, right, left, right, left," he urges them into a rhythm. "Bottom of the totem pole steers straight ahead for the doors. Right, left, right, left. Small steps. Small steps!"

Their feet resound on the barn floor in a steady rip-rap and when my pole's stalk—grand as a Parthenon column—emerges from the building, the stamping softens like the first splatters of heavy rain on dry earth.

A loon, flying just now over camp with her mate, will later recount the sight below to others of her species and report spying a cameo of her likeness on the back of a colossal, earth-swimming, speckled trout. Her story of the stunning fish gliding across the meadow—straddled by a bear and loon—will be passed from generation to generation until the legend becomes the stuff that substantiates truth.

Popeye is pushing two domed hotdog grills toward the table. A can of lighter fluid starter and half-a-dozen bags of briquettes jostle the webbing between squeaking wheels.

"Do you hear singing?" Sonja asks when Popeye reaches her.

"Sounds like 'America the Beautiful.'"

"Part of the ceremony, I suspect. Why aren't you up there helping them carry that totem pole?"

"They got plenty of people to carry it, Sonja. I'm helping Alex and Mr. Cravitz organize the raising party. That's what the rigging up there's for."

Our cook frisks him with her eyes. "You called Popeye because of your muscles?"

He crooks a wrist, flexes the bicep. "Yep." His clenched knuckles graze his nose. "And because I loves your spinach, ack kak-kak."

The singing tramps closer: "—For purple mountains majesty, above the fruited plain." Sonja adds her delicate soprano voice: "America, America—" Her singing, raised on Jamaican mento jazz, Gospel, and Eartha Kitt, pours fluid as mercury. "—God shed his grace on thee, and crown thy good with brotherhood from sea to shining sea." Sonja shoves her hands into her apron pockets. "I've sung that song a hundred times and always wonder if God's listening."

"I'm off to Stone House," Popeye says. "Why don't you come and watch the fun? The food will keep." He strides up the hill toward the lodge. Sonja pinches the aluminum foil around the serving dishes and tucks the waxed paper under the hotdog trays. She surveys the banquet table one last time and follows Popeye.

The hole, as close to the lodge's northwest corner as the rock foundation allows, measures 7 feet across and 12 feet deep. Stones dragged from the woods, the largest Alex, Popeye, and Wally could manage, bulge in two ragged heaps next to the site. A long furrow, to accept the un-carved trunk of the pole, ramps from the crater toward the lake behind Stone House.

When the exhausted crew had finished digging and sur-veyed the huge pit and its gully, Popeye—in one of his more charming moments—recalled a Superman comic book from childhood: baby Kal-el's fiery arrival in a space ship from Krypton; the space craft skidding to earth and plowing a huge channel in the Kansas corn field.

I could see his memory doting on the narrative within the bubbles above colorful pictures. My trench couldn't com-pete with its comic book, half-mile counterpart. But I felt Popeye's pride for what they had accomplished. "We dug one hell of a sink hole, a hell of a rut," he had said to Wally.

Alex told Popeye pulleys were useless in the tree business. "When a tree starts to fall, there's no guiding it. She falls according to the laws of gravity and skillful notching. But raising a totem pole is a community affair done with pul-leys, scaffolding, block, and tackle. Everything by hand."

Alex had found the pulleys in a Syracuse pawn shop. They were enormous wooden devices with double steel tracks fat as pram wheels. The proprietor said they were part of a three master's rigging "strong enough to raise a ton of can-vas." At $20 each, the owner hoped he sounded authenti-cally nautical.

"I'll need 6 of them." Alex pointed to 5 others covered in dust, hanging forgotten, and nearly buried behind a row of hedge trimmers. Besides mournful squealing from lack of oil, the pulleys seemed stout enough to upend a three-ton log.

Alex, and everyone else, will soon find out.

The totem bearers, tramping their feet in rippling syncopation, begin "The Star-Spangled Banner." Alex can sense my pole's burden. The higher pitched lyrics are breathless.

"Where exactly are we goin' with this thing?" Ratchet shouts.

Alex flags his arms directing the centipede to the rocks piled at the corner of the lodge.

"We'll swing the top end out, move the bottom end to the ramp, and slide the totem into the hole," he calls to them. The centipede's undulating legs pivot the crown toward the lake. Alex jogs alongside. "Keep the butt from digging into the dirt. Keep the log moving until it reaches the bottom of the pit." They tramp forward. No one speaks. His instructions are simple and none, not even Ratchet, doubt they can do it.

Stacked near the ramped mouth of the gully, cedar chocks await their role like luggage piled on a train platform. "Once the totem is in the hole," Alex shouts, "Popeye, Mr. Cravitz and I will need some able-bodied workers to help upend it with the chocks and pulleys."

None, not even Ratchet who makes no bones about his distaste for hippies, doubts that the man with the flummoxed blond hair and beaded, Gila monster headband, knows what he's doing. As though pulled by pixies, the centipede glides toward the sloped ditch.

Only Alex has doubts. What if the trough is too steep?

Alex guides the pole bearers to the trench. "Drop your four-by-fours at the channel's mouth. We'll use them as skids for the pole." The totem's butt cleaves the dirt lip at the mouth of the chute. The bearers ease the pole forward on its flat, chiseled back. The first skid tumbles to the furrow's edge. Foot by foot as the pole slides forward on jettisoned skids, paired carriers peel off, and relinquish the log to thin air above the yawning ramp.

Twenty feet up the pole, where the bear's shoulders finally nestle against the rim of the gully, the totem pole stirs, its tipping point roused. Alex's chest tightens with fear. Powerless to reverse the pole's languid awakening, he imagines the teetering log catapulting screaming children onto the lodge roof.

But the cedar and I are now in strong sympathy. I exhale and the pole responds. Ruby and Charlotte's avian arms—along with all the others' release our weight and our weightlessness—into the accepting sky. The totem's crown rises in a curved fluke and then the log plunges into the pit's soft dirt. It *thunks* to a sucking stop, the dense wood reverberating like a gong.

"Perfect!" Hal pronounces. His daughters clap their delicate hands and hop in their Sunday shoes. The centipede's many feet, now detached from the host thorax, scatter into paired legs and becomes human again. The bearers massage their arms and gape up at the partially buried pole slanting toward the lake like a battleship's gun barrel.

Alex's heartbeat eases from drumming into measured pounding. Too steep, he thinks, much too steep.

For the next 2 hours, Alex follows a ritual he had studied but never seen. He climbs the A-frame step ladder and attaches lines to the pole's cap, runs these ligaments through the antique pulley system that dangles like sinewy organs within the ribcage of lumber scaffolding. The totem obeys. They steady the pole's upright progress using chocks at first, then, in groups of 3, grunt two sets of lashed tripod poles into position underneath. The tripods stagger against the totem's indolent sway as the ropes and pulleys inch it upward.

It ascends, as Alex said it would, in stages. When fully upright, the adults roll and thump the larger stones into the moat around its shank. The younger campers, scurrying in small gangs, finish with smaller rocks. When the last of these clack into place, the crowd cheers. It sounds to me like frothing champagne.

My beautiful totem pole tops even the Stone House chimney, its bear and loon dazzling the cornices and lame embellishments of window trim. At the pole's peak, the sky can't contain the children's gaudy innocence. Their images float free like carnival balloons escaping ownership, escaping time.

Thank you, Myron.

Chapter Nineteen

Popeye salvaged the bamboo pole from an 18-foot screen he found rolled up and abandoned in the barn. Standing on the A-frame within the scaffolding's lattice, he could reach anywhere on the totem pole with the pointer. A crowd had assembled in a semi-circle around the pole with Shortstack's beaming parents in the front. Their ill-fitting "Can Camp Cravitz Get It Up?" sweatshirts wicked the sun's late August warmth.

"The eighth notes," Shortstack said, "stand for Debussy's Arabesque Number Two which I learned here at Camp Cravitz." The child, dwarfed by the towering pole directly behind her, curled and interlocked her fingers at her stomach. "And this painting means that I became an Otter in swimming class." Popeye tapped the bamboo's point on the questionable image of a football with blue flippers and a tail. Shortstack's parents led the applause. The girl bowed and skipped over to them for hugs.

Myron told the crowd that explanations weren't mandatory, but Haida tradition encouraged praise for makers of exceptional poles. He wanted to give everyone who had a hand in my totem's creation an opportunity to talk about the painted images and the carvings' significance. "The figures and paintings are the story of Camp Cravitz's last year," he told them.

The totem pole acknowledgement ceremony went on for another half hour in short, self-conscious speeches. Even Fanny's small white hand print "just to let people know I was here," received accepting nods.

"Deidre loved the loons on Match Lake," Mye told the group in the concluding speech. "Some nights on the veranda, we'd listen to them until dark." He regarded the bear's ecstatic grin and the loon's outstretched wings dipping beyond the bear's ears. "I listened to the bear right from the beginning," he said. "The bear guided me. And Deidre's loon approved."

Myron reached up to my initials, "D. C.," which had inexplicably appeared during the last week of carving. The crests Myron had crafted with Alex and Popeye's help hadn't included the two letters. My husband monitored the initials' three-day emergence with quiet reflection. He was convinced that I had somehow coaxed the letters from the wood, assured that they memorialized Devon and Caleb, Myron's twin calamity now tangibly pardoned.

The 13-year-old sculptor who had carved the initials had intended them to be my monogram.

"They're all at home now," Mye said to the mute and puzzled crowd.

The dancers and soloists would perform in front of the bleachers under klieg lights hastily moved from the barn. These were the same lights under which my husband had sculpted late into the night and under which Kurt Willington had carved the letters 'D C' between the bear's ears and the loon's webbed toes after Mye had gone to bed exhausted. The boy had practiced with his knife on wood scraps for weeks. The initials—serifs distinct, the indentations at the center of the "D" and "C" deep and smooth— were clearly visible from the ground. He had worked for three nights straddling the totem to finish. Sonja brought the midnight carver peanut butter and jelly sandwiches with reconstituted, powdered milk.

"I feel like Santa Claus," he told Alex.

Kurt's disappointment didn't show when Mye failed to mention the carved initials in his speech. But afterwards, Myron's sad rapture as he stood on the ladder stroking Kurt's gift touched the boy deeper than anyone—save I—knew. Kurt's single acknowledgement for his work (a wink and "nice job" from Alex) was enough. Like Bilbo Baggins, Kurt lived a double life: Hobbit by day with his jack-knife's assurance (he named it *Blade*) and—for three nights anyway—creator and guardian of a powerful secret. He loved the feeling.

Robin cornered Popeye near the totem. "So, will this thing actually stay upright?"

"So many opinions, so little faith. Why do think we rolled all those boulders into the hole?"

"Because it was easier than shoveling dirt?"

Popeye pursed his lips. "The rocks keep the pole from falling over. That thing will be there for a hundred years. Cravitz had some wild idea about inserting a steel column up the trunk's middle, but we talked him out of it. Besides," he lowered his voice, "Alex and me didn't have a clue how to put a steel shaft up the center of that monster." He glanced into the distance over Robin's head. "Sonja's waving at me. I gotta go start the hotdogs. Men are superior master-grillers, you know." He snapped his finger at her as he left.

She watched his retreating back muscles ripple under the thin shirt. "It's Alex and *I*," she said, "not Alex and *me* didn't have a clue. And women are superior grammarians, another clue of which I am sure you are unaware."

Earlier that morning, Leon and Stanley had created a make-shift theater on the beach in front of the pier. Joint-cranky from bending and stretching beyond their age limit, they had staked poles into the sand, secured rope from tip to tip, and draped curtains in dog-toothed points along the fabric's top edge. Leon assembled the cast for *Homage to Cole* and gestured to the black material. "The older Match-ettes will enter from stage right," he told his actors milling on the beach, "and the younger Matchettes from stage left."

For the next few minutes, Scotty and Rope whipped up confusion about stage right and stage left. "It's just dumb," Rope said. "I'm here facing the stage. This is my right hand. *That,*" he pointed accusingly, "should be stage right."

"Just turn it around," Megan said. "If you think it's stage right, it's stage left."

"Except when you're on-stage," Stanley said.

Scotty stamped forward. "Okay, I'm standing on the stage." With his toe, he flicked sand to his left, "so *now* that's stage left?"

"No, no," Leon said pointing, "*that's* stage right."

Thea, in a long silk neck scarf, twirled her body among them in two sweeping circles and sank down on the sand. Her scarf tips drifted to the beach.

"Where is my audience?" she called mournfully.

"Out here," Leon's voice rose above the chatter. The cast quieted.

"Theater, like dance, must have its audience to exist." Thea milked an English accent.

"I think she's doing Isadora Duncan again," Megan whispered behind her hand to Angela.

"Without your love, without your applause," Thea implored them, "life is a worthless sea shell, a shriveled-up snail, a cold, cast-away house with no one home." She cupped her left hand over her right, palms up, and extended them. "Stage left, stage right," she gestured, "are from my viewpoint as the actor on her beloved stage. These traditions will never die, but now I must. *Auf Wiedersehen,* goodbye." She sank forward, torso prone in the sand.

"Yes! Thank you, Thea," Leon clapped in a rapid, soundless flutter. "Did everyone get that? Think of stage right and stage left from your perspective as the actor on the stage facing your audience."

Scotty and Rope scampered over the squat bleachers in a game of tag. The three-tiered risers would soon hold the chorus. The audience wouldn't appreciate Leon's historical nod to Greek Theater, but when Leon first suggested it, Stanley approved. "A Greek chorus? Cultural integrity even in the woods. Well done, Leon!"

Leon warned *Homage to Cole* cast members not to overdo dinner. "There's lots of dancing," he told them, "and barfing on stage is a definite turn-off for the audience." Scotty and Rope ate 12 hotdogs between them, the 6th for each on a dare.

"I will if you will," Scotty said.

"You take the first bite." They traded mouthfuls with diminishing enthusiasm. When Rope stuffed the last of the bun between his teeth, the dough lodged there like Mr. Thurley's chomped-wet stogie. He breathed through his nose.

"Come on," Scotty challenged, "chew it up and swallow. I swallowed mine."

Rope crammed the dog down and gulped the cloying remains. "I never want to see a hotdog again." He waited for the food to rebel and released a cavernous belch.

The Thurleys spread a woolen blanket on the grass just above the beach. Holding her plate, first with one hand and then the other, Mrs. Thurley tucked and re-tucked her skirt under her calves. Her husband snored, the empty paper plate on his chest rising and falling like ocean swells. Shortstack squirmed on the blanket between her parents. She would soon change from her "Can Camp Cravitz Get It Up?" sweatshirt into her costume for *Homage to Cole* and couldn't wait to sing her solo for her mother and father.

In the evening's gloaming, Alex turned on the klieg lights which bathed the sand stage and wooden bleachers in a bright square. Jake Daryl walked into the illumination. "Well," he began with unctuous familiarity, "here we are again on the last night of another enjoyable season at the Cravitz Fine Arts Camp."

Fanny, finishing a cigarette near the boathouse, snorted smoke in his direction. "Enjoyable for you, maybe." She ground the stub into the cinder block.

"I know many of you," Jake said, "are still eating or finishing up a scrumptious dessert our young cooks created in Sonja's kitchen. Please feel free to continue eating. Before we begin tonight's entertainment, I want to again thank Miss Moffett for donating the tree for the Cravitz Totem Pole. Without her generosity—"

"That tree was mine, not hers!" Gerald Ratchet swayed on his feet at the light's edge near the bleachers. A curved flask of dark liquid sloshed in his back pocket. "The whole damn forest over there belonged to my family until her great-grandfather stole it. Dubonnet was a cheat," Ratchet punched an unsteady finger at Sally. "And so are you."

Sally, enthroned on a small dune above the beach, tapped her feet where the sand met the grass. "Sit down, Gerald, you're drunk."

"Ladies and gentlemen," Ratchet turned with two staggering steps to address the gathered crowd, "The famous Sally Moffett," he wagged an upraised finger, "is a cheater and a liar, and I can prove it."

Jake Daryl sidled up to the man from the back and put a hand on his shoulder. "Why don't you sit down, sir?"

Ratchet shrugged him off. "Take your hands off me! This is a community party. I was invited. All your little brats told their stories so now I'm tellin' mine."

Jake grabbed Ratchet at the bicep. "That's enough now."

Ratchet yanked his arm away. "I was invited!" he shouted.

"Let him talk," Sally hollered. "Let's see what he has to say about me and my family."

"Yeah!" Snake called from the audience. He smacked his lips as he finished a brownie. "Gerald's had a bug in his crotch for years about Sally over somethin' or other."

297

Jake flung his arms up and walked away from the drunk.

Ratchet smiled at the spectators—a stuporous, complacent smirk—and then leered at Sally. "At's better." He wobbled into the unflattering glare. "Sally Moffett's great-grandfather Dubonnet was a thief and a con artist. At's right! State of New York paid Dubonnet $60," Ratchet flexed a palm with five fingers splayed and then added an index finger from his other hand, "$60 each for wolf heads. At's a lot of money back then in 1830 somethin' or other. Dubonnet collects the money, steals the head back from the county clerk and brings it in for another $60!" Ratchet lurched toward the crowd. "Con artist, liar, cheat! Officials had to cut off the varmint's ears to keep liars and cheats like Dubonnet from swindlin' the government with last week's wolf heads."

Sally slapped her hands on her knees. "Gerald, why don't you tell the crowd about how your great-grandfather Rochette sold phony stock in lumber mills and railway lines to unsuspectin' investors?"

"A lie," he bellowed. "Told you she was a liar. That stock was *bona fida, bona fida*," Ratchet hammered his fist into an open palm, "an honest man makin' a living."

"Your great-grandfather," Sally said, "bought land from New York State for sixteen cents an acre and then turned around and sold it to my great-grandfather for a dollar an acre."

"An honest man makin' a living," Ratchet beamed.

"Except the railway line had already folded and there was no river for transport within two miles of that lumber mill. Stock was worthless and Rochette knew it."

"You can't prove that, Moffett."

Sally flicked her tongue. "You've been sore about losin' land to my family for years, Ratchet. Your great-granddad was a lousy poker player. He shoulda' kept the money he stole from my great-grandpappy and stayed away from games of chance."

Ratchet stepped toward her. "That card game was rigged from the beginnin', just like you rigged usin' the Evinrude in dead 'a winter." Ratchet batted bleary eyes trying to focus on Sally through the klieg light's blinding flood.

In the audience, Hal draped his arms over his daughters' shoulders. "Mr. Ratchet is inebriated. Drunk," he whispered. "People say strange things when they're drunk."

"Like when momma called you a boat without a rudder?" Ruby whispered.

"Shhhhh," Charlotte, shushed her. "I want to hear this."

"Great-granddaddy Rochette was mayor of Match," Ratchet was saying, "only it wadn't called Match back then."

"We heer'd that story, Gerald," Snake called out. "Tell us about the Evinrude."

"Forget the damn Evinrude," Ratchet yelled.

"Evinrude, Evinrude," Rope and Scotty chanted.

Sally spoke up. "I pulled a little trick on Gerald after he sold me a defective outboard engine. Cost near as much to fix it as I paid him for it."

"Wadn't a thing wrong with that outboard," Ratchet sneered.

"Except it wouldn't run," Sally said, "and you knew it wouldn't run, didn't you Gerald? And when I had it fixed the next day in Tupper, you couldn't believe it when you heard it that night cranked up on Match Lake." Sally got to her feet. "January. Lake's froze fast and Sally's running her little Evinrude. Ratchet's pickin' his nose and eatin' soft-boiled eggs at the Wild Cat. He hears the Evinrude in the distance. That a chain saw? He's thinkin.' Can't be Sally's Evinrude. Lake's froze up."

Ratchet toddled closer to Sally. "That's nobody's business."

Snake's wife, Clarice, flapped her napkin. "You've had your say, Gerald. Let her have hers."

"Ya see," Sally said to the expectant crowd, "Gerald never could figure out that I had a steel rain barrel down shore with a wood fire under it. He moseyed out to my dock— trespassin' actually—and saw the skiff with the engine on the stern, prop pulled up above the ice, where I'd put it, 'a course, after runnin' it in the rain barrel. His rusty, rye-soaked mind is tryin' to figure it out. Can't be! he's thinkin.' Engine's still warm. Lake's froze solid as used spit!" Sally began to chuckle. "You still think I'm a furry animal after dark, Gerald? Ain't human after midnight. Idn't that what you told Chief McIntyre over there?"

The fire chief rocked in his cowboy boots and smiled.

Ratchet fumbled in his back pocket for the bottle. He unscrewed the cap and flung it onto the sand. He finished the flask, Adam's apple bobbing. The cast for *Anything Goes!* had crept from backstage and were huddled at the curtain's black margin.

"Is this for real?" Betsy whispered to Colleen, "or is it, you know, the town play?"

Ratchet glared at Sally. The liquor hit his stomach and spread like lava through his gut. "Liar!" he screamed and hurled the empty bottle which fell wide landing in the grass behind the large woman.

"Your aim's not near as good as the yarns you spin," Sally drawled.

Ratchet took a sudden, deep breath and launched himself at her. His torso plowed ahead on tottering legs. Sally caught him by his overall straps and swung his fuming momentum behind her. He slid on his back in the grass and came to rest under the long serving table.

The fire chief, familiar with smoke-filled kitchens, flambéed lasagna, and the domestic quarrels that often followed, strolled to Ratchet's motionless shoes protruding in a "V" from under the table's muddle of left-over stews, casseroles, gooey desserts, lemonade pitchers, and cups.

"All right, Gerald, party's over." Underneath, Ratchet wheezed for breath, rolled over, and rose onto his hands and knees. "Lemme give you a hand, Gerald," Bruce extended his arm.

"Go ta hell!" Ratchet tried to get up and thudded against the underside of the table. It reared off its legs. He fell back to the ground. Dishes jostled as the table righted. Stunned and then enraged, Ratchet heaved himself onto his feet. His head and shoulders toppled the table with a loud crash. He swayed a moment, surprise lingering on his face, then rolled his bloodshot eyes up under his brows and fell backwards across the underbelly of the table. Luckily, his head was cushioned by a hunk of meat later discovered to be beef's tongue.

Bruce McIntyre, the only town official present, told Myron and Jake he would take Ratchet home. Before they had started down the gravel drive, Ratchet lolled his head through the open back window of the car and threw up in successive heaves.

"He's gonna have one hell of a hangover," Bruce called to Jake. "Sorry for the mess, sir."

Jake stormed Bruce's car. "I've had my fill of you townies. I've had my fill of Cravitz and this fucking camp. Cravitz is crazy. He ought to be committed." Jake slammed a palm on the car's hood. "Don't you people know crazy when you see it? If parents found out what was going on up here, they'd lock him up for child abuse." Jake cringed at the vomit splattered on the drive. "And get that bastard out of here."

The fire chief pulled away. Bruce didn't like being ordered around by our head counselor who had earlier, and falsely, identified himself as the camp's associate director. Child abuse? The children Bruce saw and spoke with that afternoon seemed happy and healthy enough.

In the back seat, Ratchet sat up. "Told ya! A damn cheat and liar!" And then passed out again in a slump.

An interesting evening, McIntyre thought. Technically, Gerald had attacked Sally. But she'd baited him. And everyone in Match knew he'd never have tried messing with her if he were sober. Sally outweighed him, and a lot of her

200 plus pounds was pretty tightly packed. Sally and Gerald had traded barbs. They'd mixed it up before.

Jake Daryl's outburst, however, troubled our fire chief. Bruce felt something was up, and it was more than one man's fury—as though the camp itself had been bitten and the sting's site hadn't yet blistered.

Without Jake's further introductions, Leon and Stanley assembled the children.

Hal escorted Ruby and Charlotte back from the toilet stalls after the ruckus. Our town's barkeep was accustomed to sloppy, inebriated crooning at the Wild Cat Bar and Grill. As the evening deepened, the children's voices from the stage drifted over the lake. When the chorus ended, Hal cued his daughters: "We're on tooooop," they squealed.

Stanley flourished his baton, turned to the audience, and bowed at the waist. Amid the applause, he gestured to the chorus members on the risers who stood erect, slouching, yawning or smiling according to their natures. The ragtag band, sitting on folding chairs next to the bleachers, lowered their instruments.

"Thank you ladies and gentlemen," Stanley said. "And now, Mr. Leon McAdam presents Camp Cravitz's own dance troupe, the Matchettes, assisted by the chorus and the Cravitz Orchestrette in our *homage* to Cole Porter with lyrics by our poet in residence, Miss Robin, and yours truly."

The older campers, led by Thea, streamed from backstage right and took their places clenching bamboo canes tipped with silver duct tape. Their sequined coat tails jabbed the audience in flashes of reflected light. The girls had angled rakish top hats, each anchored with a choking strap under the chin. Colleen, the costume coordinator, had outdone herself: black mesh stockings; blue corduroy; sequined tails; ruffled white blouses and red bow-ties, some with still-moist dots of yellow tempera.

The younger girls bustled out from stage left in flouncing tutus ("made from chicken wire, by the looks of it," Snake whispered to his wife), blue blouses, and red berets. Short-stack had added a thick appointment of lipstick to match her cap. The footwear, all approximately black—boots, pumps, loafers, tennis shoes pinned with dark crape paper—Leon had sanctioned with last minute fluster. "For God's sake, wear whatever's comfortable and allows for graceful movement!"

Freddie, her tree-trunk legs bulging in the stockings, plodded to center stage. Stanley blew his pitch pipe, and Freddie broke into song like a ruptured faucet. The chorus "Ahhhed" behind her lyrics; Freddie belted the words to a brief pause. The dancers froze waiting for Stanley to finish his four-count, and then the Cravitz Orchestrette stuttered into a dissonant chord which the clarinet corrected as Freddie wailed, "We're on Top! Like the bear and the loon, not a mop! You're a totem that croons—"

The older girls pumped their canes, "like you're pushing those lock bars on the gym door," Leon had urged. They hopped backwards sticking their fannies out and flapping their sequined tails. "Good choreography," Leon had said, "makes you proud to be human."

"—We're an Adirondack woodsy symphony," Freddie bellowed.

The smaller girls circled their palms in front of them, first to the right, then in swirls to the left, ("wash the window, wash the window"), while goose-stepping around the older girls ("face your audience, keep smiling").

"You're a silk screen wonder, and the totem's thunder behind Stone House" (three, four, one two, three, Stanley mouthed the rhythm and snapped his baton.)

Megan scooted up to join Freddie for the next verse. "On Match Lake," they sang as a duo, performing the struts, cane shaking, and sand-flinging leg kicks in unison, although Freddie's kicks were meek and labored compared to Megan's.

"We carve totems, eat peanut butter and jelly, scrambled eggs fill up our belly. We came to learn to paint, to act and never stop." The girls faced one another. "We're better, brighter kids up here—" They snapped elbows straight, stretched splayed fingers at my totem barely visible now in the faded light behind the audience, "—We're on tooooop!"

The show lasted for another 30 minutes. Shortstack hammed-up her rendition of "Friendship," squirting the lyrics at her parents, trying to mimic the qualities of her favorite actress, singer, and dancer, Shirley Temple. The audience joined in singing *Homage to Cole* during the reprise. When the musical extravaganza ended, Myron invited everyone to a bonfire on the beach.

Colleen stopped Reginald on his way back to his cabin for bug spray.

"So, did camp live up to your expectations this year, Reginald?"

"Pretty much. How about you?"

"Holding pattern until school starts."

"Yeah, I know about holding patterns."

Colleen swept sand from Reginald's shirt. "How so?"

What the hell, Reginald thought, tomorrow's the last day. If his brother couldn't be straight with him maybe someone like an older sister could. "It's just that I really wanted to find out about –"

"What?"

The boy turned toward the woods, a dark curtain at the brink of Ringer's field. "It's embarrassing."

"God, Reginald! You don't have to be embarrassed with me. Tomorrow we'll both be," Colleen mimicked her mother, "successful Camp Cravitz alums like Cousin Walter."

"Who's Cousin Walter?"

"Someone I'll never live up to." They ambled toward the woods.

"Kurt's helped me a lot," Reginald said. "You know, about understanding girls."

"Really? Well, I guess he and Angela seem to be getting along." She stopped and peered into his magnified, moon-illuminated eyes. "Does that make you jealous?"

"It's not that." Reginald removed his glasses and cleaned them on his sleeve. "This is embarrassing."

"Look, let's find a quiet place away from everybody. You can tell me all about it."

They strolled to the meadow's border and drifted toward the back of the boathouse where the ground sloped away to a huge spruce leaning into the dark.

Maria didn't know where else to turn. Myron was engaged with parents, Wally with campers. She wanted a head start in preparations for final beach clean-up the following day. Jake was backstage rounding up instruments with Stanley. The life guard approached him reluctantly.

"I think I need your help," she said curtly, "Mr. Cravitz and Wally are busy."

"Anything for our water safety instructor," Jake said. They walked to the boathouse together.

From the meadow, Fanny saw them enter the ugly building. The fluorescent work light flickered on. But Jake's wife neither saw Maria standing like a post just inside the doorway nor heard her husband's solicitous attempts to cajole the woman into the shed. In Fanny's mind, they were pressed together and groping each other. She turned away and headed for Stone House, anger throbbing in her ears.

"I can see where to put the rope from here," Maria was saying.

"Okay," Jake said. "Well, the life vests go here and the paddles are stored over there on the racks—"

When Maria had the information she needed, she thanked Jake with formal iciness and left. As she walked back to the beach, he ogled the woman's hips undulating in the moonlight. Jake smoothed his mustache and began whistling "Strangers in the Night."

"Well, at least I found out why Cheryl wouldn't go all the way with me," Reginald said. "Thirteen's a little young to be a mother."

"And a father," Colleen added.

On his back in the dark behind the boathouse, Reginald dug his heels into the thick carpet of evergreen needles. "Can you have the spasms and not get a girl pregnant?"

"You mean, can you ejaculate and not get the girl pregnant? Depends on where she is in her monthly cycle." Colleen propped herself on her elbow. "Reginald, how old are you?"

"Don't ask me that! My father does that every time I try to figure this out."

"Sorry. Wow, we're touchy aren't we?"

Reginald sighed. "I'll be thirteen next month."

"Do you know what the spasms are?"

"Yes, I know what spasms are. My father's a doctor—"

"No, not that kind of spasm. I mean have you ever ejaculated?"

"Ejaculated? You mean like in talking?" Reginald recited from his school's history book: "'I've found it! ejaculated

Balboa as he beheld the wide Pacific spread before him.'"

Her sight now accustomed to the dark, Colleen studied the boy's face. Despite the glasses, his eyes were handsome, attractively troubled. The downy moustache above his lip softened the tense mouth. "No, I mean have you ever had an orgasm?"

Colleen's voice seemed faintly magnetic to the boy, as though its flat sonority would tug the metal pen from his shirt pocket. Reginald turned on his side to face her.

"I've read that word somewhere. Spell it."

Reginald felt the extended "Ahhhhh," of Colleen's breath on his face: "O-R-G," she said fogging his glasses' right lens, "A-S-M," and fogged the left. The moon became a blurred corona of light. The tree limbs and stars disappeared.

"What does it mean exactly?"

Orgasms are the spasms you're talking about. You must have had wet dreams?"

"My brother's mentioned wet dreams to me."

Colleen frowned. "His wet dreams?"

"No, he said at night when I was—" Reginald didn't finish. He was embarrassed to admit to Colleen that he had almost wet his bed.

"So you've had wet dreams?"

"But I never actually wet the bed," Reginald blurted. "I woke up first. I stopped myself!"

"Why did you stop yourself?"

"I'm almost thirteen, Colleen. Kids my age don't wet the bed!" Reginald was uncomfortable. He started to get up. Colleen put a hand on his shoulder and eased him back onto the ground.

"Wet dreams are orgasms you have at night in your sleep."

His understanding, like his fogged sight, began to clear. The moon again became distinct, the stars orientation points: Orion's belt; the drinking gourd; the faint Pleiades—seven daughters of the sky.

"Reginald, I think it's time you went all the way. I'm not going with you, but I'll help you get there, and when you're rich and famous, remember me. Take your glasses off."

Fanny had had enough. Jake was never nice, she thought. But at first, he'd been exciting—to her anyway after suffocating under her parents' roof and endless criticism.

"It's a shame she's not prettier," her mother's voice leaked from behind her parents' bedroom door. "It's a pity she isn't smarter. If only she'd been born a boy like her four brothers. Who'll take her as a wife?"

Jake took her and she was glad. At first.

But Jake's mean streak got wider every year. One of these days, she sulked, he'll knock me senseless. And that wasn't the worst of it. She'd suspected he'd been cheating on her since last spring when the checker at the Safeway phoned him at home.

"Who is this?" The familiar female voice had asked Fanny when she answered the phone. From then on, Jake grabbed the phone for late night calls, his conversations brief and hushed. "Yes," he'd say, and "no" and "later" to disguise his treachery.

Then this summer, Maria shows up with a flimsy bathing suit and exotic eyes. Eyes much prettier than Fanny's, not to mention Maria's younger body which he stared at openly and with total contempt for Fanny's feelings. Jake's wife had never actually seen them diddling each other, but she was sure her husband's little affair had gone much farther than staring. They're probably together right now in the boathouse or behind it in the woods, she thought.

She crouched in the wooden rocker on the Stone House veranda and lit a cigarette. The match illuminated her mouth as she sucked the tobacco's yellow heat. The diluted fluorescence of the boathouse light cast shadows onto the beach; the moon sliced a broad, dark arrow into the trees by the chained rear door of the building.

Fanny rocked forward, stood up, and pulverized the cigarette under her shoe. She smoothed her white lab coat and stalked down the stairs. Crossing the meadow in the long nurse's coat, her ghostly figure skirted the bonfire on the beach and its complacent throng of singing campers huddled around the dismal flames. She was soon in the woods and within moments heard them from the blackness beyond the boathouse.

"That's right," the woman's voice urged, "let it come! You've wanted this all summer. Just let it come. See? See! I told you!" And his strangled groans.

Just let it come! Yes! Yes .... She'd find them and kick Maria's naked Colombian ass. She'd break his cheating neck ....

No. That's too good for Jake Daryl. Fanny's anger, bitter as green fruit, clawed her brain.

There are other ways of getting even, she thought. He's an ex-convict, they'll find out about that. "It's what you wanted for me, momma," she whispered to the darkness, "a woman that takes care of her husband. It won't be a crime, it'll be justice." Fanny stole away toward the lone, mournful light twinkling in the upstairs Stone House window. She'd need to plan. She'd need to think this through.

Reginald's heaving chest slowed. His breathing lengthened. Spent, he rolled onto his side to look at Colleen.

"Congratulations," she said. "See?" She wiped his still warm semen from her hands onto his naked thighs. "All the way—and then some!" Even in the dark without his glasses, Reginald knew she was smiling.

Chapter Twenty

Popeye dropped another shard into the metal pail. After 20 minutes of cleaning up, the lawn still winked broken glass. "Quite a party last night," he said to Leon whose arms bulged costumes on their way to the Stone House closet.

Leon tucked his chin into the hump of mesh stockings. "What did you think of the show?"

"Which one?"

"I'm referring to *Homage to Cole*."

"Oh, *that* show. Great, Leon, great."

"Not a bad warm up, actually, when Gerald Ratchet attacked Sally Moffett. No one was napping for our opening number."

"I think the table attacked Mr. Ratchet, Leon." Popeye plinked another casserole splinter into the bucket.

McAdam hoisted the clothes against his chest. "God, I'm so ready to get back home to community theater. The actors may not be Elizabeth Taylor and Richard Burton, but at least they have some respect for the craft." He waddled off toward the lodge.

Fanny, a dead cigarette in her fingers, stopped next to Popeye on his hands and knees in the grass. "Have you seen Jake, Popeye?"

"Saw him last near the boathouse."

"Thanks." She flicked her cigarette into his pail. Fanny steered onto the beach, shoes flinging pebbles. She stopped near the shed and composed herself before venturing inside. Jake was alone in the pallid light. "Jake, darling, I need a favor. Mr. Cravitz said he has to stay on a few days at the lodge and he asked me to make sure there was kerosene to light a fire in the fireplace. He says it starts getting cold early at night." Fanny's fingertips kneaded the valleys between her knuckles.

Jake dropped the buoys into the spider-webbed corner. "Yeah, it does. Remember Schroon Lake?"

"Those were good days," she said to the cement floor under her husband's shoes.

"Kerosene's in the storage shed," Jake said.

"It's too heavy for me to lift."

Jake probed his wife's crooked eyes. "Darling?"

"Yes?" Fanny's voice was almost hopeful.

"No, you called me 'darling.'"

She pinched a ridge of skin at her throat. "I don't want this distance between us anymore, Jake. I'm your wife."

Jake stooped to pick up a buoy by its algae-veneered cord. He slid the rope between his fingers. "In sickness and health, for richer or poorer, is that it?"

Fanny smiled weakly. "That's it, I guess."

Jake tossed the float onto a haphazard coil of stiff line. "Does he want the kerosene in the lodge?" He opened the boathouse door.

Fanny turned away. "What?" She hadn't considered that. The kerosene container would have to be where they could find it later.

"Jesus, Fanny!" Jake's impatience smacked the cinder-blocks. "Where does Cravitz want me to take the can?"

"Oh," she turned to him. "He said to leave it next to the fireplace on the stone floor."

"On the hearth?"

"Yeah, the stone hearth—place."

The large kerosene container, a relic from the 1890s with a white ironstone handle, was nearly full. Jake chuckled to himself imagining his wife dragging its weight across the gravel drive, bumping and spilling its contents up the porch steps and along the gritty wooden floor of the lodge. Why on earth would Cravitz ask a woman to do a man's job? he thought. But then, Cravitz wasn't thinking very clearly these days.

Jake heaved the can off the ground, kicked the storage shed door open with his boot and carried the sloshing canister into the bright morning. After a few dozen steps, he set the container down on the drive to change hands, careful not to spill liquid from the small, curved spout protruding from the top.

Leon and Stanley, on their way to the dining hall, stopped next to him and peered down at the antique. "Looks heavy," Stanley said.

"What is it?" Leon asked.

"Lemonade." Jake picked up the cylinder with his rested

hand. Leon and Stanley watched him carry the bucket to Stone House.

"It doesn't smell like lemonade," Leon said.

Cars arrived and left all morning. By mid-afternoon, the traffic had slowed to mostly late-model, air-conditioned vehicles filled with affluent parents. The parents' lives had remained largely unchanged since dropping off their children at the start of the season. Many of their sons' and daughters' lives had changed, however. While their children's letters home—portions of which parents occasionally paraphrased to Myron (along with condolences for my death)—often complained, they also expressed a refined appreciation for the typical home-cooked meal and bragged of newly acquired skills and friends. After two months, most campers were ready to depart, easily morphing from one environment to another. Some younger, more impressionable teenage girls resisted. They hugged their new best friends and cried while embarrassed parents waited. As they drove off, the children leaned from car windows waving and sobbing. Their friends waved back and shouted promises to write.

Myron and I had seen this exodus repeatedly through the years. And now, Myron was seeing it for the last time. He hoped he would also transition easily from this setting into a new one. He was convinced our totem pole was secure, that the woods now belonged to me and our children. Standing on the worn wooden porch of the lodge, Mye gazed at the quieting hubbub and for the first time since my death, I could feel a peacefulness settling into him.

Mr. Thurley thudded up the Stone House stairs. His wife's high heels clacked behind him. "Just want to thank you for all you've done for Maura—I mean Shortstack." He removed his cigar with a stout thumb and middle finger. "It's a shame she can't come back next year."

Mrs. Thurley brushed Myron's arm. "We were so sorry to hear about your wife, Mr. Cravitz."

"What are your plans, sir?" Mr. Thurley chomped the stogie.

"It's for sale," Mye said. "Maybe it'll remain a camp. Might be a better one, next year."

"Well, I doubt that," the woman patronized. "Maura's learned so much. Thank you again." Mrs. Thurley extended a limp hand which Mye shook.

Other parents chatted with him on the porch. A large man in a Panama hat inquired about the camp's asking price. When Mye told him, the man pulled out his wallet and peered into it. He counted the bills. "Sorry, just don't have the cash on me at the moment!" A lame joke, but Myron chuckled with him.

Wally tapped my husband's shoulder. "Mr. Cravitz, telephone call. Said it was urgent."

Mye had not yet cleaned his office. No rush. He picked the receiver off his desk, stretching the tightly coiled cord.

"Myron," the familiar voice said, "Emile Barr. Sally Moffett has accepted our counter-offer. I've got the earnest money sitting on my desk. All I need is your signature. I'm in Albany. Won't take but an hour or two to get there. What do you say?"

My husband kept silent for a moment, and then said, "yes."

Late that afternoon Sally Moffett, curmudgeon of Match Lake, met with Myron and his attorney. Sally and Myron signed the lined document where Emile Barr indicated with his index finger: "Miss Moffett there, Mr. Cravitz here, Miss Moffett here, Mr. Cravitz there ..." By late afternoon Sally owned 50 of the most beautiful acres of Adirondack real estate in New York.

"Eight weeks of chaos." Robin drained her beer. The poet had lost count after the first three. The Wild Cat Bar and Grill was crowded, typical on a Saturday night.

"Pretty much the same thing as last year, Robin," Alex said, "except for Deidre."

"Yeah," Robin said. "That lady knew her stuff." The others who had known me nodded. I could feel their private losses at my passing. It was oddly reassuring. Robin steadied her weaving hand and laid the Genesee Ale bottle on its side. She spun it in the center of the table. "R I P," she said.

Popeye coaxed a fog-shrouded tone from the mouth of his bottle. "I still can't believe we got the monster up." He blew again across the opening. The low resonance made the three men in the next booth look over at them.

"Yesterday's extravaganza," Lila Mae flourished the word, "felt like high school graduation and *mardi gras* mixed together," Her cheek bones' skin reflected the muted light in the tavern.

Robin upended her empty bottle and raised it. "A toast to

good 'ol Deidre. A woman after my own heart." The counselors raised their bottles.

Popeye waved to the bartender. "Hey Hal, my fine fellow, another round for all!"

"Not for me." Alex removed the beaded headband and resettled it like a crown on his brow. "I'd sure like to know what happened to Brad."

Lila Mae put her bottle to her lips without drinking. She saw Alex watching, swigged then swallowed a mouthful. "Me, too," she lied.

"You went on the canoe trip, Lila Mae," Robin said. "What happened?"

"Nothing happened. Your typical canoe trip. Singing around the campfire, budding romance, grizzly bears, thunder and lightning. Typical. Only for once, the food was *delicious!*"

"Yeah, I heard about the steak shish-ka-bobs, you lucky ass-kissers," Popeye said.

Lila Mae said, "You could've signed up."

"All the slots were gone after they posted the menu." Popeye drooled spit into his empty bottle.

"If Maria had signed up," Robin said, "Jake would've thrown a camper overboard to go." She tried to copy Popeye's pure tone. Breath from her pursed lips washed over the bottle top in a faint *whoosh.*

"And, Jesus, what happened to Cravitz?" Alex scratched his chin stubble. "The last few weeks—"

"Talk about absentminded," Popeye said.

"Maybe it's the ringing in his ears?"

"He definitely got freaky."

Alex stared at the table top. "I wonder what's in store for him now that he's sold the camp?"

The counselors contemplated the future. Now what? The kids had gone home. The staff's winter jobs or fall semesters would soon grind into gear. Each of them had a final paycheck, one more night on sagging bedsprings and by this time tomorrow, they'd be scattered like field thistle.

Hal, dressed in his typical white shirt and black pants, brought another round of beers. "It's ten o'clock. I have to close in 30 minutes." His voice reminded me of his life. Quiet. Reserved.

"I'll miss Reginald," Robin said. "That's one smart kid. Good poet, too." She wrapped her hand around the bottle's neck.

"Sketches good as Rembrandt." Popeye plugged his beer. "Well, maybe Rembrandt's little brother."

Lila Mae furrowed two lines in the sweat of her glass. "I'll miss Freddie and Kurt. They both grew up a lot this summer."

"Pullin' the no-go out of those horses, that's what I dug," Popeye said.

"No more driver's lash for me," Lila Mae lifted her head in song. The rest joined in, "No more, no more!"

Alex stood up. "I guess I'm driving back to camp. The rest of you are completely wasted. I'm only half-wasted."

Laughter from the booth next to them. "Hey, hippie," one of the three men called to Alex, "where's your necklace and ear rings, pretty boy?" They laughed again and the one who had spoken to Alex said, "I asked you a question, pretty boy."

Alex, who had once with the heel of his hand rammed a Vietnamese soldier's nose into the soft recesses of his brain, was better at questions than answers. He swung his leg over the back of his chair and stepped over to the table in the adjacent booth. "May I have this dance?" He asked the overweight man who had baited him.

The fat man looked at his friends, smacked his fist on the table, started—and then stopped—laughing. He sucked a swift gulp of beer. "What did you say?"

"It could be our song."

The big man smiled and snorted. Then he frowned. "What the hell kind of queer-cake answer is that?"

"It's not an answer. It's an invitation."

"Get lost, pretty boy."

Alex leaned in close and honed his words into a whisper, "I ask again, sir, do you really want this dance?" From the tavern's dim corner, a triangle of pool balls cracked.

The man turned away. "Shit, no, not with you, anyway," and then to his friends, "Crazy queer-cake." His pudgy hand, strangling the neck of his beer, trembled.

Alex straightened up. "Maybe next time," he said and headed for the door. Popeye, Lila Mae, and Robin followed him out.

In the parking lot, surrounded by the ghosts of white birches, Alex helped the two women into the pick-up truck. He put Lila Mae in the bench seat's center, Robin next to the door. Her sandal slipped off the footrest. She fell giggling into Lila Mae's lap.

Popeye leapt over the tail gate, missed his footing and tumbled into the back. He pushed himself up against the cab wall. "Oh, beautiful for spacious skies," he crooned, "for amber waves of," and then he bellowed, "Grain!" His ragged voice muted a frogs' chorus rising from the dark creek. Although he hadn't seen it, Popeye heard from Alex that the totem pole levitated as though commanded by 80 voices. He closed his groggy eyes for the ride back to camp.

My husband left his office in Stone House that night at 10 o'clock for coffee in the dining hall. As he mounted the wooden steps, Leon opened the screen door and started down.

"Turning in, Leon?" Mye asked.

The middle-aged man wore his weariness like a mist. "Not even Sonja's coffee can keep me awake."

"Homage to Cole was terrific last night," Myron said. "Great choice of songs. The costumes were priceless."

"Yes, a memorable ending to the season, thank you." The drama coach trudged down to Myron's step. "I know I haven't been fully cooperative. My frustration reared its balding head more than once."

"What are you talking about?" Myron said.

Leon studied the placid, moon-lit face. "You're an interesting man, Myron."

"As are you." Mye waited for an explanation.

"Goodnight, Myron." The two men shook hands.

When Myron pulled the door open, Sonja was drinking coffee in the empty dining hall and reading a letter from her son, Bernard. The vapid odor of stale food surrounded Mye as he sat down with her.

"Bernard's quoting Lao Tzu again," she said. "Listen to this: 'If you realize that all things change, there is nothing you will try to hold on to. If you are not afraid of dying, there is nothing you cannot achieve.'" Sonja dropped the letter on the table. "Now what would a twenty-five-year-old know about dying?"

"Didn't you tell me he was a medical student?"

"Student. Medical *student.* I suppose he'll find out about death soon enough, though."

"Can I have some of that coffee?"

Sonja brought him a chipped ceramic cup and filled it from the coffee pot. She patted his forearm. "You got the totem pole done, Mr. Cravitz."

Despite the camp's harsh assessment of Sonja's cooking, I appreciated the tenderness of her reproaches for what she considered my husband's delusions.

Fanny Daryl's mind was predictably dim and unimaginative. I never liked going there, but our story (which is nearing its end) demands it. While Jake's thoughts were fast and thin, his wife's—reflected from a darker mirror—were slow and thick. I once shared her gender. Now I share her fury as the story requires.

Fanny had finished urinating in the acrid stall 10 minutes earlier, but she was still hunched in the girls' toilets, underwear and pants crumpled around her ankles. A single bulb glared in the evening's twilight. Moths swarmed the light, nicking the bulb in a restless flutter. Fanny's rage had accumulated like the tiny black flies' incessant summer pricks. If she could, she'd pop each blood-satiated nit and force the man who twice betrayed her to swallow the specks one by one. *It's still only a game in my head, a fantasy,* she thought. *I could forget the whole thing. No one will know one way or another,* she reasoned. But the memory of the slut's insistent voice lodged like taffy in a bad molar. Fanny didn't know much Spanish, but she knew *si!* meant *yes!* She knew what Maria's lewd urgings and Jake's adulterous gasps meant. "Let it come. Yes!" the Latin whore had said. "You've wanted this all summer. Yes? Yes!"

Fanny unrolled a length of tissue from the wire hanger, folded it into a square and wiped her eyes. "I loved you once, Jake Daryl," she whispered into the gloom. "But you never loved me. You wanted a housekeeper you could screw, and I wasn't even good at that. All you had to do was like me." She blew her nose and pulled up her pants. "You had it easy, husband. I would have made your bed and washed your clothes until we shriveled up together. Not now. The second offense for arson's worth a couple years at least. I'll visit you in prison. Bring the almond cookies you say taste like newspaper. You'll change your tune about my cookies." Fanny watched the moths' flurried excitement around the naked light bulb." If that were fire," she said to them, "you'd burn up."

She hurried from the toilets, snuck up the outside veranda stairs into the dark commons room, and then crept to their second story bedroom. From the window, the dining hall's screened interior where Myron drank coffee glowed. Just like Christmas, she thought. An on-shore, evening breeze rustled the spruces. She yanked one of Jake's T-shirts from the dresser.

"Shall I make some more coffee?" Sonja asked Myron.

"No, I've had enough, thanks. We should both probably get to bed."

As Sonja rose to take their cups to the sink, headlights flashed through the dining hall's slatted windows. Jake Daryl's sedan careened down the road. "Great Balls of Fire" wailed from the radio through the open window. He pounded out the rhythm with his palm smacking the car's door frame.

"Jake doesn't drink," Myron winked at Sonja, "and when he does, no telling what'll happen. Let me help you clean up," he said.

The car's headlights swept across Fanny's Stone House bedroom windowpane. Her quickening heartbeat startled the thin fabric of her blouse. She watched the light glide across the wall. Jake's car skidded to a halt at the lodge entrance. He stumbled out, vamping and staggering to the porch in an inebriated jitterbug.

Upstairs, Fanny heard the lodge screen door snap shut in the empty commons room. She tucked his shirt under her arm and headed to the end of the hall, removed her shoes and stole down the west stairs with them in her hands hoping her clumsiness wouldn't betray her. Jake tripped up the east stairwell.

In the commons room, she crouched next to the fireplace. Fanny ripped two lengths of cloth from Jake's T-shirt. She tied the rest into a spongy ball, dropped it on the stone hearth and then wrapped the shirt's torn strips around her hands to mask her fingerprints and retain his on the ironstone handle. Balanced on its bottom rim, she tilted the heavy kerosene can until the thin stream soaked the material. The sodden lump dribbled as she crossed the lodge floor with it. Fanny opened the wooden corner cupboard and shoved the drenched fabric against the tongue and groove panels.

She lit a match and watched the glow flare and die in a strand of smoke.

I can stop it right now, she thought. I can drop his T-shirt in the trash bin outside. She lit another match. When it came close to scorching her fingers she snuffed it. Jake would pass out upstairs. Their room was on the opposite end of the hall. No one else was in the building. They'd discover the fire quickly. It would only burn the corner of the lodge. No one would get hurt.

She dragged the red tipped head along the matchbook's dark rasp. Fanny's third torch lit like a small burst of wind. She flicked the flame into the wet bundle which instantly ignited. The fire lapped at the cupboard's underside and spread quickly up the yellowing, shellacked pine. Fanny stepped back from the growing heat.

"Free at last," she whispered. "Thank God almighty, I'm free at last." She didn't remember who said it, but figured it was a woman, and knew exactly what she meant. Fanny turned her back on the fire, slipped into her shoes, and then descended the veranda stairs. On the beach, she walked west along the water's coast—away from camp, away from Jake, away from life as she knew it.

Nearly 5 minutes passed before Sonja saw the glow and then the flame's tatters. She hurried to Myron who was wiping down the tables. "Mr. Cravitz! The lodge is on fire!"

My husband dashed to the dining hall's door and yanked it open. A blazing beam, leaning like a storm-whipped flag from the upstairs corner of Stone House, toppled and wedged against the totem pole. Sisiutl, Reginald's carved serpent, opened its eyes and stared at him.

"My God," Myron said.

Fire danced down the timber's length and blistered the new paint. The soffit under the roof dripped fiery globs, then gave way and tumbled into a heap at the totem pole's base. Flames spread up the tree into the bear's teeth and leapt onto the spindly, two-by-four scaffolding.

"No!" Myron screamed, "Deidre! No!" He clattered down the dining hall steps.

Sonja started after him. "Mr. Cravitz, for God's sake, don't!" The screen door slammed in her face. She scurried to the kitchen wall phone and frantically dialed the operator. "Fire!" she yelled into the receiver, "Camp Cravitz is on fire!"

Up the main road near the camp entrance, Alex down-shifted the pick-up and sniffed the air. "Something's wrong," he said to Lila Mae next to him in the cab. Robin, six beers under, snored against Lila Mae's shoulder. No one in the truck was sober. Alex turned into the camp entrance. A faint blush, like a sunset, burnished the horizon.

"Something's really wrong," he said again. They bumped along the drive and peered through the windshield at an orange sky.

Sprawled in the truck's bed, Popeye turned over and crouched to his feet. As the pickup crested Ringer's Field, the fire accosted all of them like a scream in the night. Lila Mae grabbed Robin's hands and startled her awake.

"We 'a camp?" Robin slurred. Flames gyred from the shattered windows.

Alex sped up and slid to a stop near the mess hall. "We've got to get a hose down there fast. Call the fire department!" He butted the car door open and dashed back to Popeye who staggered from the truck and reeled after him toward the storage shed.

Myron had ripped off his light jacket and was flogging tongues of flame at the base of the totem.

Robin floundered up the stairs and fell into the dining hall.

Lila Mae sprinted toward Myron. "Mr. Cravitz, we've called the fire department. You can't put it out by yourself!"

The totem's bright paint sizzled within the fire's roar. Mye thrashed at the blaze with his jacket; its sleeves exploded into torches. "No!" he yelled. "Deidre!"

Glowing specks of fabric swirled onto his shoulders. The fire ate into his shirt and flared at his collar. Like a hungry serpent, the blaze licked his ears and began to devour his hair. "Deidre?" shrieked in agony, was the last word he said. Myron's body, silhouetted in the flames, crumpled against the totem pole.

Screaming, Lila Mae stumbled toward him. "Somebody please help him!" She retreated from the scaffolding's quickening blaze and pulled her arms against her chest. He was beyond rescue, but not beyond the witness she could bear at his passing. "Pity this good man," she whispered.

Two vintage fire trucks—sirens pulsing, lights flashing— wallowed up the rough drive. Men in yellow mackinaws clung to the engines' rear decks. Alex and Popeye, wrestling tangles of garden hose from the shed, scattered as the fire trucks bore down on them. Bruce McIntyre leapt from the lead engine and flung orders at his men. "Get the hoses and pump down to the lake. You three, gear up and head inside."

Two firemen reeled hoses from the truck's huge spindles and jogged them to the lake. Four others pushed a massive wheeled pump into the shallows and swore the engine to life in a cloud of exhaust. They twisted and locked the hoses' metal flanges onto the engine and engaged the pump; it snapped the canvas tube rigid as a python. Three men with fire axes pounded up the Stone House steps and disappeared inside. Two others, helmets glistening, swept lake water from the hose onto the corner of the lodge, the totem pole, and its rigging. As the dampened fire steamed, the scaffolding's scorched carcass cracked and knelt. Pulleys swung out into the charred night tugging and then snapping timbers into shallow, fire-reflecting puddles.

In the gravel drive, Lila Mae rocked on her knees and wept, her disbelieving hands knotted at her chest.

A firefighter leaned over her. "Lady, are you alright?"

Face contorted, she pointed. Through thinning smoke, the fireman could just make out the image of her despair: at the end of cindered arms, the ravaged body's seared palms were fused flat against the totem pole. From my husband's husk, scrimshawed wisps of flame curled into the haze.

Oh, Myron my love!

But he couldn't hear me anymore.

A gray morning. Perched on the butt-numbing hump of granite, Bruce McIntyre sipped his cold coffee and watched the mist shimmer in tendrils above Match Lake. During his watch as fire chief, no one had ever died in a fire. Witnesses told McIntyre that Myron raced at the flames and, with his jacket, tried to beat out the secondary blaze that attacked the pole. The fire chief stared at the placid water. How could Cravitz have hoped to staunch that kind of firestorm with a flimsy jacket? His passion for the totem pole was well known, but why hadn't the man waited for the fire department? McIntyre's crew contained the blaze within minutes. The pole had been blackened, the lodge's northwest corner would need repairs, but it hadn't been a large fire. Such a tragic and needless death.

Arson? Suspicion cut through the fire chief's melancholy. The incident could have started in a cupboard. One of the broken cups on the lodge floor contained flakes of singed fabric. He had recovered a kerosene container on the commons room hearth.

"If it *was* deliberate," Bruce said to himself, "the Watertown arson squad will be all over us." McIntyre resettled his calves against the cold stone. Something was amiss. He tossed his coffee dregs onto the sand. What could anyone have gained by deliberately starting this blaze?

Epilogue

Reginald Farrouk, now 50-years-old and President of FAE, Inc.—Farrouk Architectural Enterprises—employs hundreds of architects and support staff in offices around the world. His company's prestige has crescendoed to enviable stature. But the glass-encased, mid-town Manhattan headquarters where he works with diminishing regularity has become too predictable for him: same ol' same ol'; no pizzazz. Some days he wonders if his presence doesn't hamper his senior staff's well-oiled efficiency.

He prefers to work at home. The albums on his bookshelf, his quiet, 29th floor penthouse and the Hudson's silver beard at dusk—these are all he really needs to stir the creative pallet. His latest design prickles the diorama on his desk carousel.

Reginald turns the miniature complex to regard its brambling structure among the sponge and twig landscape. The stained glass windows on the model's south side—portals into a pine-fringed lake and meadow—acknowledge the countryside's filigree of evergreen canopies. The four intricately leaded panes will cost his client, Blade's elderly mother, Sally Moffett, nearly $20,000 each. With his fingertips, he traces the roofline of the main building to its off-center and playful point.

The old woman had insisted on calling the main edifice a convocation center, not the embarkation hall or, God forbid, the administration building. Reginald is particularly proud of the winding granite promenade inspired by nautilus shells. Grand, but not overwhelming. All the children in his focus-groups had said as much.

"Colleen ... ? Colleen ... ?" he says under his breath. "Can't remember your last name." But he hasn't forgotten the warm night behind the boathouse when his first orgasm overwhelmed him like a flash flood. The CEO briefly shuts his eyes and returns to his Adirondack summer and its certainty that a child's life cannot end.

Reginald strides to his favorite chair overlooking the Hudson. There are several new voice mails on his phone. He listens to Blade's. "Hey, Reginald. I got your message about Thursday's meeting, but I've got to reschedule. Sorry, the director called a re-shoot for that morning, something about my co-star's wardrobe. I should have produced and directed this one. Anyway, everything's set from our end. We're ready to go over the final details before the papers are signed. Mom's hanging in there, but the docs warned me it could be any day now. She's still lucid, though. I hope I'm as sharp in my old age. Let's get together upstate at the old bar and grill on Friday."

The actor's voice is low and husky. Although her long illness hasn't interfered with his public persona (Blade had been charming the previous night on the Jay Leno Show), his mother's suffering is wearing him down.

Reginald knows many famous people—clients, neighbors. Some are even friends but none are as self-effacing. "Acting let's you be whomever you want—without reality's hard knocks," Blade once told a *People Magazine* reporter. Unlike most of the wealthy people Reginald knows who use their money to spin third party reviews of good deeds and corporate beneficence, Blade gives back quietly, often anonymously. During the 37 years of their friend-ship, Blade has always been different. Reginald checks his Rolex. Too late. He decides to call Blade in the morning. He hopes his friend's mother will live long enough to see it all happen.

Hal's younger daughter, Ruby, is 45 today. Although many years have passed since she last saw him in person, when Blade walks into the Wild Cat, Ruby immediately recog-nizes the boy, Kurt. He is probably 50, but he doesn't look it. Movie stars can afford to take care of themselves, she thinks, and this one certainly has. The man with him is elegantly gray at the temples, tummy slightly bulging the waistband of his knit-shirt. She swirls the damp cloth needlessly on the already clean table and glances at Blade. "It's my birthday," she reasons and walks over to the two men.

"Excuse me. I don't mean to interrupt. I couldn't help but recognize you." She twists the rag. Water drips from her elbow. "I've seen all your movies. And your latest one about the blind boy and his brother is just, well, it's just wonderful."

Blade smiles, his pleasure transparent. Even after years of being stopped on the street, interrupted in restaurants and tracked down during vacations, he still marvels at—and appreciates—his fans' eagerness. "Thank you, that's very kind." He tugs a paper napkin from the dispenser on the table. Reginald slips the Monte Blanc pen from his polo shirt pocket and hands it to his friend. "With gratitude for your loyalty," Blade writes and signs the bulky square. He hands the autograph to Ruby.

"Thanks, what a great birthday present!"

"Your birthday? Gimme that," Blade says in the voice he uses to play Detective Nordquist. "What's your name," he growls taking the napkin. When she answers, he drops the accent. "You're Hal's daughter?"

"Yeah. How did you know?"

Blade smiles and adds 'Happy Birthday, Ruby!' to the napkin, dates it and, showing all his capped teeth, hands it back to her.

"Wow!" Ruby slips the napkin into a large pocket on her apron and backs away. She turns to tend her tables, recalls something important and comes back. "Sorry," she gushes, "I forgot your order!" Ruby flicks the damp cloth onto her shoulder. "What can I get for you?"

"Reginald, how about a tuna fish sandwich?"

"And some coffee," Reginald says and scans the room. "I still can't believe Sally's gone." He regards his friend who looks at his hands.

"She was one-of-a-kind." Blade leans back in his chair and digs in his front pants pocket. "I've kept this guy on me ever since I took Blade as my professional name." He lays the knife on the table. Its brass caps are mottled, the blade lock long since sprung.

"Fond memories," Reginald picks up the relic and turns it in his hands. "What was that older girl, Colleen's, last name?"

"Big boobs? Bossy? I've forgotten," Blade says remembering instead a thin girl named Angela, a young man named Brad and a canoe trip. "I heard from Brad Stringer a few years ago, lives in Winnipeg. He contacted my agent. We catch up on Facebook occasionally." The two men drift on separate memories.

"After the adoption, Sally used to bring me in here all the time," Blade says. "There was a pool table over there where the video games are now. She taught me to play until I got pretty good. I could beat her every time. And then one day, she says, 'Son, now that you've learned to win, you need to learn to lose.' She cleared the table!"

Ruby returns with their order. "I forgot to ask, I hope you don't mind. It's wheat, not white bread. I'll change it if you like."

"Wheat's perfect," Blade says.

Ruby's face shines in gratitude. She carefully sets the sandwich plates by each man and fills their coffee cups. Her hands tremble. "I remember when your mother brought you here to play pool." Ruby puts a hand to her mouth. Her shoulders slump forward. "Oh, forgive me for not mentioning it sooner. I was so sorry to hear of Ms. Moffett's death."

"Thank you," Blade says. "Mother Moffett lived a very full 86 years."

"Let me know if you need more coffee," Ruby says. She tries to smile but her mouth turns mournful and she leaves.

"If the foundation's matching grant can't cover the construction costs, we can make up the difference with appreciated stock," Blade says. "Easy as going to sleep with the lights on."

His freckles have mostly faded, but the glint in Blade's eyes reminds Reginald of the red-headed kid he shared his summer with in 1969. "Sally would have wanted some bells and whistles," Reginald says.

Blade grimaces. "Bells and whistles are fine on a building. But children need a community, a little down-home love, and encouragement." He raps the table. "I visited a place in California where four- and five-year-olds didn't know their own names because nobody talked to them." He snorts. "California. The enlightened coast."

"More coffee?" Ruby appears with a silver thermos. She unscrews the black top.

"I'm done," Blade says.

She peers down at their half-eaten sandwiches. "Is the tuna fish okay?" Her face is tight, coiled for rejection.

"An aquatic wonderment, Ruby." Blade takes a large bite.

"*¡Exactamente!*" says Reginald.

Later that afternoon before the meager dinner crowd arrives, Ruby's sister, Charlotte, walks into the Wild Cat. "Happy birthday, Sis."

Ruby grins her appreciation, then bolts upright. "You'll never guess who came into the tavern today!"

"George Clooney."

Ruby is taken aback, then realizes her sister is joking. "No!" she scolds, "but almost. Blade Moffett! Just sauntered in with his famous architect friend. They were at Camp Cravitz together. It's all in today's Bugle."

"You're in today's paper? Since when—"

"No, Blade Moffett is in today's paper, along with his friend, Reginald somebody." Ruby carefully pulls the signed napkin from her apron pocket. "My name and everything, see?"

Charlotte is impressed. "Don't get that wet."

Ruby tucks the paper napkin into her apron and reads the newspaper's headline: "'Gift largest in history of region.' Imagine that! 'The town of Match will be the site of a state-of-the-art children's home.'"

"They've been talking about that for months at the VFW."

"I know, and they're finally breaking ground this Saturday." Ruby lifts the paper and snaps the sheets in half. "'Local philanthropist, the late Sally F. Moffett pledged through her foundation thirty-two million dollars to match a similar gift from the New York-based Rockhurst Trust.'"

"Thirty-two *million* dollars?"

"I know, I *know!* Thirty-two million dollars 'for a world-class children's living center in Match township.' Here it is, here it is! 'Popular stage and screen star, Blade Moffett," she nods knowingly at Charlotte, "'who is the philanthropist's surviving son and was, himself, an orphan, credits his adoptive mother with his own success. 'Mother Moffett taught me to be a winner,' he told this reporter using an endearment reserved for Ms. Moffett. 'But she also taught me to remember my roots and help others along the way—'"

339

"Sally could've scooted some money our way. We could've used the help."

Ruby rustles the paper. "'—The Sally Moffett Center for Children, designed by internationally renowned architect, Reginald Farrouk, will break ground this Saturday in Match on 50 acres of lakefront property that Miss Moffett purchased in 1969.'"

"Don't ya just love it?" Charlotte says. "Break ground. The bigwigs get a silver-plated shovel that never touched dirt. The photographer gives 'em spick-'n-span hard hats for the photo op –"

Ruby snaps the paper in irritation and creases it. "'The site was once a tourist lodge and later a fine arts camp. All evidence of the former structures, now crumbling with neglect, will be demolished with the exception of a thirty-foot totem pole erected by the camp director, Myron Cravitz, in memory of his wife, Deidre, and their two children, Devon and Caleb.'"

Charlotte gazes at the paper in her sister's hands. "That was one whiz-bang of a day." She's contemplative and then animated. "We sang. Remember, Rue?" Charlotte reaches to smooth her sister's hair. "What did we sing, Sis?"

"I've forgotten." Ruby lays the paper on the table, "But I remember when that totem pole *dove* into the pit like it was going home." She covers her sister's fingers with her own. "Thanks for remembering my birthday, Charlotte."

For eight generations, my favorite loon family has prospered. A returning female swoops with her new mate over Match Lake for the first time this late spring season. Below them, the silver water stretches southeast to the Salmon River. On the lake's coast, Stone House has crumbled, its caved-in roof now home to hoot owls. The totem pole's shadow leans across the remnants of our chalky drive.

Toward town, the hardware store's new asphalt parking lot is a black square by the winding gray roadside. Condos are spilling from the north, crowding billboards to the south. In a shabby tavern camouflaged among pines, two sisters remember the centipede—a colossal, earth-swimming speckled trout and the bear and loon that straddled it. Farther up the lake shore, chimney smoke puffs from the late Sally Moffett's cabin. Inside, Reginald's wife reads *The Hobbit* on an old couch that sucks her into the story like a thumb. Draped over the old six-sided table next to her, today's *Tupper Bugle* is open.

I wing into the dim comfort, settle invisibly on the sofa's shoulder and read our tale's last lines: *Although blackened in a long-ago fire, the Cravitz totem pole will endure on the grounds of the Sally Moffett Center for Children. Blade Moffett has promised to restore the monument.*

My story's done. I'm flying away.

Acknowledgements

This novel owes its existence to more folks than can be remembered. I apologize if I have omitted anyone. My thanks go to: Chrissy Ward, who kept the faith—even through the book's "first, awful draft"; Susan Biles, for broad sweeps of intelligent revision suggestions; Jeanne and Dan Proctor, for input and probing questions which—when addressed—made for a better book; the late Bob Chrisman, who provided a line-by-line, page-by-page close edit—a special thanks, and farewell, to you, Bob; Michael Pritchett, for enthusiastic and helpful criticism; Brian Shawver, whose suggested cuts at first alarmed and then charmed me; Catherine Browder, for understanding how fiction works and helping me understand it as well; Bob Stewart and the late James McKinley, for early chapter edits; Frank Higgins, who, in his play *Black Pearl Sings,* introduced me to songs of the abolitionists; Denise Low, for sensible and sensitive reflections on Native American culture; Katie Madigan who kept my French in line; The Kansas City Writers Group, for listening and responding to numerous drafts; Debra Shouse, Mary-Lane Kamberg and Dawn Downey, for their tireless interest in my prose; readers Susie McRoberts, Katherine Heilman, Devin Proctor and Thom Proctor, who gave me honest, first-impression input; James Garbarino, for believing in the book; and, most of all, my wife, Susan Proctor—you never gave up on me, even when you probably should have. Thanks again to all my readers, cheerleaders and editors.

About the Author

Mr. Proctor has written and published short fiction, essays, humor, and poetry for nearly 50 years. A memoir, *The Sweden File: Memoir of an American Expatriate*, which he co-authored with his late brother Bruce Proctor and published in 2015, received a featured review in *Kirkus Reviews* and was selected as a 2015 "literary star" by the *Kansas City Star* newspaper. *Adirondack Summer, 1969*, is his debut novel. Mr. Proctor lives in Kansas City, Missouri with his wife, Dr. Susan Proctor and their cat, Beans.

Alan Robert Proctor
(photo by Dr. Susan Proctor)

Made in the USA
Middletown, DE
19 January 2019